## Suicide Mission

"We have a lot of details to sort out," Nighthawk said.

Kinoshita observed him thoughtfully. "You don't seem overly nervous."

"Should I be?"

"Well, you're about to take on four million soldiers with a handful of untrained men, and to try to assassinate the best-protected politician on the Inner Frontier," replied Kinoshita. "That would make most men a little nervous."

"Most men," agreed Nighthawk.

"But not you?"

"Not the Widowmaker."

ALSO BY MIKE RESNICK

*The Soul Eater*
*Eros at Zenith*
*Lucifer Jones*
*Stalking the Unicorn: A Fable of Tonight*
*Ivory: A Legend of Past and Present*
*Bwana/Bully*
*Second Contact*
*Soothsayer*
*Oracle*
*Prophet*
*Paradise: A Chronicle of a Distant World*
*Purgatory: A Chronicle of a Distant World*
*Inferno: A Chronicle of a Distant World*
*A Miracle of Rare Design*
*The Widowmaker*

# The Widowmaker Reborn

*Volume Two of the Widowmaker Trilogy*

# MIKE RESNICK

BANTAM BOOKS
New York Toronto London Sydney Auckland

THE WIDOWMAKER REBORN
A Bantam Book/August 1997

ISBN 0-553-57161-3

*Published simultaneously in the United States and Canada*

Bantam Books are published by Bantam Books, a division of Bantam
Doubleday Dell Publishing Group, Inc. Its trademark, consisting of
the words "Bantam Books" and the portrayal of a rooster, is Regis-
tered in U.S. Patent and Trademark Office and in other countries.
Marca Registrada. Bantam Books, 1540 Broadway, New York, New
York 10036.

PRINTED IN THE UNITED STATES OF AMERICA
OPM 10 9 8 7 6 5 4 3 2 1

*To Carol,*
*as always*

◆ ◆ ◆

*And to Richard Potter*
*and Andrew Rona,*
*two of Hollywood's Good Guys*

# Prologue

*In a small, dimly lit room a mile beneath the glittering sur-face of Deluros VIII,* the capital of mankind's sprawling Oligarchy, Jefferson Nighthawk opened his eyes.

"Good evening, Mr. Nighthawk," said a slender man wearing a white tunic. "How do you feel?"

Nighthawk gradually became aware that he was lying on a long, narrow table, staring at the ceiling. He tentatively lifted an arm, made a fist, and then began slowly opening and closing his fingers.

"Pretty good," he said, surprised.

He brought his hand up to his face and stared at it as if it were some alien object he had never seen before.

"It looks normal," he said at last.

"It is."

"Then I'm cured?"

"Well, yes and no," replied the man in the white tunic. "It's a complex situation."

Nighthawk eased his legs over the edge of the table and slowly, carefully, sat up.

"Yeah, I feel all right," he said. "I guess the clone did his job."

"You're getting ahead of yourself, Mr. Nighthawk," said another voice, and Nighthawk turned to see a stocky, bearded, middle-aged man dressed in gray staring at him.

"Who are you?" demanded Nighthawk.

"Marcus Dinnisen, a senior partner in the firm of Hubbs, Wilkinson, Raith and Jiminez." He smiled. "I'm your attorney."

"That's right," said Nighthawk, nodding his head slowly. "You told me the last time you woke me up that Raith was dead."

"He died more than three-quarters of a century ago," said Dinnisen. "His great-grandson worked for the firm until a few years ago."

"Okay," said Nighthawk. "You're my lawyer." He turned to the man in the white tunic. "I assume you're my doctor?"

"In a manner of speaking" was the reply. "My name is Egan. Gilbert Egan."

"I think I've met you before."

"Just over two years ago," said Egan.

"So what year is it now—5103?"

"5103 G.E.," Egan confirmed.

"Then this means you've come up with a cure for eplasia sometime during the past two years," said Nighthawk.

"No, Mr. Nighthawk, I'm afraid we haven't."

Nighthawk frowned, confused. He carefully touched his face with his fingertips. "But I'm cured," he insisted. "There's not a mark on me!"

"You're not cured," said Egan gently. "In fact, you're in the very earliest stage of the disease. It won't manifest itself for another year."

"What are you talking about?" demanded Nighthawk. "Look at me. The disease is gone!"

"Maybe *you'd* better look at you," said Egan, handing him a mirror.

Nighthawk carefully scrutinized his handsome, unblemished face, looking more and more puzzled.

"What the hell is going on?" he said. "I look thirty-five!"

"Our best estimate is thirty-eight," answered Egan.

"But that's crazy! I was sixty-one years old when I checked in here more than a century ago."

"Calm down, Mr. Nighthawk."

"*You* calm down!" said Nighthawk, and something about his manner made both men draw back. "*I* want to know what's happening, and I want to know now!"

"Certainly, Mr. Nighthawk," said Egan, stepping forward again. "You've been injected with tranquilizers to ease the shock. I hate to think of what might happen if . . ."

A hand shot out, grabbed Egan by the collar, and pulled him close.

"I'm not feeling very tranquil, Mr. Egan," said Nighthawk coldly. "Now talk."

"*Doctor* Egan," said Egan, pulling loose from Nighthawk's grasp and brushing the rumples from his tunic. He stared at Nighthawk uneasily. "You know, I've spent the past two days wondering just how to tell you—and I still don't know where to begin."

Nighthawk looked annoyed. "Try the beginning."

"All right," said Egan. "It's a matter of record that Jefferson Nighthawk, also known as the Widowmaker, a well-known lawman and bounty hunter on the Inner Frontier, contracted eplasia and voluntarily submitted himself to freezing in the year 4994 of the Galactic Era. His instructions were that he was not to be awakened until science had developed a cure for his disease."

"I'm right here," said Nighthawk. "You can stop referring to me in the third person."

"Please let me continue in my own way," said Egan. "We had every intention of honoring Jefferson Nighthawk's wishes, but a financial crisis arose two years ago. Due to an inflationary spiral in the economy of Deluros VIII, the interest on Nighthawk's principle was no longer sufficient to cover the very high cost of this facility. We were faced with the possibility of awakening a diseased, aging man and turning him out, when an offer made to Mr. Dinnisen's office provided us with an unique alternative: a world on the Inner Frontier required a man of the Widowmaker's talents, and they were willing to pay seven million credits for those talents. We could not use the real Nighthawk, of course; he was almost dead when he first came here, and he couldn't survive, unfrozen, for another month with the disease. But we could and did create a clone that cost about half of the amount offered, which allowed us to add more than three million credits to Nighthawk's principle."

"I know," said Nighthawk. "You woke me to sign a release allowing you to clone me."

"That's correct," continued Egan. "We cloned you and sent the clone out to the Frontier."

"I know," said Nighthawk. "What happened?"

"He did what he was paid to do," said Dinnisen, "but he was seriously flawed."

"He had the disease?"

Egan shook his head. "No. He was a perfect replica of the twenty-three-year-old Jefferson Nighthawk, with all of Nighthawk's physical abilities. But because of the urgency of the situation, we sent him out only two months after he was created. He was a remarkable killing machine, but that was the only thing he knew how to do, and emotionally he was only two months old. He proved totally unable to cope with his abilities. In the end, he was killed trying to help a woman possessed of what I shall term questionable character and loyalties."

"Get to the point," said Nighthawk.

"The point is that the government has not managed to control inflation. Furthermore, for reasons with which I strongly disagree, Colonel James Hernandez, the man who commissioned the clone, refused to make his final payment. Most of the money we received was spent creating the clone; the profits we anticipated did not materialize." He paused. "Science is very close to developing a cure for eplasia, but it's still two or three years in the future, and once again the interest on the Nighthawk account is insufficient to pay for this facility."

"If you're trying to tell me I'm a clone, you've picked a lousy audience for a very bad joke," said Nighthawk. "I can remember everything I've done, every man I've killed, every woman I've had."

"I know," said Egan. "Because the initial clone *did* accomplish its mission before its untimely death, Mr. Dinnisen's office has had more offers. He has winnowed them down and come up with the most lucrative. But based on our first experience, we felt that we couldn't send another physically perfect but emotionally immature specimen out to do the job. So we hired some of the top men and women in the field of genetics and have finally managed to create a clone—yourself— that possesses all, or almost all, of the memories of the host."

"I don't believe it," said Nighthawk.

"I didn't really expect you to," said Egan. He studied Nighthawk carefully. "Do you feel strong enough to stand?"

Nighthawk eased himself down to the floor. A sudden weakness swept over him, and he clutched for the table.

"What's the matter with me?"

"Nothing," said Egan. "You're just using muscles you've never used before. You may also experience some dizziness." He waited until Nighthawk was able to stand without using the table for support. "Can you walk now?"

"I think so."

"Then come this way, please," said Egan as Nighthawk and Dinnisen fell into step behind him. As they left the room they came to a slidewalk, which they rode down a long, dimly lit corridor.

After passing a number of doors, the slidewalk brought them to a security checkpoint, then stopped until Egan's ID badge and retina had been scanned. It began moving again, only to stop once more at a second checkpoint fifty yards farther on.

After another two hundred yards the corridor branched off, and Egan chose the slidewalk that veered to the right. The doors came more frequently now, as did the checkpoints, but finally they came to a halt in front of a door that appeared no different from any of the others.

"This is it," announced Egan, allowing the scanner above the door to verify his retina and palm print.

The door slid open, revealing a circular chamber with a number of large drawers built into the wall.

"Drawer 10547," ordered Egan, and a drawer slowly emerged from the wall, stretching to its full eight-foot length. A human body was discernible beneath the transluscent covering.

"The true Jefferson Nighthawk," said Egan, touching a control that turned the covering totally transparent.

Nighthawk peered into the drawer, and saw an emaciated man whose flesh was hideously disfigured by the ravages of a virulent skin disease. Patches of shining white cheekbone protruded through the flesh of the face, knuckles pierced the skin of the hands, and even where the skin remained intact it looked like there was some hideous malignancy crawling across it and discoloring it.

"That's the way I remember it, all right," he said, turning away.

"I realize what a shock this must be," said Egan sympathetically.

Nighthawk tapped his head. "But these are *my* memories. I *know* they are. They're *real!*"

"They're real, but they're not yours," interjected Dinnisen. "I know it's difficult to accept, but today is your birthday, in the truest sense of the word." He paused a moment while Nighthawk wrestled with the concept, then continued: "Physically you're thirty-eight years old, and free of the disease that brought you here."

"*Almost* free," corrected Egan. "It's there, but dormant."

"I didn't contract it until I was in my late fifties," said Nighthawk. "Why do I have it now, twenty years earlier?"

Egan shrugged. "You have a genetic weakness that invites the disease. Because we were able to get blood and tissue taken before the original Nighthawk developed eplasia, the first clone possessed nothing more than a tendency to the disease. We used that same sample with you, but you are almost twice that clone's physical age, and it has begun developing within you. Very likely it is due to the laboratory process that aged you so rapidly." He paused. "I should add that now that you are alive, you will henceforth age at a normal rate."

"The last clone never developed the disease?"

"No, but he died very young," answered Egan. "He would surely have contracted it if he'd lived long enough. Given your particular genetic makeup and immune system, it seems inevitable."

"All right," said Nighthawk. "Next question: why am I in my late thirties? I—*he*—is sixty-one."

"We were able to make you any age we wanted," replied Egan. "We decided to create you at the peak of your powers."

"I was quicker and stronger at twenty-three."

"Too many hormones," said Dinnisen. "They proved your undoing last time. We want the Widow-maker, not the Testosterone Kid."

"Okay," said Nighthawk. "Let's cut to the bottom line. What happens to *me* after I make enough money to keep *him* alive?"

"You assume a new identity—it's essential to maintain the original Nighthawk's legal claim to investments and personal property—and live a long and prosperous life. No one will mistake you for him, since he hasn't been seen in more than a century."

"What about my eplasia?"

"If science can cure his, it can cure yours," said Egan.

"And you should certainly possess enough skills to earn whatever it takes to effect a cure," added Dinnisen.

"How much will it cost?"

"For the next few years, maybe half a million credits. Within a decade, perhaps a hundred thousand. In a quarter of a century, we'll be immunizing fetuses for about ten credits apiece."

Nighthawk was silent for a long moment. Finally he turned to Dinnisen, who felt uncomfortable under the gaze of his almost colorless eyes.

"You know what I think?" said Nighthawk.

"What?"

"I think you're full of shit."

"I beg your pardon?"

"I may be a century out of date, but it's a big galaxy out there. There are still thousands of killers and bounty hunters on the Inner Frontier, and even more on the Rim and in the Spiral Arm."

"I don't follow you, Mr. Nighthawk."

"If whoever is paying for my services went to the time and expense to clone the Widowmaker when he had thousands of others to choose from, I would imagine the odds are so stacked against me that the smart money says I won't last a week."

"He wanted the best," replied Dinnisen, looking distinctly uncomfortable. "That's you."

Nighthawk fell silent again for a long moment. Then he looked up at Egan.

"Give me something sharp," he said.

"Sharp?" repeated Egan, puzzled.

"A knife, a scalpel, something like that."

Egan examined his pockets with no success.

"Never mind," said Nighthawk. He walked to the edge of the still-open drawer, pressed his thumb against it, and pulled it across the edge, leaving a deep gouge in the skin.

"Scanner?" he demanded.

Egan merely pointed at the glowing red mechanical eye.

Nighthawk walked over, wiped the blood from his thumb, and held it up to the scanner.

"Have I got an official name or number around here?" he asked.

"Just Jefferson Nighthawk Clone Number Two," answered Egan. "Serial number 90307."

"Good. Tell the machine that this is the thumb-print of Jefferson Nighthawk Clone Number Two, serial number 90307. The scar will differentiate it from any other Nighthawk clone you may be tempted to create in the future."

"It's listening. It knows," said Egan.

"Fine. Now I want you to go tell whoever is paying for me that our price just went up half a million credits. When he agrees—and he will, or he would have settled for a man with lesser credentials—tell him we want it in advance. Then put it in an account that can only be opened by my voiceprint and thumbprint."

"We've already agreed on a substantial price," said Dinnisen. "Holding him up for more at the last minute isn't ethical."

"You worry about ethics," said Nighthawk. "I'm worrying about getting enough money to cure my eplasia while it's still in the early stages—and I'll want cosmetic surgery so I don't resemble *him* too much."

"He'll be the one having the cosmetic surgery," said Egan. "Look at him. We can't let him go out in public looking like *that*."

There was a tense silence.

Dinnisen finally nodded his agreement. "I'll do what I can, Mr. Nighthawk."

"I'm sure you will," replied Nighthawk. "Or I *won't* do what I can."

"Is that some kind of threat?" asked Dinnisen.

"Not at all. Just a statement of fact."

Another silence.

"I hope you won't be offended by my observation," said Dinnisen, "but your predecessor was much easier to deal with."

"Of course he was," replied Nighthawk. "He was a newborn baby in the body of a man. *I'm* the Widowmaker."

"I know you are. That's precisely why you have to fulfill this contract. Our client put up millions of credits just to create you."

"Then he can put up another half million to keep me alive after I finish this job."

"And if he won't?"

Nighthawk smiled. It was a smile that sent a chill down Dinnisen's spine. "If he had someone who could make me do something I don't want to do, he wouldn't need me in the first place."

"A point well taken," said Dinnisen, nervously returning his smile.

"I'm glad we all understand each other," said Nighthawk. "As soon as the money's been deposited, you can sit down with me and tell me just how many hundreds of men I have to kill for it."

"Possibly no one," said Dinnisen.

"That's the upside," said Nighthawk. "What's the downside?"

"I think you've had enough surprises for one day," said Dinnisen. "Especially considering that it's the first day of your life." He rose and walked to the door of the chamber. "We'll talk again tomorrow."

"Shall we go too?" asked Egan as Dinnisen left the chamber.

"In a minute," said Nighthawk, walking over to look at the original Widowmaker. "Jesus! I—he—looks awful."

"Eplasia is an awful disease."

Nighthawk stared down at the disfigured, skeletal body. "You've waited a long time," he said softly. "I know what it means to you. I won't let you down."

He stood in silence for a moment, then turned to Egan. "Okay, let's go see the world."

# Chapter 1

*Jefferson Nighthawk stood two hundred yards from the burning targets, a laser pistol in his hand, and grimaced.*

"Six shots, five hits, elapsed time 4.13 seconds," announced Ito Kinoshita, the small, wiry man who was standing near him. "Very good."

Nighthawk shook his head. "It stinks. Set 'em up again."

"You're sure you don't want to rest? We've been at this for over an hour now."

"Not until I get it right." He looked around at the rolling green countryside. "It's not as if we're bothering anyone. I'd be surprised if there's a neighbor within five miles."

"You hit one hundred percent with your Screecher

and your bullet gun," said Kinoshita. "And you've got the laser up from fifty percent to five out of six, and doubled your speed. I'd call it a good morning's work."

"The laser's the one I'll use the most often," answered Nighthawk, frowning at the targets. "Makes the least noise, lightest in weight. And that's not five out of six targets I just burned. It's five out of six armed men; the sixth one just killed me."

"You're a perfectionist."

"In my business you don't live much past twenty if you're not."

"How often did you practice when you were . . . ?" Kinoshita paused, trying to find the right word.

"Alive?" asked Nighthawk wryly.

"Actively engaged in business, let us say."

"Not regularly. But I was used to my body and my weapons. They haven't made any major changes to these pistols"—he indicated the various weapons that were laid out on a table beside him—"but they're a little lighter in weight. It makes a difference. As for my body," he continued, "it's in perfect shape, and *that* requires adjustments."

"That's a problem?"

"Absolutely."

"Why?"

"I broke my hand when I was twenty-eight," explained Nighthawk. "I didn't realize it until now, but it made a difference in the way I held a gun. Not much of one, but enough to throw my aim off. Also, I'd taken a few burns and bullets in my younger days; that made me hold my body differently. A tiny difference, to be sure . . . but the difference between a kill and a miss can be pretty small, too."

Kinoshita gave a brief order to his control board, and six more targets flashed into existence.

Nighthawk stared at them for a moment, then aimed and fired the laser pistol again. There was a soft humming noise, and an instant later all six targets were ablaze.

"Time?" he asked.

Kinoshita checked the automatic timer. "3.86 seconds."

Nighthawk laid the laser pistol down next to the other weapons. "Better. Not great, but better." He turned to Kinoshita. "Let's get something to drink. This afternoon we'll try again, and tomorrow we'll work on fast draws. Blowing away six targets in three seconds won't do you much good if it takes you a couple of seconds to get your gun out of its holster."

They stepped onto the carefully manicured sliding trail that took them past the large angular main house at the center of the compound. Dozens of impressive-looking machines were caring for the grounds, sweeping up fallen leaves and atomizing them, mowing the vast lawn to a height of exactly two inches, dispensing insecticides. A robot maid exited one bungalow and made its way to the next.

"How many people can this place accommodate?" asked Nighthawk.

Kinoshita shrugged. "Twelve bungalows plus the main house. Maybe forty people. Any given day there are usually three or four members of the firm and their mistresses of all genders, and I've seen up to three hundred at their parties." He paused. "Of course, it's empty now except for you and me and the chef. I don't think they want anyone trying to buy you away."

"Is this where you trained the last clone?"

"No. Dinnisen's firm only bought this place about a year ago." They reached the door to Nighthawk's bungalow, which slid back after identifying them. Kinoshita immediately walked into the kitchen. "What would you like?"

"Water or coffee," answered Nighthawk.

"We have beer and whiskey."

"I don't drink alcohol when I'm working. Besides," he added, "I don't know how my body will react to it, and I'd rather not experiment until all my reflexes are up to par."

"It's your own body. How can you not know?"

"It's never had any liquor before. The last time I was this age, I'd probably consumed a swimming pool's worth. I have a feeling that makes a difference to a body's tolerance."

Kinoshita nodded in agreement. "I'm beginning to see why you lived so long," he said. "You're a very cautious man. You think of everything."

"There's more to being a bounty hunter or a lawman than being good with a gun," answered Nighthawk as Kinoshita ordered the kitchen computer to prepare two tall glasses of ice water. "Especially out on the Frontier. Which reminds me: when will Dinnisen be here?"

"Any time now. Late morning, he said."

"Good."

"Is there a problem?" asked Kinoshita, carrying Nighthawk's drink to him.

"Could be."

"What is it?"

"I don't buy his whole bullshit story," replied Nighthawk. "I've got a lot of questions for him." He downed half his glass of water in a single swallow, then stared at Kinoshita. "Unless *you'd* like to answer them?"

"Not me" was the reply. "I'm just your trainer. Which," he added, "is ridiculous. You're already twice as good as I am, and you know your body far better than I do."

"Did you train the last clone?"

"Yeah . . . but he was a baby with your body. I had to teach him how to shoot a gun, how to break a skull, everything." Kinoshita looked at Nighthawk with open admiration. "There's nothing I can teach you, Widowmaker."

"Sure there is," said Nighthawk. "There's a computer in the next room. They've changed a lot in the past century. I don't even know how to turn it on."

"What do you need from the computer?"

"The Widowmaker file. I'm sure it's protected, but you work for the organization. You ought to know how to access it."

Kinoshita frowned. "Why?"

"This organization sent a clone out two years ago, and as near as I can tell, he did what they asked him to do, and no one in Dinnisen's firm lifted a finger to save him. That's not going to happen to me. If I find they can't be trusted—and I suspect they can't—then I don't plan to ever put myself in a position where I need their help. I want to learn everything I can about the last clone: what he did, where and how he did it, who killed him, and why."

"I doubt I can access all that," answered Kinoshita. "But I'll be happy to bring up my own file. The problem is that it stops the day he left for the Frontier."

"I suppose it's better than nothing," said Nighthawk. "Will you get in trouble for letting me read it?"

"I don't think there's anything all that sensitive in it," said Kinoshita, walking to the next room. "Besides, if push comes to shove, I'd much rather be in trouble with Dinnisen than with you."

Kinoshita opened the file, then left him alone until Dinnisen showed up.

Nighthawk looked up from the computer as Dinnisen entered the bungalow. He deactivated the machine, then walked across the glowing carpet, which was woven from exotic alien filaments. When he reached a form-fitting chair that floated a few inches above the floor, he sat down.

Dinnisen and Kinoshita soon joined him in the small, cozy room. Dinnisen sat down opposite Nighthawk, while Kinoshita remained standing.

"Well, how are you coming along?" asked the lawyer.

"A couple of more weeks and I'll be ready."

"That long?"

"Just making sure I can properly protect your investment," said Nighthawk.

"*My* investment?" asked Dinnisen, puzzled.

"Me."

"I thought I explained that time was of the essence."

"Surviving is of the essence," said Nighthawk. "Time is secondary."

Dinnisen turned to Kinoshita. "Does he really need two more weeks?"

"It's not his decision," interrupted Nighthawk.

"Your predecessor was a much more pleasant person," said Dinnisen, making no attempt to hide his annoyance.

"That's probably why he's dead."

"I don't like your attitude, Mr. Nighthawk."

"I couldn't care less, Mr. Dinnisen. I'm not going out until I'm ready."

"I'm told that you put all three of your sparring partners in the hospital yesterday. How much readier do you have to be? Couldn't you at least have pulled your punches?"

"He *did* pull his punches," interjected Kinoshita. "That's why they're still alive."

Dinnisen stared at Nighthawk for a long moment, then shrugged. "All right," he said at last. "Two weeks." He took a deep breath, released it slowly, and made another attempt to be charming. "How do you like the facilities?"

"They're fine," said Nighthawk. "And Selamundi seems a nice enough world."

"And it's only two systems removed from Deluros, which is quite convenient," noted Dinnisen. He leaned forward. "Do you need anything? Different weapons? Protective clothing? Anything at all?"

"Yes, I need something."

"Just name it."

"Answers."

"I beg your pardon?"

"This cock-and-bull hunt you're sending me out on," said Nighthawk. "It reeks."

"I assure you—"

"Spare me your assurances," said Nighthawk. "I want the truth."

"I told you what you need to know."

"You haven't begun to tell me what I need to know, and I'm not putting my life on the line until you do."

"I'll go over it again," said Dinnisen irritably. He pulled out a tiny, pen-sized holo projector and cast an image of a slender young blonde woman in the middle of the room. "Cassandra Hill, the daughter of Cassius Hill, governor of Pericles V, has been kidnapped by a revolutionary named Ibn ben Khalid." The holograph of a ruggedly handsome man in his early thirties replaced the woman's image. "I have supplied you with dozens of holographs of each of them, and told you that he is presumed to be on the Inner Frontier. You have been given a considerable amount of money to draw from for whatever you need. You'll have your own ship. Ito will accompany you until you're comfortable with the changes that a new century has brought about. What more could you possibly want?"

"Plenty," said Nighthawk. "For starters, why me?"

"You're the best," said Dinnisen. "Or, once upon a time, you *were*."

"Not good enough," said Nighthawk. "The governor of Pericles V has the entire resources of his planet at his disposal. He can send out the Navy, and post a reward that will attract hundreds of bounty hunters. After all, he'll only have to pay one of them." He paused. "But someone has already paid to create me—and they've paid more than the girl is worth. I want to know why."

"Rescuing Cassandra Hill is only part of your mission," said Dinnisen, looking just a bit uncomfortable. He paused almost imperceptibly. "The other part is killing Ibn ben Khalid."

"*He's* what's worth all those millions, not *her*," said Nighthawk. Then, sardonically, "My sympathies to the grieving father."

"He *is* a grieving father," said Dinnisen.

"Sure he is," said Nighthawk. "But if the only way to kill him is to kill her too?"

Dinnisen sighed. "Then you kill them both."

"Yeah, he sure loves his daughter, this politician,"

said Nighthawk. "How comforting to know that nothing's changed in a century." He paused. "Hell, if I were her, I'd choose Ibn ben Khalid over Cassius Hill every time. Maybe she wasn't kidnapped at all."

"Look," said Dinnisen, "he would much prefer that you rescue his daughter and bring her back to him in one piece. That is the ideal scenario."

"You've been a lawyer too long. You couldn't utter a simple factual sentence if your life depended on it." Nighthawk lit a smokeless cigar. "All right, we'll overlook all the nuances of the father's motives. My job is to rescue her and kill him, and that's what I'll try to do." He paused. "Now, he's enough of a revolutionary that his death is the most important part of this assignment. How big is his army?"

"I don't know," said Dinnisen. "Big."

"So big that Cassius Hill doesn't really expect anyone to try to earn the reward?"

"If someone can find the girl, by herself, of course they'll claim it."

"But they won't go up against Ibn ben Khalid." It was a statement, not a question.

"I doubt it. He's got informants all over the Frontier. It would be almost impossible for anyone to infiltrate his organization." Dinnisen stared at Nighthawk. "Anyone but *you*. That's one of the reasons Hill made us the offer. Not only are you the best at what you do—but you haven't been around for a century. His agents won't know who you are, won't spot you as a bounty hunter or an employee of Cassius Hill."

"You undercharged," said Nighthawk.

"What?"

"If Hill's afraid to go up against Ibn ben Khalid's

men with his own planetary forces, you're not charging him enough."

"It's not a matter of fear. It's a matter of legality and cost. Pericles V has no authority on the Inner Frontier, and even if it did, equipping such a mission could cost billions."

"All the more reason to demand triple what he offered. If the alternative was putting billions into a military operation, with no guarantee of seeing his daughter alive again, he'd have paid."

"You're not going to hold him up for more money *again*?"

"No, I'm getting what I want," said Nighthawk. "But for a smart lawyer, you're a lousy bargainer, Mr. Dinnisen. It makes me wonder why."

"I assure you—"

"So you've said. Now let's get back to the business at hand. Has there been a second ransom demand?"

"No. Nothing since the tragedy on Roosevelt III."

"Let me make sure I've got this straight. Ibn ben Khalid contacted Hill through intermediaries, explained that he'd kidnapped his daughter, and demanded two million credits for her return. Hill sent his bag man to Roosevelt III with the money, as instructed. Once the man landed, he was killed and the money was stolen. Right?"

Dinnisen nodded. "Right."

"Is there any proof that Ibn ben Khalid was responsible for it?"

"Who else could it be?"

"Anyone who wanted two million credits in cash."

"It was *him*, take my word for it."

"I don't take your word for anything," replied Nighthawk. "In fact, until you tell me how Hill knew that Ibn ben Khalid had his daughter, I don't even take your word that he kidnapped her. He could just be an opportunist who heard she was missing and tried to pry a couple of million credits from a grieving father while she's shacked up somewhere with a lover. It wouldn't be the first time a smart man has pulled a bluff like that."

Dinnisen reached into a pocket, pulled out a small computer cube, and tossed it to Nighthawk.

"Here's a holo duplication of the first ransom demand. I just got it this morning."

"Okay, I see Ibn ben Khalid," said Nighthawk, looking at the cube. "Are you sure the girl's not an actress or a double?"

"The voiceprint checks out. It's her."

"I'll look at it later," said Nighthawk, placing the cube on a table.

"If we get anything further, I'll of course see that you get a copy."

"Fine. And I want everything you have on Hill."

"You have it."

"The father, not the daughter."

"Cassius Hill?" said Dinnisen, surprised. "Why?"

"He's involved. Why not?"

Dinnisen shrugged. "Whatever you say. I'll have it sent here this afternoon." He paused. "Do you have any more questions?"

"When I do, you'll be the first to know."

The lawyer turned to Kinoshita. "How's his progress?"

"He's the fastest and most accurate shot I've ever seen with every weapon he's tried," replied Kinoshita. "I should add that he's very disappointed in his performance. He's the Widowmaker, all right."

"That just means he's an exceptionally able killer."

"And you're an exceptionally able lawyer," said Nighthawk. "Ironic, isn't it?"

"What?"

"You get guilty people off the hook," said Nighthawk. "And eventually I get paid to hunt down your triumphs."

"You haven't liked me from the first moment you opened your eyes," said Dinnisen. "Why? What could I possibly have done to you in your four days of life?"

"To me? Nothing."

"Well, then?" demanded the lawyer.

"You sent my predecessor out without preparing him for what he would face."

"Nonsense. He knew what he had to do."

"Oh, he knew who to kill. But he didn't know how to live, and you didn't give him enough time to learn. That may work here in the heart of the Oligarchy, where you have laws, and lawyers, and more social safety nets than you can count—but out on the Frontier, that's a death sentence. And I think you knew it. I think you were fully prepared to kill him if he made it back alive."

"Kill him? Hell, we'd have rented him out again. He was a valuable commodity!"

"Well, I'm a human being and not a commodity," said Nighthawk. "Do you think you're going to rent *me* out after this assignment?"

"The firm of Hubbs, Wilkinson, Raith and Jiminez would be happy to enter into any such arrangement as your representative," said Dinnisen. "But I suspect you're too independent. I truly don't foresee us having a working relationship with you."

"You bet your ass."

"Have you any further questions before I leave?" asked Dinnisen.

"Just one," said Nighthawk. "You mentioned that I would have my own ship."

"That's right," replied the lawyer. "Mr. Kinoshita will handle it until you're able to fly it alone."

"Where is it?"

"It's due to be delivered either this evening or tomorrow morning."

"Good. Once we take off, I'll let you know where we're going."

"Your destination will be Innisfree II," said Dinnisen.

"Eventually," said Nighthawk. Both men looked at him questioningly. "I have some unfinished business to take care of first. It won't take long."

"Unfinished? After one hundred and nine years?"

Nighthawk dumped the nub of his smokeless cigar, lit another, and ignored the question.

# Chapter 2

· · · · · · · ·

*"You're sure you want to come with me?" asked Nighthawk,* surveying the spaceport as their ship touched down.

"I feel like I've got a vested interest in you," answered Ito Kinoshita.

"I hardly know you."

"Then let me amend my statement," said Kinoshita with a smile. "I feel like I've got a vested interest in the clan of Jefferson Nighthawks." He paused. "I'm your biggest fan, as well as being your instructor in a previous incarnation."

"Then you know why I'm on this world?"

"It doesn't take a genius to guess."

"All right. Let's go."

They left the ship and took a shuttle vehicle to the

spaceport's main terminal. When they arrived, Nighthawk approached an empty Customs booth, while Kinoshita sought out another.

"Name?" asked the computer's electronic voice as it scanned Nighthawk's retina, dentation, and skeletal structure.

"Jefferson Nighthawk."

"Passport?"

Nighthawk handed over the titanium disk.

"Purpose of visit?"

"Tourism."

"There was another Jefferson Nighthawk with an identical retinagram and—except for a scar on your thumb—similar fingerprints, who visited the Solio system two years ago, but he was sixteen years younger."

"That's no concern of mine," replied Nighthawk.

"My programming tells me that two men possessing the same names and retinagrams approaches the statistically impossible," responded the machine.

"Is the other Jefferson Nighthawk still here?"

"He died on Solio II."

"Then it couldn't have been me, could it?"

"I never stated that it was," answered the computer. "Still, the similarities are remarkable."

"What now?" asked Nighthawk.

"I am authorized to make value judgments after accessing my sixth-level programming. I am doing so now."

Nighthawk stood patiently as the computer buzzed and beeped while making its decision.

"How long will you be here, Mr. Nighthawk?" asked the machine after a moment's pause.

"Perhaps a day, possibly two."

"That is a very short visit for a tourist," noted the machine.

"Are short visits forbidden?"

"No, they are not," said the computer. It paused. "Your credentials are in order. Please note that we accept only Oligarchy credits. If you have any Far London pounds, Maria Theresa dollars, or New Stalin rubles, you may exchange them at the spaceport bank. All other currencies, including Kenyatta IV shillings from our neighboring system, should be left in your ship, as they are illegal currencies in this system, and our banks post no exchange rates for them."

"Understood."

"The penalty for selling or purchasing illicit drugs in any quantity, however minimal, is death. No legal appeal will be allowed."

"Understood."

"The atmosphere is seventeen percent oxygen, eighty-one percent nitrogen, two percent trace elements, and the gravity is 1.06 times Earth Standard. If you have any medical condition that will be affected by continued exposure to our air or gravity, please state so now and the proper life-support system will be supplied."

"None."

"Then you may be admitted. Welcome to Solio II."

The door at the far end of the booth dilated, and Nighthawk stepped through it. Kinoshita was waiting for him.

"What took you so long?"

"I'm not the first Jefferson Nighthawk with these retinas or fingerprints to land here," replied Nighthawk.

"Do you think you set off any alarms?" asked Kinoshita. "Will Customs send word ahead that you're here?"

"Why?" said Nighthawk. "I must be the last guy in the whole damned universe anyone expects to encounter. After all, Jefferson Nighthawk died here a couple of years ago; I can't imagine that the Customs computer has been programmed to keep an eye out for me."

"So where to now?"

"Now, since I don't feel like walking into the government building that houses Security headquarters and facing hundreds of guns, I find out where Hernandez lives, where he eats, where I can find him alone or nearly so." He paused. "I assume that megalopolis five miles east of here is the capital city, since this is the only spaceport on the planet. We'll go there, I'll spread a little money around, and before too long someone will tell me what I want to know."

"As simple as that?"

"The direct approach is usually the best."

Nighthawk and Kinoshita began walking through the spaceport. When they came to an exit, they caught a shuttle bound for the nearby city, and a moment later they were skimming a few inches above the ground as the shuttle raced across the flat, barren, brown landscape.

They got off in the middle of the city, a forest of angular steel-and-glass buildings with the streets crisscrossing in regular patterns. As he had predicted, it took Nighthawk less than an hour to get the information he sought. He soon stood before a small, elegant restaurant that was located just off one of the main thoroughfares.

"Are you really going in there?" asked Kinoshita.

"Why not?" responded Nighthawk. "It's lunchtime. Either he's here now, or he soon will be." He paused. "Do you know what he looks like?"

Kinoshita shook his head. "I never dealt with him. I've never even seen a holograph."

"It doesn't matter," said Nighthawk. "This place caters to businessmen and bureaucrats. If he's in uniform, I'll spot him."

"And if he doesn't eat here every day?"

"Then I'll pay him a visit at his home tonight," said Nighthawk. "But I'd much rather meet him here."

"There are more witnesses here," said Kinoshita.

"True. But the security's poorer."

"Are you sure?"

Nighthawk walked to the door. "Pretty sure," he said. "Still, there's only one way to find out."

"There are close to fifty men and women in here," whispered Kinoshita as Nighthawk paused in the doorway. "Some of them have got to be armed."

Nighthawk shrugged. "There's nothing I can do about it," he said, scanning the restaurant. Finally he stared intently at a uniformed man who was sitting with two other officers at a table in the farthest corner. "*That* has to be him."

"You've never seen him before," said Kinoshita. "How can you know?"

"He's the highest-ranking officer in the place," said Nighthawk. "Get a table halfway between him and the door and keep an eye on my back."

"I don't understand."

"This is the most powerful man on Solio II," explained Nighthawk. "Believe me, he'll have more than two bodyguards. Kill anyone who reaches for a gun."

"But—" said Kinoshita, but Nighthawk was already walking calmly through the room. Finally he stopped at the officer's table. "Do you mind if I join you?" he asked, sitting down before receiving a reply.

"Do I know you?" asked the officer, staring intently at him.

"That all depends," replied Nighthawk. "Are you James Hernandez?"

The man nodded. "You have the advantage of me, sir."

"Still a colonel, I see. You haven't advanced very far in the last two years."

Hernandez continued to stare at Nighthawk. "We met two years ago?"

"In a manner of speaking." Nighthawk leaned forward. "Look at me closely, Colonel Hernandez."

"*Nighthawk!*" exclaimed Hernandez after another moment had passed. Suddenly he turned to his two companions. "Leave us alone for a few minutes."

"But sir—" protested one.

"It's all right," Hernandez assured him.

The two officers got up reluctantly and moved to a nearby table.

Hernandez turned to Nighthawk and lit a Cygnian cigar. "You're much older," he noted. "I approve." He paused. "I suppose your friends on Deluros sent you here about the money?"

Nighthawk shook his head. "I'm on my own."

"Really?" said Hernandez. "Good. I can use a man like you, Jefferson Nighthawk."

"The way you used the last one?"

"He was a child masquerading as the Widowmaker," said Hernandez contemptuously. "You're the real thing—or at least you appear to be." He smiled. "We can do business together."

"Slaughter whole planetary populations?" asked Nighthawk, returning the smile.

"We'll start with three or four people who have been causing me problems lately and work our way up from there."

"Only three or four?"

"Do I look *that* beleaguered?"

"I'd rather expected you to be a general by now. There have to be more than three or four men standing between you and what you want."

"I found a properly malleable puppet to be governor," replied Hernandez. "Let *him* get the headlines and attract the assassins. I am content to rule the planet in obscurity." He grinned. "That's why I'm not a governor *or* a general."

"Very intelligent."

"So," said Hernandez, "can we do business?"

"Actually, I'm here on business," said Nighthawk.

Hernandez frowned. "I told you: if your people have sent you here about the final payment . . . "

"They haven't."

"Then why are you here?"

"Think hard, Colonel Hernandez. What is the very last thing you did to my predecessor?"

"I killed him," responded Hernandez. "But surely you know he was trying to kill *me* at the time." He paused, then added incredulously: "You're not going to tell me that you feel any loyalty to a clone you never met, a clone that was killed two years before you were created?"

Nighthawk stared coldly into Hernandez's eyes. "You didn't kill my father, or my brother, or my son," he said at last. "You killed someone even closer. You killed *me*. A younger, more innocent version, but me nonetheless." He continued staring at the colonel. "You never intended that I would survive my mission. You used me and set me up and when the opportunity presented itself, you killed me."

"Not *you!*" insisted Hernandez. "I killed a version of you that you never even knew!"

"It was a Jefferson Nighthawk—and I take it personally when Jefferson Nighthawks are killed."

"Fine. I won't kill you or that hideous monstrosity they cloned you from."

"You don't understand," said Nighthawk. "I'm not here to extract promises; I'm here to extract *payment*. And there is only one way you can pay for killing Jefferson Nighthawk."

Hernandez glanced quickly around the room. "You'll never make it out of here alive."

"You're not going to live long enough to know whether I do or not."

"Look, we can reach an accommodation," said Hernandez smoothly, his dark eyes seeking out the bodyguards who were spaced around the various tables. "Your principals think I owe them a few million credits. Come back to my office with me and we can work something out."

"I told you: I'm here for myself."

"Then I'll deal with *you*."

"I don't want your money," said Nighthawk firmly.

"Then why all the talk? Why didn't you just walk in and shoot me?"

"I wanted you to know *why*. In your last second of life, I wanted you to know that your death was neither a mistake nor an accident. It was because you used and betrayed and finally murdered Jefferson Nighthawk." He paused, then added with a sense of finality, "And now you know it."

Nighthawk got to his feet, pulled out a laser pistol in a single fluid motion, and as the weapon hummed softly with power, he burned a sizzling, bubbling hole between Hernandez's eyes. The officer slumped over, dead, as a woman shrieked. In the same motion he turned and killed the two officers at the next table.

Then, as Kinoshita watched, transfixed, Nighthawk, the one calm island in a sea of confusion, picked three more men from the crowd and burned them away. He surveyed the room, couldn't spot anyone else with the urge to be a hero, and walked through the restaurant, taking the stunned Kinoshita by the arm and heading for the door. As they stepped outside, he turned and melted the lock with his laser pistol, effectively sealing the staff and customers inside.

"You're everything they said you were!" remarked Kinoshita as they crossed the street and rounded a corner. He stopped and stared admiringly at Nighthawk. "I never saw anything like that!"

"Keep walking. There'll be a back entrance—and it'll only be a matter of minutes before someone remembers."

"So what do we do now?"

"We go back to the spaceport," answered Nighthawk, spotting a shuttle at rest and increasing his pace to reach it. "By the way," he added sardonically, "thanks for protecting my back."

"I never saw any guns," said Kinoshita defensively.

"You wait until their guns are out and you're dead. A man with that much clout figures to hire only the best."

"So he had some guardian angels spread around the restaurant in civilian clothes. How did you know which ones they were?"

"I didn't."

"But—"

"Anyone who ducked or sat still was a civilian.

Anyone who reached inside his tunic or jacket was an enemy."

"And if they were just reaching for their wallets?" asked Kinoshita as they reached the shuttle.

"Then I'd say they timed it very poorly," replied Nighthawk as the shuttle doors opened.

"Are you saying that—?" began Kinoshita.

"Shut up," said Nighthawk. Kinoshita looked at him questioningly. "This isn't the time or the place for this discussion."

Kinoshita fell silent, but his active imagination played out thirty or forty scenarios, each grimmer than the last. To his amazement, they reached the spaceport without incident and were soon racing out of the Solio system at light speed.

The instructor poured himself a drink, stared at his calm, relaxed companion for a long moment, and began to understand, for perhaps the first time, exactly who and what he was traveling with. It had just been a morning's work for Nighthawk, nothing to get excited about, nothing to celebrate, nothing to turn into song or fable.

Just *business*.

Suddenly Kinoshita was very glad that he was not one of the Widowmaker's enemies.

# Chapter 3

*Nighthawk sat at the control panel, sipping a mutated* fruit drink and staring at the viewscreen. Finally he looked across at Kinoshita.

"What planet do you want me to put you off on?" he asked.

"Do you think you're able to run the ship yourself?" responded Kinoshita.

Nighthawk smiled. "The panel looks different, and the galley cooks better meals, but if they've made a meaningful improvement in the past century, I sure as hell haven't been able to find it. You still say 'Take me to Binder X,' and then you relax for two days while the ship does what you ordered."

"Oh, they've made a few changes. Nowadays if it

spots an ion storm or a meteor swarm coming up on its flight path, it won't bother you for instructions. It'll avoid them on its own and then recalibrate its course."

"Big deal," said Nighthawk. "As far as I'm concerned, an ion storm is one of the few things that keeps you from being bored in deep space."

"They also fly a little faster."

"You could cross the whole damned galaxy in less than a month back in *my* time, and if you didn't want to look out the portholes or play games with the computer, you could go into DeepSleep, so what the hell difference does it make that it can do it in twenty-seven days instead of twenty-nine?"

"Not much," admitted Kinoshita. "But when an object approaches maximum performance, any improvements will seem small."

"Fine," said Nighthawk. "You still haven't answered my question: where do you want me to put you down?"

"Nowhere."

Nighthawk stared at him.

"I'd like to come along," continued Kinoshita.

"As a watchdog for Marcus Dinnisen?"

Kinoshita shook his head. "I've been in the Oligarchy too long. It's time I got back out to the Frontier."

"You're crazy," said Nighthawk. "If the odds weren't hundreds to one against pulling this job off, you don't think they'd have cloned me, do you?"

"I have confidence in you."

"Bully for you." Nighthawk paused. "I don't take partners. Anything I earn is already earmarked for me or for my dying double."

"I have enough money," said Kinoshita.

"No one has enough money."

"Look, I'll explain it as simply as I can. I used to be

a lawman and a bounty hunter. A damned good one, if I say so myself. I took enormous pride in my accomplishments." He paused, awkwardly trying to stake out a position halfway between admiration and hero worship. "You're the best I've ever seen, maybe the best there ever was. I want to watch you work."

"I'll have enough trouble protecting *me*. I won't be able to worry about you."

"I can take care of myself," said Kinoshita. "And I can be useful to you."

"Like you were at the restaurant?" asked Nighthawk with a sardonic smile.

"I'd never seen you in action before. I wanted to see just how good you really are, so I decided not to help unless you needed me." He paused. "It takes a hell of a lot to impress me, but I'm impressed. You're even better than the history books make you out to be." He looked into Nighthawk's eyes. "Next time I'll back you up. It won't happen again, I promise."

Nighthawk stared at Kinoshita until he shifted nervously in his seat. At last he said, "It damned well better not."

"Then am I coming along?" asked Kinoshita.

"For the time being."

"Thanks. I owe you."

"Fine," said Nighthawk. "Start paying."

"I beg your pardon?"

Nighthawk tapped his head with a forefinger. "I've got a lifetime of memories in here, but they're a century out of date." He paused. "For example, I *think* the biggest whorehouse on the Inner Frontier is Madame Zygia's on Tecumseh IV, but for all I know it's been out of business for ninety years."

"I see what you mean," said Kinoshita.

"So does Madame Zygia's still exist?"

"Madame Zygia's?"

"That's what we're talking about."

"I don't know," said Kinoshita. "I never heard of it."

"Find out," said Nighthawk. "And if it's not there anymore, find out where the biggest whorehouse *is*."

"I've heard that there's a huge one on Barrios II."

"Multispecies?"

Kinoshita shrugged. "I really couldn't say."

"Find out," repeated Nighthawk.

"All right," said Kinoshita. Then: "Why this sudden interest in whorehouses?"

"It's not sudden, and we're going to one."

*"Now?"*

"Now."

"Why don't we just stop at the next oxygen world? I don't suppose there's a world anywhere on the Inner Frontier that doesn't have a whorehouse."

Nighthawk shook his head. "I'm not looking for your everyday whorehouse."

"I'll find a luxurious one," Kinoshita assured him.

"That's not what I asked for. I need the biggest, not the best."

"Just what are you looking for?"

"I already told you," said Nighthawk, leaning back comfortably in his chair, putting one foot up on the panel, and closing his eyes. "Now let's see if you can find it."

"Is this some kind of test?"

"Just do it."

Kinoshita sighed and had the ship's computer start poring through its more esoteric data banks until he found out that Madame Zygia's was nothing more than a memory, and that the biggest brothel on the

Inner Frontier was indeed the Gomorrah Palace on Barrios II. He directed the ship to set a course for the Barrios system, then went off to the galley to get some lunch, all the while wondering why, if the Widowmaker was addicted to interspecies sex, his multitude of biographies never made mention of the fact.

# Chapter 4

*The Barrios system was perfectly placed, on the main* route between Terrazane, the huge world at the outskirts of the Oligarchy, and the Inner Frontier's vast Quinellus Cluster.

There were fourteen planets in all. Eight were gas giants. Four more were mining worlds that had long since been abandoned. The thirteenth boasted an ammonia atmosphere. But Barrios II was a bustling center of activity. It had started out as nothing but a refueling station. Then plutonium had been discovered, and it became the proudest of the system's mining worlds. When the plutonium ran out, it metamorphosed into an agricultural world, becoming the breadbasket for half a dozen nearby systems. Finally, thanks

to its favorable location and its constantly increasing
population, it became a major financial world, dealing in
thousands of rare commodities from the Inner Frontier,
and handling literally hundreds of different currencies.

One of Barrios II's landmarks was the Gomorrah
Palace, easily the biggest brothel on the Frontier, and
quite possibly the oldest as well. This was not a swank,
elegant temple of luxury like the fabled Velvet Comet,
which drew its clientele from the wealthiest men and
women in the galaxy. Instead, it was an efficiently run
operation, specializing in service rather than expensive
fantasy. From its meager beginnings almost a century
ago, it had undergone a series of facelifts and five addi-
tions, and now took up an entire city block. Some of
the locals objected to it, as had their parents and grand-
parents, but since the Gomorrah Palace brought in
more hard currency than any business on the planet
except for the branch of the Bank of Deluros VIII, no
one in authority ever seriously considered shutting it
down as long as it paid its taxes.

Nighthawk looked at the front entrance to the
Palace as he and Kinoshita approached it on foot.

"Not as impressive as one might expect, is it?" he
remarked dryly.

"I told you it wasn't," replied Kinoshita defensively. "We could have stopped at Pollux IV."

"I was observing, not complaining. This is the
place I want."

"I can't imagine why."

"Because the biggest whorehouse will have the
biggest selection."

"Just as the best whorehouse will have the best
selection," grumbled Kinoshita. "And the best whorehouse is about forty-five hundred light-years behind us."

"This'll do just fine."

"Whatever perverse needs you have, you could have taken care of them in much more luxurious surroundings on Pollux IV."

"I doubt it," said Nighthawk.

"Well, it may suit *your* tastes, but it sure as hell doesn't do much for *me*."

"Just as well. We won't be here long enough for you to avail yourself of their services anyway."

Kinoshita stared at him curiously.

"Just stay in the bar and have a drink or two. I expect to be through before you're done."

"Maybe you're right, after all."

"About what?" asked Nighthawk.

"If you're that fast an operator, a whorehouse like the one on Pollux IV would be wasted on you."

Nighthawk allowed himself an amused smile as they reached the front door, which melted before them and reconstituted itself after they had passed through to the large lounge. There were prints and holos—no originals—on the walls, and a long, gleaming bar along one wall. A few men were discreetly sitting inside "lineup booths," selecting their companions for the evening.

A once-beautiful and still strikingly handsome middle-aged woman, obviously the madam—or one of them, at least—walked up to Nighthawk and Kinoshita after they'd each ordered a drink.

"Welcome to the Gomorrah Palace," she said. "I don't recognize either of you."

"It's our first visit," said Kinoshita.

"Did you have anything special in mind?" she asked.

"Not really."

"How about any*one* special?" she continued with a knowing grin.

"It's possible," replied Nighthawk. "What have you got?"

"We have too many girls to do a live lineup," answered the madam. "But we can show you holographs of each of them."

"Fine," said Nighthawk. "Let's see them."

"Most men prefer the privacy of a booth when making their selection."

"My friend's just here to drink, and I'm not shy."

The madam shrugged. "Whatever you say."

She touched a small control on her bracelet, and suddenly a holograph of a gorgeous redheaded woman, no more that a foot high, floated a few inches above the bar. Nighthawk made no comment or gesture, and after a moment the holograph was replaced by another.

By the time the fortieth holo had appeared without eliciting any reaction from Nighthawk, both Kinoshita and the madam were wondering just what he was looking for. He found it in the forty-first holo.

"Stop."

Kinoshita stared at the holo in disbelief. "You're kidding!" he exclaimed at last.

"Why should you think so?"

"She's got to weigh three hundred pounds. And look at her features: she's not even human."

Nighthawk turned to the madam. "She's the one I want."

"I'm afraid that's not possible. She's in hospital."

"Have you got any other—?"

"—Balatai women?" She completed his sentence. "Just one other. They're quite rare, you know."

"So I've been told."

"And consequently they cost extra."

"How much?"

The madam stared at him, as if sizing him up. "Twelve hundred credits?" It was as much a question as an answer.

Nighthawk stared at her without speaking, and she became visibly uneasy.

"This your first time here, right?" she asked at last.

"Yes."

"Hell, make it an even thousand. I wouldn't want you to be unhappy with us." She paused. "We'll also take payment in Far London pounds, Maria Theresa dollars, or New Bombay rupees. There's a five percent conversion charge. If you have any other currency, you'll have to exchange it at a bank."

"A thousand credits is acceptable."

She turned to Kinoshita. "And how about you? Are you sure we can't find someone to interest you?"

"I'm sure you can," said Kinoshita bitterly. "But I'll just stay here at the bar and wait for my friend."

The madam shrugged. "Whatever makes you happy."

"Being happy's got nothing to do with it," muttered Kinoshita.

"Lead the way," said Nighthawk. "And put my friend's bar bill on my tab."

"Happy to," she replied, as Nighthawk followed her down a long, dimly lit corridor. A doorway dilated and they entered another building, then took an airlift to the third level.

"Here we are," said the madam, coming to a stop in front of an unmarked door. "You'll pay me now. Any tip you arrange will be paid directly to the lady of your choice."

She pulled out a pocket computer, which registered

Nighthawk's retina and thumbprint, paused for about ten seconds, and flashed a credit approval code.

"Enjoy," said the madam, turning and walking back to the airlift.

Nighthawk looked for a handle or a knob, couldn't find one, and finally said, "Open." The door slid back into a wall as he stepped through, then closed behind him.

Lying on a bed in a corner of the room, wearing something black, lacy, and skimpy, was a female. At first glance she appeared to be a normal human woman, but there were enough differences so that even the casual observer would quickly realize that while she had come from human stock, her branch of the Tree of Man had been evolving and changing for more than a few generations.

Her ears were round and lobeless. Her fingers were all of the same length. She had only four toes on each foot. Her pupils were not round but vertical slits. Her knees and elbows seemed somehow exaggerated, almost swollen.

Nighthawk stood where he was, carefully observing her. At first the woman struck a provocative pose, then another. Finally she stared at him, studying him as carefully as he was studying her.

"All right," she said after a minute had passed. "What's going on here?"

"I just bought you for the night."

"Why?" she said. "You don't want me."

"I want you very much," said Nighthawk.

"You know you can't lie to me. I'm a Balatai woman."

"I know."

"Well, then?" she said. "Why did you pay for my time if you don't want to have sex with me?"

"Because I have a business proposition for you, and I didn't know how else to contact you."

"I don't know what you're talking about," she said. "You've already made a business proposition, and the house has accepted it. Otherwise you wouldn't be here."

"That was business with *them*. Now I want to talk business with *you*."

She frowned. "What the hell are you talking about? You have no more desire for me than I have for you."

"Less, probably," said Nighthawk. "Now, are you going to listen to me or not?"

"You've paid for my time," she answered with a shrug. "If talking is your notion of a good time, go ahead. And watch your temper; you're starting to get angry."

"Irritated," he corrected her.

"Irritated, angry, what's the difference? They both wind up with me getting beat up."

"I'll never lay a finger on you," said Nighthawk. "Consider it carefully. You should be able to tell if I'm lying."

She stared at him curiously for a long moment. "Okay, you're not lying," she said at last. "Go ahead. You do the talking, I'll do the listening."

"My name is Jefferson Nighthawk. Does that mean anything to you?"

"No. Should it?"

"Not necessarily. In some places I'm also known as the Widowmaker."

"I remember reading stories about the Widowmaker when I was a little girl."

"That was me."

"It couldn't be," she said, sitting on the edge of the bed and staring at him with a mixture of curiosity and disbelief. "He died a century ago."

"Check me out. Am I lying?"

She frowned. "No." A thoughtful pause. "But that doesn't mean you're not crazy. A crazy man might believe that he's the Widowmaker, and I couldn't tell he was lying because he'd truly believe it."

"Fair enough," said Nighthawk. "When I start acting crazy, activate that alarm by your headboard and call for the bouncers. But in the meantime, why not assume I'm sane and hear me out? After all, I've paid for your time."

She continued staring at him, more curious than frightened. "All right, Jefferson Nighthawk, let's hear what you've got to say."

"To begin with, I'm a clone of the original Widowmaker."

"I thought clones were illegal."

"Most of them are."

"Including you?"

"Probably," said Nighthawk.

"Okay, you're a clone," she said, walking to the bar and pouring herself a drink. "So what?"

"I'm a clone with a difference. I was given the original's memories."

She looked him up and down, as if appraising him. "Can they do that?"

"They can." A pause. "They did. I've got 'em."

"So who's after you?"

Nighthawk smiled. "*I'm* after someone."

"Me?" She put the drink down, suddenly tense. "What did I ever do to you?"

He shook his head. "No, not you. I've been commissioned to rescue a woman who's been kidnapped, and to terminate her kidnapper."

"Terminate?" she repeated. "You mean kill him?"

"Right."

"I still don't understand: what does all this have to do with me?"

"The kidnapper is a revolutionary," said Nighthawk. "He's got an entire army protecting him and the girl. That means I can't approach him directly. I'm going to have to infiltrate his forces to get to him." He paused. "I had to infiltrate a gang of smugglers in 4986 . . . "

"You?"

"No, I mean the original me," said Nighthawk irritably. "Sometimes I get confused separating us." He grimaced. "He's the one who did it, but I'm the one who remembers it."

"What about it?"

"I used a Balatai woman," he said. "I think it's time to use another."

For the first time the woman's face came alive with interest. "You used one of us?"

"Yes," answered Nighthawk. "I think I would probably have been killed if I hadn't."

"What was her name?"

"I couldn't pronounce her real name. She had a human name she used, but it wouldn't mean anything to you."

"How interesting," mused the woman. "Someone actually had the good sense to use one of us for something meaningful, instead of games in a whorehouse." She paused and scrutinized him intently. "But why did you seek me out here? Why not go to my home world?"

"I don't know where it is."

"She never told you?"

Nighthawk shook his head. "It was a well-kept secret a century ago. If it's been made public since then, I wouldn't know about it."

"It hasn't," she answered. "We have enough problems without being exploited."

"Seems to me you're being exploited right here."

She shook her head. "I have my reasons for working here."

"What are they?"

"Personal."

Nighthawk sat down on the room's only chair. "I just paid a thousand credits for your time. How much of that do you get?"

"Three hundred, plus whatever tip we agree to."

"Come with me and I'll pay you two thousand a day for as long as the job takes."

She smiled at him. "You'll pay more than that, Widowmaker. Someone went to a lot of expense to create you. They can spend a little more and protect their investment."

"Twenty-five hundred," said Nighthawk.

"Five thousand."

"Don't get too greedy," he said. "That's a raise of almost seventeen hundred percent."

"Maybe I'm only worth three hundred credits a night here, but I'm worth a hell of a lot more than that to you. After all, who else but a Balatai can tell you if your cover has been penetrated, if your identity is known, if your enemy is aware of your presence?" She paused. "Of course, if you think you can get some other Balatai cheaper . . . "

"Maybe I can, maybe I can't," said Nighthawk. "But I don't have the time to find another one."

"There's another consideration," she said. "I have a contract with the Gomorrah Palace."

"Don't worry about it."

"Why not?"

"For the same reason the bouncer who's monitoring this conversation won't try to stop you from leaving." He paused. "Would *you* go up against the Widowmaker because some prostitute decided to break her contract?"

"No, I don't think I would." She paused and then smiled. "Have we got a deal, then?"

He shrugged and nodded. "What the hell, it's not *my* money I'm spending."

"You shouldn't have said that, Mr. Nighthawk," said the woman. "That'll cost you another thousand a day."

"Forget it. You named a price, I agreed to it. I don't renegotiate."

"If you don't, I'll stay here."

"Then stay," he said, walking to the door.

"You're bluffing."

He turned and faced her. "Am I?"

She stared at him for a moment. "No," she said slowly. "No, you're not."

"Well?" he said. "Am I leaving alone or with you?"

"Give me a moment to get dressed." She got to her feet and walked to a closet, then turned to him. "Mr. Nighthawk, you've bought yourself an empath."

# Chapter 5

"*Why not a telepath?*" asked Kinoshita after they had taken off and were heading deeper into the Inner Frontier.

"Find me one and I'll hire him," responded Nighthawk, relaxing in the pilot's chair.

"They say the Domarians are telepaths."

"They're aliens."

"They have less reason to fear or distrust you than most humans."

"Swans swim with swans, ducks swim with ducks," answered Nighthawk.

"What the hell does *that* mean?"

"It means I'll attract enough attention with a Balatai."

Kinoshita turned to the Balatai woman, who was sitting near the navigation tank, watching holographs of the ship making its way among the stars of the Inner Frontier. "I meant no offense," he said. "But my fortune is intertwined with his, so I want him to have the best chance."

"I know," she replied. "You don't believe it, Mr. Kinoshita, but reading your emotions isn't very different from reading your thoughts."

"It isn't?"

"Nine times out of ten."

"And the tenth time?" asked Kinoshita.

She smiled. "That's why he's the Widowmaker. Because the tenth time can get messy."

Kinoshita stared at her for a long moment and finally nodded his approval. "You'll do," he said decisively. "What's your name?"

"What name do you like?" she responded.

"I didn't realize it was up to us."

"Choose one."

"Melisande," said Nighthawk.

"Fine," she said. "Then I'm Melisande." She paused. "Who was she?"

"Nobody very important," said Nighthawk.

"Your emotions say you're lying," said Melisande. She turned to Kinoshita. "Perhaps *you'll* tell me."

"She was the woman who betrayed his predecessor," said Kinoshita.

She turned to Nighthawk. "Do you expect me to betray you?"

"No."

"Then why—?"

"It's a pretty name. I thought you might redeem it."

"In that case, I'm honored."

Kinoshita studied Nighthawk carefully, and finally spoke. "First Hernandez and now Melisande. I think you'd be better off if you forgot about the previous Nighthawk's life and concentrated on your own."

"I'm an orderly man with an orderly mind," answered Nighthawk. "I'm just taking care of the things that affect *all* Jefferson Nighthawks."

"I'd concentrate on Ibn ben Khalid if I were you."

"If you were me you'd be six inches taller and a hell of a lot faster with a gun—and you'd be an orderly man."

"It seems to me that an orderly man wouldn't proceed without a plan. How do you intend to make contact?"

"The simplest and most efficient way possible."

"Jeff—your predecessor—shot up a bunch of the Marquis of Queensbury's men and offered himself as their replacement," noted Kinoshita. "I seem to remember from the reports that he also fought the Marquis to a standstill."

"My predecessor was two months old," said Nighthawk. "He can be forgiven for his methods."

"So what do *you* plan to do?"

"I plan to use the tools at my disposal."

Kinoshita frowned. "Your weapons?"

"God gave you a brain," said Nighthawk irritably. "You offend Him when you refuse to use it."

"Why don't you just tell me what tools you're going to use and stop insulting me?"

Nighthawk stared calmly at him. "I'm going to use you and Melisande, of course."

"How?"

"She'll enter a bar or a restaurant and sit down alone. A few minutes later you and I will come in and sit elsewhere. After we've had a drink or two, we'll start discussing Ibn ben Khalid, and we'll make sure we're overheard. I'll praise him to the skies, you'll argue that he's the worst kind of slime—and Melisande will read the emotional reactions. When she finds one that's strong enough, we'll assume he's working for Ibn ben Khalid and I'll follow up on it."

"If he doesn't kill me first," added Kinoshita ruefully.

Nighthawk shrugged. "You want to come along. That's the chance you take when you play for high stakes."

"I'm *not* playing for them," Kinoshita reminded him.

"Of course you are," said Nighthawk. He leaned forward on his seat and stared intently at the smaller man. "Do you really think I haven't figured out that you're here to keep an eye on me for Dinnisen, and that you're to report to him the second it looks like I might wander off the reservation?"

"There no sense denying it," said Kinoshita. "Sure I'm being paid to keep tabs on you—but I just look on it as found money. I can't stop you from doing anything you want to do. Hell, I wouldn't if I could. Like I told you, I'm a fan."

"I know that," said Nighthawk. "But you'd better understand that there'll come a day when you'll have to choose between me and your employer."

"Easy choice. Dinnisen can't kill me; you can." Suddenly Kinoshita grinned. "You see? I *do* have an orderly mind."

"In the meantime," continued Nighthawk, ignoring his companion's attempt at humor, "I'll dictate your reports back to Deluros VIII."

Suddenly Melisande spoke up. "You're *good*, Widowmaker!" she said admiringly. "You don't need me. Hell, you don't need anyone!"

"I'm flattered that you think so, but I know what I need. My job is to kill Ibn ben Khalid. Let's suppose, just for the sake of argument, that he has a million followers; that's just a tiny drop in the bucket when you consider that there are almost two trillion Men abroad in the galaxy. But it means the odds are a million to one against me. If you can lower the odds, then I'll use you."

Melisande broke in. "So where are we going?"

"I'm not sure yet. Deeper into the Frontier."

"Any world in particular?"

Nighthawk shook his head. "I don't suppose it makes much difference—except that I don't want to set down on any world where my predecessor landed."

"Why not?"

"Just in case he wasn't as efficient as I am."

"I don't follow you."

"He may have left some enemies alive. I won't know who they are, but some of them might recognize me. That's a suicidal situation, and if the Widowmaker was suicidal, he would have taken his life when he contracted eplasia rather than freezing himself on the slight chance that someone would effect a cure."

"You have eplasia?" she asked, backing away.

"Do I look like I have eplasia?" he asked.

"Your flesh says no, your emotions say yes."

"That's because my flesh doesn't know it yet," replied Nighthawk. "It's in the very early stages. You won't be able to notice it for another year or two—and by that time I'll be dead or cured."

"You should have told me before I agreed to come with you," said Melisande.

"It's like cancer used to be—deadly, but not contagious. You may contract it someday, but you won't catch it from me."

She stared at him for a moment, then relaxed. "Okay, you're telling the truth." She paused. "As you know it, anyway."

There was a high-pitched beeping sound.

"What was that?" she asked, as Nighthawk got to his feet and walked to the galley.

"Time for another shot of whiskey," he said, pulling out a bottle and taking a swallow.

She frowned. "You have to remind yourself to drink?"

"As a matter of fact, yes," answered Nighthawk.

"I don't understand."

"I woke up a month ago in a body that had never had a drink of alcohol. I work in a profession where a lot of information gets traded in taverns. The first few times I took a drink I was giddy and uncoordinated for an hour afterward. I'm trying to get my system used to it, so a few shots of whiskey won't affect my judgment or my reflexes."

"You're a very careful man."

"The graveyards are full of careless ones."

"Someone ought to collect your little homilies and put them in a book," she said with a smile.

"Are you volunteering?"

"Not me. My talents lie in other directions." Suddenly she looked around. "Where do I sleep?"

"We'll probably be two or three more days before we touch down," said Nighthawk. "How about a Deep-Sleep machine?"

She shook her head vigorously. "I don't trust them."

"I can vouch for at least one of them working for over a century."

"Not interested."

"All right," replied Nighthawk. "There are two cabins. You can have mine, and either Ito or I will sleep out here in the control room."

"Thank you," said Melisande. "Where is it?"

"You've already been to the head. Mine is the door just past it on the left."

"Just making sure. I wouldn't want to open it and find myself bumping into the nuclear pile."

She walked to the door, waited for it to melt before her, and walked into the cabin while the door quickly reconstituted itself behind her.

"You know," said Nighthawk, sitting down and ordering his chair to fold around him, "I could use some sleep myself."

He closed his eyes, and was soon breathing regularly.

*I don't know*, thought Kinoshita, looking at the Widowmaker with concerned eyes. *This guy is obsessed with the first clone. He seems stable enough, but I wonder . . .*

Suddenly he was aware of Melisande, standing in the doorway to her cabin.

"I read your concern," she said softly.

"It's a legitimate one," answered Kinoshita.

"Then let me address it: Jefferson Nighthawk is as normal and well adjusted as any man I've met."

She turned and went back into her room.

*That's a pretty comforting statement*, thought Kinoshita. *Until I remember just what kind of men you've been meeting . . .*

# Chapter 6

*The Blue Dragon wasn't a typical Frontier bar. For one* thing, it was run by its namesake. For another, it catered to Men and aliens in almost equal percentages. For a third, it offered no sexual services. For a fourth, it didn't have any gaming tables.

It was also one of the few leads provided by Cassius Hill on the possible whereabouts of Ibn ben Khalid.

It was that first item, though, that made its reputation. The owner was a blue-skinned alien, covered with octagonal scales, with a face almost as elongated as a Shetland pony's. He stood erect and had opposable thumbs. He also possessed vestigial wings from an earlier point in his race's evolution when his progenitors either flew or, more likely, rode high upon the thermals.

His chest was angular and oddly shaped, as if once, a few thousand generations ago, his wings were much stronger and were manipulated by a coil of muscles that was clearly visible around his rib cage. He had a short, flat tail, one that in eons past had functioned as a rudder.

His eyes were the palest blue, and his teeth were a rich violet. He had two sets of nostrils, separated by a couple of inches, on each side of his long face. There were no ears, just pulsating slits on the side of his head.

He wasn't the only member of his race, but he was, so far as anyone knew, the only member that had migrated to a human-occupied planet in the Inner Frontier. Whenever anyone asked the name of his race, or the name or location of his home planet, he answered them promptly and truthfully—in his native language, which was an assortment of guttural clicks, grunts, and whistles.

He called himself Blue Eyes, and pretty soon so did everyone else.

"Good evening, good evening," he crooned as Nighthawk and Kinoshita entered his bar on Sylene IV, which circled a dull yellow sun, dragging two moons with it. "I don't think I've seen you here before."

"Probably we all look alike to you," answered Nighthawk wryly, looking around until he spotted Melisande nursing a drink at a table in the darkest corner of the place.

Blue Eyes threw back his head and hooted.

"Is that a laugh?" asked Nighthawk.

"You think only Men have a sense of humor?" shot back Blue Eyes. "Where are you two from and where are you heading, and how long can I entice you into staying on Sylene?"

"Don't tell me—you own the hotel, too."

"Okay, I won't tell you."

Nighthawk stared at Blue Eyes for a moment. "Never saw an alien like you before."

"Never will again, either," said Blue Eyes. "But let's keep in mind that on this world, you're as much an alien as I am."

"You speak the language very well," continued Nighthawk. "No accent, and no formality—your slang sounds very natural."

"Languages are easy for dragons," said Blue Eyes. "Giving up virgins—now *that* was hard." He threw back his head and hooted again.

"As long as you feel compelled to entertain us, the least I can do is buy you a drink."

"I never drink with the customers, but I'll be happy to sit with you for a while." He turned to the bar. "Nicholas, bring me my chair."

A young man, underweight and carelessly dressed, immediately stood up, walked over to a strangely configured chair, and carried it over to the empty table where Blue Eyes was waiting.

"Thank you," said the dragon. "Gentlemen, this is Nicholas Jory. He has spent the last three years recording everything I say in my native tongue and trying to create a dictionary of my language."

"How far along are you?" asked Kinoshita.

"About thirty words," said Nicholas. "Maybe thirty-two."

"In three years?"

"That's more progress than is made on a lot of alien tongues in the same period of time," replied Nicholas. He frowned thoughtfully, then continued. "The biggest problem is determining whether the alien is intelligent. A lot of nonsentient animals communicate by vocalizing."

"How long did it take you to learn Terran?" Kinoshita asked Blue Eyes.

"About a week." The dragon smiled—as much as he *could* smile, anyway. His jaws parted and his eyes narrowed. "It's a knack."

"The government could use you in the Alien Affairs section," remarked Nighthawk.

"The Oligarchy doesn't hire nonhumans, or hadn't you noticed?" said Blue Eyes.

"They used to," said Nighthawk.

"Not since the Domarian Rebellion," answered the dragon, as Kinoshita put his heel atop Nighthawk's toe and leaned on it.

*All right, it happened in the past hundred years and I'm supposed to know about it. Now leave my toes alone.*

"*I* used to work for them," volunteered Nicholas. He grimaced. "Until we had a slight disagreement about taxes."

"Oh?"

Suddenly Nicholas grinned. "They said taxes were mandatory, and I said they were voluntary. So I came out to the Frontier where there aren't any taxes at all."

"So let's all sit down and get to know one another," said Blue Eyes, finally lowering his bulk onto the chair Nicholas had brought. He signaled to the bartender, who brought over a bottle and three glasses.

"Sounds good to me," said Nighthawk, as he and Kinoshita sat down across from him.

"Try to get him mad," said Nicholas, picking up a chair from a nearby table and carrying it over.

"Why?" asked Nighthawk, curious.

"Because when he gets mad, he curses in his native language. The rest of the time he speaks Terran, just to annoy me."

"Be careful, my friend," said the dragon. "If you annoy me enough, I'll start speaking in dead tongues like English or Swahili and *really* drive you crazy."

"Can you really speak dead human languages?" asked Nighthawk.

"Of course," answered Blue Eyes. "Languages are easy. Giving up drugs is hard."

Nighthawk saw what he hoped was a small opening, and plunged in. "How about Arabic?"

"Arabic's a very broad word, Mr. . . . ah . . . you know, I never did catch your name."

"Nighthawk. Jefferson Nighthawk. And this is Ito Kinoshita."

"You know, I used to hear stories of a Jefferson Nighthawk," said the dragon. "He had quite a reputation."

"I've heard 'em too. But *that* Nighthawk lived more than a century ago."

"So they say," replied Blue Eyes. "Where were we?"

"We were talking about Arabic."

"And I was about to explain that what we know as Arabic probably covers a couple of hundred dialects. To say that two people are similar because they both speak Arabic is like saying that the Raphinites and the Yorbans are the same simply because they both breathe chlorine."

"Point noted."

"Still, I'm curious to know why you were interested in Arabic."

"Simple enough," said Nighthawk, finally pouring

himself a glass of blue-tinted whiskey and taking a swallow. "Ibn ben Khalid is an Arabic name. If he has to issue orders and he's not sure that his communication system is secure, he can do it in an Arab dialect, and probably no one monitoring him would have any idea what he's saying."

"An intriguing thought," admitted Blue Eyes. "But I suspect Ibn ben Khalid is as ignorant of dead languages— including that one—as you yourself are."

"Still, it's an interesting idea," interjected Nicholas. "Maybe I'll suggest it to him the next time I see him."

Nighthawk wanted to ask, *Do you see him often?*, but fought back the urge.

"Lots of death tonight," remarked Blue Eyes. "Dead languages, dead gunfighters."

"Lot of death on the Frontier," responded Nighthawk.

"Maybe a little less than there used to be."

"Why should you think so?" asked Nighthawk.

"You brought up the reason—Ibn ben Khalid."

*Speak up now, Ito, or you're going to find out what getting your toes ground under someone's heel really feels like.*

"I hear he's nothing more than a kidnapper," said Kinoshita, as if he had somehow heard Nighthawk's thoughts.

"Actually, he's a *lot* more than a kidnapper," answered Blue Eyes. "I assume you're referring to Cassius Hill's daughter."

"They say he's holding her for ransom," continued Kinoshita. "That sure sounds like a common kidnapper to me."

"There's nothing common about him," said the dragon.

"I say he's a kidnapper and a murderer!" shouted Kinoshita, wondering just how far he could go before someone simply pulled a weapon and shot him.

"True," said Nighthawk. "But those aren't necessarily bad things to be when you're fighting for a just cause."

"When is murder ever good?" demanded Kinoshita.

"When your enemy is even worse," answered Nighthawk. "Maybe it's not pretty, but you do what you have to do."

"Let's not lose our tempers," said the dragon. "Ibn ben Khalid has never wronged anyone at this table."

"Damned right," chimed in Nighthawk. "And if he was here right now, I'd tell him so." *Damn! I wish I could look at some other faces in here. Are we loud enough, Melisande? Are they reacting?*

"In fact," added Blue Eyes, "I can tell you all a story about Ibn ben Khalid to prove my point."

"Spare us another of your meandering stories," said Nicholas.

"Yeah," added Kinoshita. "I don't need to hear you apologize for him."

"As you wish," said the dragon with a shrug that made every scale on his body shimmer.

*Thanks a lot, pal. Don't overplay your goddamned role, okay? We need all the information we can get.*

"So, Mr. Nighthawk, where do you come from and what do you do?"

"I come from out there," answered Nighthawk, waving his hand carelessly in a motion that encompassed roughly half the galaxy. "And I'm a troubleshooter."

"Trouble walks in and you shoot it?" asked Blue Eyes with another reptilian grin.

"That's perhaps a bit too literal," said Nighthawk. "I fix problems."

"What kind of problems?"

"What kind have you got?"

Blue Eyes sighed deeply. "It's been a long time since I've been with a lady dragon."

Nighthawk chuckled. "That kind isn't exactly in my line."

"I had a feeling it wasn't," replied Blue Eyes ruefully. He turned to Nicholas, who was pouring himself another drink. "Hey, go easy on that stuff. You've had half a bottle already."

Nicholas got up and staggered off without a word. Then, just in case his indignation had been missed or misinterpreted, he walked back, picked up his chair, tried to remember where he'd gotten it from, suddenly looked very confused, and sat down on it again.

"Did you have a nice trip?" asked Blue Eyes.

"Not bad, not bad," replied Nicholas. Suddenly he leaned forward until his head was on the table, and began snoring.

"I guess that's the end of today's language lesson," said Blue Eyes. Suddenly he uttered a totally incomprehensible sentence in his native tongue. "Just so you can tell him what he missed." He turned to Kinoshita. "I haven't yet asked you what *you* do, Mr. Kinoshita?"

Kinoshita jerked a thumb in Nighthawk's direction. "I'm with him," he said. "Until he decides to get us both killed by Ibn ben Khalid."

"I'm not going up against him," said Nighthawk. "Hell, I'm on his side."

"That's what I meant," said Kinoshita. "You can't trust a killer."

"I'd watch what I said about him if I were you," said Nighthawk ominously.

"Gentlemen, gentlemen," said Blue Eyes, rising to his feet. "I will not permit any altercations in this establishment."

Kinoshita made a vague gesture with his hand which could have meant anything from defiance to acquiescence, then also stood up.

"Okay, I know when I'm not wanted. I'm out of here." He turned and started walking to the door.

"Has he got a place to sleep?" asked Blue Eyes.

"That's not your problem," replied Nighthawk.

"You're absolutely right." He sat down again, staring at Nighthawk through his pale blue eyes. "I like you, Mr. Nighthawk. Tell me some more about yourself."

"There's not much to tell."

"Oh, I think there is. There's something about the way you carry yourself, something about the way you choose your words . . . something *dangerous*. Forgive an indelicate question, but how many men have you killed?"

"Forgive an indelicate answer, but go fuck yourself."

"I can, you know," answered Blue Eyes. "That's why I haven't spent my savings on a lady dragon."

"I don't want to destroy your self-confidence, but whether you can actually fuck yourself or not is a matter of complete indifference to me."

The dragon hooted his laughter again. He made a brief signal with his hand, and a moment later the bartender brought over a spherical bottle and a tall, thin glass. Blue Eyes opened the bottle, filled the glass halfway, then reached for the whiskey and filled it to the top. It began smoking and sizzling.

"I thought you didn't drink with the customers," noted Nighthawk.

"You were a customer when I said that. Now you're a friend."

"What *is* that stuff?"

"I suppose it really needs a name, doesn't it?" said Blue Eyes thoughtfully. "I first encountered it in the Deneb system. A mixture of Bilotei rum—it isn't really rum at all, but that's what they call it—and pure Sirian whiskey. Wonderful stuff." He took a sip. As he did so his eyes rolled back until only the whites showed, but Nighthawk couldn't tell if that was a reaction to the concoction or an inadvertent physical reaction caused by swallowing. "I think we'll name it after you, Mr. Nighthawk."

"A Nighthawk?"

"A Widowmaker."

"The Widowmaker died a century ago."

"All the more reason to find ways to keep his memory alive." He took another sip. "Though of course there are more meaningful ways."

"Oh?"

"That is, if your skills lie in the same direction."

"It's possible."

"How long will you be on Sylene, Mr. Nighthawk?"

Nighthawk shrugged. "How long do you want me to be here?"

"Another day, perhaps two, while I check you out."

"You won't be able to."

"Why not, pray tell?"

"I took this name less than a year ago. At the same time, I had laser surgery on my retinas and I had fingerprint grafts. I'm not on file anywhere, not with the Oligarchy, not with anyone else."

"A man who's not on file with the Oligarchy?" repeated the dragon. He threw back his head and hooted.

"What's so funny?"

He hooted once more, then finally managed to control himself. "What could possibly say more about your skills than that?"

# Chapter 7

"Well?" demanded Nighthawk.

They were back on the ship, sipping coffee made from hybrid beans that had been imported from the green slopes of Peponi's mountains.

"Most of them didn't react at all," answered Melisande. "They couldn't care less about Ibn ben Khalid."

"Who *did* care?"

"The one you call Nicholas Jory," she replied. "Every time Ito would slander Khalid, it was all he could do to keep from showing his rage."

"Is there any way you can tell if he simply admires Khalid or if he knows something more, like where he is or how to reach him?"

She shook her head. "No, he was drinking too heavily. It was just rage."

"What else *could* it have been?" asked Kinoshita curiously.

"Fear. Worry. Concern. Either at the thought of you going after Khalid—"

"That's silly. He's got an army to protect him."

"—or the mention of Cassandra Hill, who could conceivably be stolen back from him."

"Ah," acknowledged Kinoshita, nodding. "What about Blue Eyes?"

"I can't read aliens well enough to tell you with any degree of certainty."

"He seemed just like us beneath the admittedly hideous surface."

"Absolutely not!" she responded. "Never make that assumption. What you saw was protective coloration. He has very little more in common with you than an insect does." She turned to Nighthawk. "So what is your next step?"

"I wait for Blue Eyes to check me out while I'm doing the same to him, and when he finds out that what I've told him is true—he can't find me in any computer in the Oligarchy—then I hope he'll try to recruit me."

"Oh, there's no question he wants to recruit you," agreed Kinoshita. "But for what? I think rum-running is at least as likely as serving in Ibn ben Khalid's army, such as it is."

"Probably you're right," said Nighthawk. "That's why we're not about to put all our eggs in one basket." He turned to Melisande. "I passed the local jail on the way back to the ship. There can't be ten cells there, and I'm sure they're not all occupied. Have the ship's computer print you up some credentials saying that you're with some charitable organization. Then buy some desserts at a local bakery, take 'em over to the jail, and explain that they're for the prisoners. The guards will want to harass you—until you give 'em a couple of cakes or pies, that is. Then they'll let you through."

"But my credentials are no good. Anyone can print them up."

"Right. And the guards will check anyone who wants something—but why should they check on someone who's giving things away?"

"And if I'm jailed?"

"Kinoshita will be right outside. If you're not out in an hour, he'll pay your bail or pay off any guards who need it in order to get you released."

"All right," said Melisande. "Once I'm in, what do I do?"

"Simple. Give a present to each prisoner, and mention Ibn ben Khalid and Cassandra Hill to each of them. Then remember if anyone reacts."

"Why?"

"Do *you* know where they are?"

"No, of course not."

"Well, neither do I. But if you get the kind of reaction from one of the prisoners that convinces you *he* knows, we'll spring him and take him with us."

"I thought *I* was what you needed."

"What I need is protection and insurance, and I plan to get all I can of both."

"What will you be doing in the meantime?"

"Sleeping," answered Nighthawk.

"Sleeping?" she repeated, half-amused and half-outraged.

"Who knows when I'll get another chance? In this

business, you grab it when you can. The computer can put together Blue Eyes' profile for me while I'm asleep."

"If Melisande finds what you're looking for, do you want me to bail him out?" asked Kinoshita.

Nighthawk shook his head. "No, that'll be my decision."

"Why? Look at the time I could save you."

"Because if we guess wrong and he winds up trying to shoot us or warn Ibn ben Khalid, I'd hate to have to kill you for getting us into such a jam."

"Right," said Kinoshita promptly. "Your call."

"I'm glad we see eye to eye on things," said Nighthawk dryly.

# Chapter 8

As Nighthawk walked back to The Blue Dragon, he got the distinct impression that he was being followed. He knew enough not to turn and look directly, but he could see swift, subtle reflections of motion in the store windows and on the metal doors of vehicles that he passed.

If someone wanted to kill him, they would have fired their weapons already, so he assumed that his shadow either wanted to talk with him or find out where he was going. And since there wasn't much doubt where he was going—it was the only place he'd gone the night before when he'd left the ship, and it was nighttime again—he decided that his tail wanted to talk.

The only question remaining was: make it easy, or

make it hard? If they were recruiting a killer, he'd be well advised to duck into an alley—or whatever passed for alleys in this crazy-quilt checkerboard of human and alien streets—and lie in wait for his tracker, disarm him, possibly rough him up a little, and then find out who sent him. It would be an impressive display.

But he was pretty sure Ibn ben Khalid had more killers than he knew what to do with. This was juvenile thinking, the kind the younger Widowmaker clone was prey to.

No, the more he thought about it—and he thought very rapidly, given the circumstances—the more he was convinced that someone simply wanted to talk to him. Now, *why* someone should want to talk to Jefferson Nighthawk—for the Widowmaker had been dead a century, and no one here knew otherwise—was a mystery to him, but one he decided to solve.

He came to an alien restaurant that catered to Canphorites and Lodinites, looked in the window until he saw another flash of motion reflected in it, and then entered. The headwaiter, a furry orange marsupial of the Kragan race, looked terribly distressed when confronted by a Man, but managed to control itself long enough to lead Nighthawk to a table.

"We are pleased to serve you," it said into a T-pack that translated its voice into cold, unemotional Terran words and tones, "but I must advise you that you will be unable to metabolize most of the items on our menu."

"I'm game if you are," responded Nighthawk.

The Kragan listened to the translated words, then uttered a squawk loud enough to attract attention from the nearby tables—those few that weren't already staring at Nighthawk with hostility.

"I am not a game meat!" said the little marsupial. "You cannot eat me! We cannot eat each other!"

"Bad translation," said Nighthawk. "You really should learn to speak Terran."

"I suppose it never occurred to you to speak Kragan."

"No, it never did. I don't want your money; you want mine. That means you must make the accommodation."

The Kragan stared at him for a long moment. "You do not wish to eat me?"

"It will cheer you to no end to know that I find the thought totally repugnant."

"Good," said the Kragan. "What will you order?"

"Just water for the moment. I'll be joined very shortly, and then you can explain your menu to us."

"I see no other human," remarked the Kragan.

"I didn't say it was a human."

"Then what is it, so I can be alert for it when it enters?"

"That's not your concern," replied Nighthawk. "Whatever it is, it will find me."

"True," agreed the Kragan. "If you have an instinct for protective coloration, it is not functioning."

"Thank you for that observation. Now please get my water and then leave me alone."

"There is one more thing I must tell you," said the Kragan. "We do not accept Oligarchy credits."

Nighthawk pulled out a handful of gold Maria Theresa dollars and laid them on the table.

"Good enough?" he asked.

The Kragan looked, blinked, wrinkled its nostrils—which was as close as it could come to a satisfied smile—and left to get Nighthawk his glass of water.

When it came back, it placed the water down on the table and reached for the dollars.

Nighthawk slapped its furry hand.

"Not until after I've ordered and eaten," he said.

"How do I know you won't pick up all the dollars and walk out with them?" asked the Kragan in what Nighthawk was sure were petulant tones prior to the T-pack's translating them into a dull monotone.

"How do I know you won't poison me?" he shot back.

The Kragan stared at him for a long moment, as if this was a fascinating new idea that bore serious consideration, and then waddled off.

Nighthawk sipped his water and looked around. There were seventeen Canphorites, eight Lodinites, a couple of Kragans, all trying very hard to pretend there wasn't a Man in their midst. One small Lodinite child, perhaps four years old and only two-thirds grown, stared at him openly, as if he'd never seen a Man before. He had, of course, but Nighthawk thought it was a fair bet that he'd never seen one inside an alien restaurant.

Finally he looked up at the walls. His first impression was that they were covered with works of non-representational art—but as he studied them more carefully, he saw certain themes and color schemes reappearing time and again, and decided they were probably *very* representational to the beings that frequented this restaurant.

Suddenly a tall alien—sleek, red, humanoid, almost gleaming in the dull light of the restaurant—entered and walked directly to Nighthawk's table.

"May I join you?" it asked in harsh, grating syllables.

Nighthawk nodded. "I assume you got tired of waiting for me to come out."

It was the alien's turn to nod. Its ears, though no larger than a man's, flopped wildly with the motion, reminding Nighthawk of nothing more than the re-creations he had seen of African elephants.

"Why are you here?" asked the alien. "You cannot consume this food without becoming ill."

"I thought you'd rather speak to me here than at The Blue Dragon. But if I'm wrong, we can go there right now." He half rose from his chair.

"You are not wrong."

Nighthawk settled back down. "Have you got a name?"

"Everyone has a name, Jefferson Nighthawk."

"Would you care to tell me what it is?"

"In due time."

"All right, then—at least tell me what race you are?"

"It is I who shall ask the questions," said the alien.

"That's a matter of some debate," replied Nighthawk calmly. "It is I who has his gun trained on your belly beneath this lovely table."

The alien tensed, but chose not to verify the statement by looking.

"You cannot pronounce my name, but another Man I worked with many years ago called me Friday, and that is the name I use when dealing with Men. I am a member of the Projasti people of Czhimerich, which Men call Marius II."

"And I'm Jefferson Nighthawk, as you already seem to know. Now state your business, Friday."

"You are the Widowmaker," said Friday. "You are

the most remarkable of all Men, for your appearance has not changed in more than one hundred Standard years."

"You saw me over a century ago?"

Friday nodded his head, setting his ears to flapping again. "My race is very long-lived. I saw you kill seven men without aid of any kind on—"

"—Dimitri IV," concluded Nighthawk.

"Then it *is* you."

"In a manner of speaking. But my question remains: why have you sought me out?"

"Where the Widowmaker goes, Men die. And now, after being gone for a century, you are back, and Men will die again." Friday paused. "For almost a century I have worked in the mines across the Inner Frontier, opening them when they were discovered, sealing them when they were played out. My specialty is explosives, and I tell you that there is none who knows them better. But one of the problems with a life span as long as the Projastis' is that eventually one becomes bored, even in a field where one has no equal." It paused and stared into Nighthawk's eyes. "I am tired of using my explosives on inanimate mines, Widowmaker. I wish to work with you."

"You don't even know who or what I'm up against."

"It makes no difference to me."

"What if I've been commissioned to blow up Marius II?" asked Nighthawk.

"*Have* you been?"

"No."

"All other worlds are equally unimportant to me."

"You just want to play with your explosives, right?" said Nighthawk.

"I want to kill *Men*."

"Why should I help you?"

"Why not? You will kill them for money and I will kill them for pleasure, and in the end, what difference will it make which of us does the killing?"

"How do I know you won't kill me, too?"

"*Can* you be killed?"

"Not by you."

"There you have it."

"How much do you propose to charge me for your services?"

"Nothing," responded Friday. "I will save you from failure and you will save me from boredom. It will be a fair trade."

Nighthawk stared at him for a long moment, waiting for a gut instinct, pro or con, to kick in. Finally it did.

"Okay," he said at last. "You're working for me now."

"When do we leave?"

"A day or two. You know which ship is mine?"

"I followed you from it."

"Right. Okay, then . . . vanish for a day and then come to the ship."

"I will go there right now."

"Do what I say. You might terrify one of the occupants, and the other might shoot you."

"All right, then: one day from this moment," agreed Friday.

"Aren't you curious to know who's on the other side?"

"I already know," said Friday.

"Oh?"

"You make war with Ibn ben Khalid."

"Why should you think so?"

"Against who else would the Widowmaker need

my expertise?" answered Friday. "Have you been commissioned to kill him, or merely to rescue the human girl?"

"Both. You know where I can find them?"

"I have no idea. I did not expect to be at war with him until I recognized you." Friday paused. "How very exciting this is! Not only has the Widowmaker returned, but I am working for him, and together we shall kill millions of Men!"

"Try not to get *too* excited about wiping out my race."

"I will try," promised Friday with a dubious expression on his alien face.

# Chapter 9

*Blue Eyes looked up from his pocket computer as Nighthawk entered The Blue Dragon.*

"Welcome back, my friend," he said. He deactivated the computer. "Numbers," he said. "I hate numbers."

"You don't look like you're losing money."

"I wasn't cut out to be a business owner."

"Then why don't you stop pretending to be one?"

Blue Eyes stared at Nighthawk for a long moment, then threw back his head, rolled his eyes, and hooted.

"You're *good*, Widowmaker! How long did it take you to find out?"

"Less than a day."

"That's all? And I've managed to keep it a secret for almost ten years."

"Maybe nobody else cared," suggested Nighthawk.

"While you were checking me out, I was doing the same to you."

"And?"

"You don't exist."

"I seem to remember explaining that to you."

"Let me finish," said Blue Eyes. "You don't exist— but you did once."

"I told you . . . "

"I know what you told me. But the Master Computer on Deluros VIII says you have the same fingerprints, voiceprint, and retinagram as the original Widowmaker. I'll wager that if you let me draw some blood or take a skin scraping, you've got the same DNA, too."

"Coincidence," said Nighthawk with a shrug.

"If you thought I'd believe that, you'd also think I was too stupid and gullible to work with."

"The Widowmaker was born more than a century and a half ago," said Nighthawk. "Do I look that old to you?"

"You look maybe two months old," said the dragon with as much of a grin as his facial structure allowed. "I pulled some strings and found out that the original Widowmaker has been frozen for more than a hundred years. He's still there." He stared at Nighthawk. "I've never seen a clone before. They did a fine job, Widowmaker."

"Better than the last one," agreed Nighthawk.

"They've cloned you more than once?" asked Blue Eyes, surprised.

"One other time."

"And that clone is . . . ?"

"Dead."

"Good. I don't think I'd feel comfortable in a galaxy with hundreds of Widowmakers on the loose."

"It's not going to happen. Cloning a human being is a felony on every world in the Oligarchy." Nighthawk walked over to the bar, reached down behind it, and brought up a bottle of Cygnian cognac. He opened it and took a swallow.

"Careful with that stuff!" cautioned Blue Eyes. "It costs me two hundred New Bombay rupees a bottle."

"It doesn't cost *you* a thing," replied Nighthawk. "Now that you know who I am, I think it's time you told me who pays the two hundred rupees, and why you're fronting for him."

"Haven't you guessed?"

"I never guess. *I* pulled some strings too, and my creators have a lot of strings to pull. It's Ibn ben Khalid."

"Right the first time," said Blue Eyes. "All the profits go into maintaining his organization."

"How many bars does he own across the Frontier?"

"Bars, restaurants, assay offices, hotels, boarding-houses—maybe three hundred, maybe a little more."

"Does he travel under his own name?"

"Depends on his mood."

"Does he ever show up here?"

"Once every few years."

Suddenly the dragon was staring into the cold muzzle of a sonic pistol.

"Have you told him I'm after him?"

Blue Eyes reached out and gently pushed the pistol aside. "If I had, you couldn't have made it from your ship to The Blue Dragon without being attacked."

"I was followed."

"Not by anyone connected to Ibn ben Khalid," said Blue Eyes. "And that's a fact."

"All right," said Nighthawk. "You work for him. *Why* haven't you warned him?"

"Look at me and tell me what you see."

"A dragon who's closer to getting blown away than he knows."

"The operative word, my friend, is 'dragon.' Not Man. What do *I* care if Ibn ben Khalid overthrows some human government and starts giving orders himself? What do I care if he doesn't? None of it affects me."

"I begin to appreciate your position," said Nighthawk. "The only thing that affects you is his death. Then The Blue Dragon gets a new owner, right?"

"Where does it say that greed must be confined to the race of Man?"

Nighthawk took another swallow of the cognac. "As long as it's not yours yet . . . " He closed the bottle and put it back behind the bar. "Are there likely to be any other claimants to The Blue Dragon and the hotel?"

"It depends on the circumstances of Ibn ben Khalid's death," replied Blue Eyes. "And how much of his organization remains."

"I couldn't care less about his organization. I just plan to do my job and get the hell out."

"Then yes, there will be claimants. Why?"

"I just want you to know that as long as you're willing to help me, I'll back up your claim." He paused. "I can be a pretty useful ally to have on your side."

"That's very thoughtful of you," said Blue Eyes. "And what if I decide at some point not to help you after all?"

"Then I'll mourn at your funeral."

"So much for a relationship based on mutual trust," said the dragon.

"Would you rather I lied to you?"

"I'd rather you didn't begin our partnership with a threat."

"First, I didn't *begin* with a threat; I *ended* with one. And second, I don't have any partners. You're working *for* me, not *with* me."

"I don't know if I'm all that pleased with this arrangement."

"You don't have to be. You'll be pleased when it's over and you can get obscenely rich from The Blue Dragon."

"First let's see if I live long enough, and if no one tries to take over the business while I'm gone," muttered the dragon. "You know, a million to two isn't a lot better odds than a million to one."

"Actually, it's a million to five."

"Well, that's a start. How many more are you going to recruit before you go after him?"

"None."

Blue Eyes possessed four separate and distinct stomachs. At that instant, he was sure all four were coming down with ulcers.

# Chapter 10

"*Did you find anyone?*" asked Nighthawk, when he, Melisande, and Kinoshita were all together on the ship again.

"I found four men who believe in his cause, but no one who knows how to find him," answered Melisande. "Do you want to interview them further?"

"No. There are millions of men and women who came to the Frontier because they hate the Oligarchy. Most of them will believe in Ibn ben Khalid's cause. What I need is someone who knows where he is." He paused. "It's possible that I've got a couple. We'll have to find out."

"Who?" asked Kinoshita.

"The dragon and that linguist—what's his name?—

Nicholas Jory. Blue Eyes admits that Khalid owns the bar and hotel, and Jory actually said that he'd seen him before."

"If that's the case, why did we waste our time at the jail?" demanded Kinoshita.

"Because I believe in being thorough. Since Melisande can't tell us for sure if the dragon's lying or not, we can never take his word for anything. And it's more than possible Jory was lying, building himself up. Why should a dead-broke drunken linguist have access to the most powerful revolutionary on the Frontier?"

"Now I'm confused again," said Kinoshita. "You just said you might have a couple of people who know how to find Ibn ben Khalid. Now you've all but eliminated them. So do they know how or not?"

"I plan to find out before we leave."

"Are you going to have Melisande check Jory out?"

"If it's convenient. Given that she seems to have trouble reading drunks, it probably won't be."

"Then how—?"

"There are ways," said Nighthawk so coldly that Kinoshita decided he didn't want to know what the ways were.

"So when do we plan to leave?"

"Tomorrow. I've recruited a couple of aliens to our team: Blue Eyes, and one you haven't met yet called Friday. They'll both show up about an hour before we take off."

"Do you trust them?" asked Kinoshita.

"I don't even trust *you*," responded Nighthawk.

Kinoshita looked offended, but chose not to argue, and a few minutes later Nighthawk got to his feet.

"Wait here," he said. "I've got to go out."

"We're not leaving for another day," protested

Kinoshita. "Why should we have to stay in the ship until then?"

"So I'll know where to find you."

"You're getting awfully dictatorial."

"I'll let you know when this becomes a democracy," replied Nighthawk. "Either you take orders from me, or you walk. There's no third way." He put his hands on his hips. "Well?"

"You know the answer," said Kinoshita. "I'm staying. But you don't have to be such a goddamned dictator. You could ask instead of ordering."

"Waste of time."

"Why?"

"You might say no, and then I'd just have to order you."

Kinoshita smiled in spite of himself. "You've got a unique way of looking at things."

Nighthawk left the ship without returning his smile. It was dark, and there was a thick ground fog. He walked to within a block of The Blue Dragon, then sat down in the recessed entryway to a boardinghouse, his back propped against the wall, and waited.

Men and women came and went, aliens passed within feet of him without ever knowing he was there, and still he sat, absolutely motionless. If anyone *had* seen him, they would have thought he was asleep. They'd have been wrong. He was waiting for his quarry as patiently and silently as a jungle beast waits for *its* prey—and eventually his patience was rewarded.

He got to his feet and stepped out onto the pavement so quickly that the man he had been waiting for almost collided with him.

"I'm sorry!" said Nicholas, pivoting awkwardly and almost falling to the ground. "I didn't see you."

"That's all right," answered Nighthawk. "*I* saw *you*."

Suddenly the young man's eyes widened in recognition. "Nighthawk!" he exclaimed. "What are you doing here?"

"Waiting."

"For what? Or who?"

Nighthawk made no reply.

"For *me*?" said Nicholas at last. "Why?"

"We have to talk."

"About what?"

"Ibn ben Khalid."

"I don't know any more about him than you do," said Nicholas nervously.

"I've got a Balatai woman back on my ship," said Nighthawk. "She can tell me if you're lying."

"Bring her along. I've got nothing to hide."

"You said you would speak to Ibn ben Khalid next time you saw him," continued Nighthawk. "That implies you've seen him before."

"You misunderstood me!" protested Nicholas. "I meant that if I ever saw him, I'd speak to him."

Suddenly the cold muzzle of a sonic pistol was pressed against Nicholas' head.

"Let's try again," said Nighthawk.

"But I *told* you: I've never met him!"

"I know. But I don't believe you."

"You can't shoot me down in cold blood!" said Nicholas. "Blue Eyes told me all about you. You were a lot of things, but you were never a murderer!"

"I'm an officer of the law," said Nighthawk. "My credentials may be a century old, but they're still valid. And you're a tax evader."

"That's a goddamned misdemeanor!"

"But resisting arrest isn't."

"It'll be your word against—"

"Against what?"

Suddenly Nicholas froze. "All right. What do you want to know?"

"Where can I find him?"

"I don't know. He's stopped by The Blue Dragon twice in three years." Nicholas paused to regain his composure. "He and Blue Eyes go into the back room and come out a few minutes later. Then he has a drink and leaves. That's all I know!"

"Where does he come from?" asked Nighthawk. "Where does he go?"

"How the hell should I know?" shot back Nicholas. "He has to file a flight plan somewhere. Why don't you check the spaceport and leave me alone?"

"I already did. The spaceport doesn't have a record of Ibn ben Khalid landing here. He must have used another name. What was it?"

"I don't know!"

Nighthawk took the safety off the sonic pistol. "This will scramble your brains as if they were eggs over a campfire. It's not a death I'd wish on anyone." He paused. "I'm only going to ask once more: what name did he use?"

All the life seemed to go out of Nicholas. He slumped and seemed to sink within himself.

"I'm all out of answers," he said wearily. "I don't know what name he used. You might as well shoot and get it over with."

Nighthawk stared at him for a long moment, then put his pistol back in its holster.

"Go home."

"Soon," said Nicholas. "But first I'm going to The Blue Dragon for a drink."

"No. I mean, go *home*—back where you came from."

Nicholas frowned. "Are you ordering me off this planet?" he asked, puzzled.

Nighthawk shook his head. "No. But I'm taking the dragon with me tomorrow. You won't have anyone left to study."

"How long are you taking him for?"

"For as long as it takes to find Ibn ben Khalid."

"Finding him should be the easy part," observed Nicholas. "What comes next is harder." He paused, as if considering his options. "Still, you're the Widowmaker. You might actually pull it off. I think I'll wait until I hear you're dead before I leave the planet."

"I thought you wanted Blue Eyes, not me."

"If they can kill *you*, they'll have already killed *him*."

Nighthawk shrugged. "Do what you please."

"I'm free to go?"

"Yes. And tell Blue Eyes that I expect him to show up on time."

Nicholas scurried off into the fog.

Nighthawk walked around the area for another hour, not searching for anything in particular, but not without purpose. He looked at buildings, vehicles, Men, aliens, shadows, all with the uneasy feeling that something was wrong, that as careful as he'd been he had overlooked some tiny detail that could come back to haunt him. It was nothing he could put his finger on, but the feeling persisted, and he had learned in his previous incarnation never to ignore his instincts. So he walked, and searched, and walked and searched some more.

Finally he returned to the ship without having

satisfied his doubts. He played every possible scenario over and over in his mind, but couldn't spot whatever it was that his subconscious felt he had missed.

Finally, after a couple of hours, he lay down on his bunk and drifted off to a troubled sleep.

# Chapter 11

*Friday ate insects. Preferably live ones.*

Nighthawk, who in his prior life had spent a lot of time on the Inner Frontier with aliens, paid no attention. Kinoshita, who was sharing the control room with Nighthawk while the aliens shared his cabin, thought the habit was disgusting and said so. Blue Eyes found it amusing. Melisande took one quick peek at Friday's emotions, got a truer reading than she wanted or expected, and spent the rest of the voyage in her own cabin, trying not to read the emotions that were there for the perusing.

"Just how many of those things did you bring along?" asked Nighthawk as Friday withdrew a large, hairy, spiderlike insect from a pouch and started biting off the legs one by one.

"Enough," answered the alien.

"What do *they* eat while they're waiting to be eaten by you?" continued Nighthawk.

"Each other."

"Disgusting!" muttered Kinoshita for perhaps the tenth time.

Friday looked at him calmly. "You eat fish, which my race considers sacred."

"It's not the same thing at all," said Kinoshita. "At least everything I eat is dead before I eat it."

"Ah," said Friday. "I see now. It is moral to slaughter animals in a building constructed for that purpose, or to let a fish gasp for air for hours before it dies, as long as you yourself do not have to kill it."

"I've had about enough of you," muttered Kinoshita.

"Calm down," said Nighthawk.

"Damn it," complained Kinoshita. "Have you been watching and listening to him?"

"That's the way he's built. Try to treat him like an equal."

"Equals don't pull the legs off bugs and eat them!"

"This one does," said Friday, pulling another leg off the insect.

"What do we have him along for anyway?" persisted Kinoshita.

"He's our explosives expert."

"Do we need one?"

"I don't know," admitted Nighthawk. "But if we do, I don't want to have to go out searching for one."

Kinoshita stared at the impassive alien and fell

silent. When Friday continued nibbling on the insect, he got up and left the galley.

"Touchy friend you've got there," said Blue Eyes, who had been an amused but silent observer of the little contretemps.

"He's not my friend."

"That's right—I forgot. You don't have any friends, do you?"

"None that I'm aware of," answered Nighthawk.

"Well, at least you've got a lady, which is more than the rest of us have."

"She's a part of the team, just like you."

Blue Eyes grinned. "You mean you don't rut in the muck and then stand guard while she lays her eggs?"

"Is that how blue dragons do it?"

"Probably not," answered Blue Eyes. "It's been so long, I can't remember exactly *how* we do it."

"Is he here for any reason other than to keep you amused?" asked Friday, biting through his insect's carapace with a sickening crunching noise.

"He's here to help me find Ibn ben Khalid."

"That's what *I'm* here for."

Nighthawk shook his head. "I'll need you *after* we find him." He turned back to Blue Eyes. "You'd better be right about Cellestra IV."

"I know he's been seen there a number of times," said Blue Eyes. "Maybe he's got a camp there, maybe he doesn't—but he sure passes through a lot."

"We'll be there in about five hours. Once we land, where do we go?"

Blue Eyes shrugged. "I've never been on Cellestra, remember? How would I know where someone like Ibn ben Khalid would be?"

"When he came to your world, what did he do?" asked Nighthawk.

"Took all the money out of my safe and left."

"He didn't get drunk, or stop by a drug den or a whorehouse or a bank?"

"Not to the best of my knowledge. He came in, ordered a drink, refused to pay for it, and after a couple of minutes he'd make me take him to my office and open the safe. Then he'd fill a bag with cash and walk out as bold as you please."

"Who saw him on Cellestra?" persisted Nighthawk.

"Beats the hell out of me," answered Blue Eyes. "Miners. Gamblers. Bounty hunters. Who knows? Not a lot of people announce their line of work when they come into my tavern for a drink." The dragon paused, then continued. "As for the governor, forget it— Cellestra doesn't *have* a governor. That's why there are so many bounty hunters there. *Some*one's got to enforce the law."

"What law?" asked Friday. "If there's no government, who made it?"

"A telling point," said Blue Eyes. "The minimal law as perceived by Men." He turned to Nighthawk. "I believe it comes from your holy book. Thou shalt not kill, thou shalt not steal. There's something about not coveting your friends' wives, too, but no one pays much attention to that."

"Sounds like just the kind of place I used to find work," commented Nighthawk.

"It's just the kind of place where Ibn ben Khalid can walk the streets with impunity," replied Blue Eyes. "No law."

"There's a million-credit price on his head. He

starts walking down any street that's got a bounty hunter on it, he's a dead man."

"Perhaps they aren't all as opportunistic as you are."

"What's that supposed to mean?"

"Just that he's a hero on the Frontier. Maybe even the bounty killers believe in his cause."

"More likely, they know what will happen to them before they can leave the planet," put in Friday.

"You think he's that popular?" asked Nighthawk curiously.

"Empirical evidence would seem to confirm it."

"Empirical evidence?"

"He's still alive," said Blue Eyes.

"Maybe he's just lucky."

"Do you believe in luck?" asked Friday.

"No," admitted Nighthawk.

"Neither do I," said Friday.

"*I* do," put in Blue Eyes. "That's why I don't allow gambling in my establishment." He threw back his head and hooted in amusement, then sobered just as quickly. "Your friend Kinoshita's been lucky so far, too."

"Oh?"

"Yeah," said Blue Eyes. "He's lucky Friday hasn't killed him."

"Why is he here?" asked Friday. "I know why you and I have come, and the female is an empath, and this one"—he gestured disdainfully at the dragon—"may have information and at least knows what our prey looks like. But what does Kinoshita bring to the team?"

"He may be the most important cog," replied Nighthawk.

"Why?"

"When this is all over, assuming I live through it, I don't plan on going back. He'll know how my creators will react, who they'll contact, where they'll search for me."

"Your creators?"

Nighthawk made no reply, and the alien let the matter drop.

The ship altered course a few minutes later to avoid a meteor swarm, and Kinoshita emerged from his cabin to see what was happening. Friday promptly reached into his pouch and pulled out two more spider-like insects, taking a bite of one and offering its squirming companion to Kinoshita.

"Get that away from me!" snapped the little man.

"I was just being friendly," said the alien calmly, putting the insect back.

"You mean you were just being Friday," said Blue Eyes with a hoot.

"Mind your own business, dragon," said Friday coldly.

"Who elected *you* leader?" demanded Blue Eyes. "I'll say what I want whenever I want."

"And I'll back him up!" snapped Kinoshita.

Suddenly Melisande emerged from her cabin and stood in the doorway to the galley, looking pale and nervous.

*"You've got to stop!"* she said weakly.

"Stop what?" asked Kinoshita.

"You know I'm an empath. I'm trying not to get involved, but there are too many savage emotions here. You could drive me insane before we ever encounter Ibn ben Khalid."

"I thought you couldn't read blue dragons," said Nighthawk.

"I can't," she said. "It's the other two."

"You can read my emotions?" asked Friday with open curiosity.

"Not all of them, and not clearly," replied Melisande. "But you have such hatred for Ito . . ."

"I *knew* it!" growled Kinoshita. He turned to Friday. "Do you want to have it out here or later? It makes no difference to me."

"That's enough," said Nighthawk. He looked at his motley crew. "Like it or not, you're a team. I chose you, I assembled you, and if anyone's going to do any killing around here, I'll be the one to do it. You don't have to like each other. You don't have to like *me*. You just have to remember that you're a team, and the first one who forgets it has to answer to me—and I promise you won't enjoy it. Is that clear?"

Kinoshita grudgingly nodded his agreement.

"What about you?" demanded Nighthawk of Friday.

"I will not strike the first blow in anger."

"Not good enough," said Nighthawk. "If you strike *any* blow, first, second, or three thousandth, in anger or in jest, you'll wish you hadn't. Do you understand?"

Friday nodded his head.

"That's not good enough. Say you understand."

"I understand," muttered the alien.

Nighthawk turned to Blue Eyes.

"Don't look at *me*. I'm the most peace-loving dragon you ever saw. I don't even carry a weapon."

"You could bite either of their heads off with that mouth," said Nighthawk.

"If I do, *then* you can threaten me."

Nighthawk stared into the dragon's clear blue eyes until the latter finally looked away.

"This is not a court of law, you have no legal

rights, and I am not a compassionate man," said Night-hawk. "Try to keep that in mind."

"May I go back to my cabin now?" asked Meli-sande. "Or do you want to warn me too?"

"You know if I was telling the truth or not. That's enough. You can leave."

"Thank you," she said, turning and walking back the way she had come.

Nighthawk considered making Friday and Kinoshita shake hands, but he didn't know if that was a meaningful gesture for the alien, and he could tell that the thought of touching Friday made Kinoshita's flesh crawl.

*This is some crew*, he thought wryly. *I wonder if we can avoid killing each other long enough to find Ibn ben Khalid?*

# Chapter 12

Cellestra was a dirty brown world without much in the way of natural resources. But it was an oxygen planet, and it possessed potable water, and it existed at a midpoint in the starlanes between the major Frontier worlds of Palinaros III and New Kenya. So, when it turned out that the soil wasn't rich enough for it to become a farming world, and that what lay beneath the soil wasn't really worth extracting, it became a trading world, a small but bustling center of commerce.

It was here that subspace messages were received from the Oligarchy and redirected farther into the Inner Frontier. A trio of import-export companies competed for the business of anyone shipping to or from the Frontier worlds. Thousands of preserved animal carcasses were shipped to the taxidermists who plied their trade on Cellestra. Banks traded in Oligarchy credits, New Kenya shillings, Maria Theresa dollars, Far London pounds, New Stalin rubles, Pukkah IV rupees, and a dozen other currencies, with the exchange rates changing and adjusting every ten seconds.

The population was close to twenty thousand Men, and perhaps three thousand aliens of various races, mostly Canphorites, Lodinites, and Mollutei. Almost all of them were involved in some form of interstellar commerce.

As Nighthawk's ship entered orbit around Cellestra, his radio came to life.

"Identify yourself, please," said a cold, almost mechanical voice.

"This is the *Olympus 6*, planet of registry Deluros VIII, commanded by Jefferson Nighthawk, two Standard days out of Sylene IV."

"Purpose of visit?"

"Commerce."

"Type of commerce?"

Kinoshita made a negative gesture.

"None of your damned business," answered Nighthawk.

"We are loading landing coordinates into your ship's computer," said the voice without missing a beat. "Enjoy your stay on Cellestra."

Blue Eyes hooted and Kinoshita grinned.

"You've never been here before," said Melisande. "How did you know we could get away without telling them our reason for landing?"

"Nighthawk *gave* him our reason for landing: commerce," answered Kinoshita. "This is the Frontier, not the Oligarchy. He had no authority to ask us what kind of business."

"That doesn't make sense. It's his world, after all. It must have laws."

"If you're a trading world, probably half of the goods that pass through are contraband. You don't attract a lot of business if word gets out that you're asking embarrassing questions."

"The voice also didn't ask if you had any non-humans in your crew," added Friday. "That was another departure from Oligarchy procedure."

"They're still doing that?" asked Nighthawk.

"They've been doing it for four millennia," answered Friday. "Why should you think they have changed?"

Nighthawk shrugged. "Men are outnumbered thousands to one in the galaxy. You'd think we'd start making accommodations."

"The race that is in the ascendancy never makes accommodations," said Friday. "Fortunately, the galaxy has a long memory. Today Men possess the greatest technology and weaponry, and this has made an arrogant race even more arrogant. But you did not dominate the galaxy in times past, and the day will come when you do not do so in the future. I would not wish to be a Man on that day."

"I don't think you have to worry about it," said Kinoshita sardonically.

"I don't. As long as I can kill Men now, I am content."

"How about you?" asked Kinoshita, turning to Blue Eyes. "Do you feel that way too?"

"Absolutely not," answered the dragon with an amused hoot. "Man is the only race that believes in gratuities."

"So he wants us dead because we have the best weapons, and you want us alive because we're the biggest tippers?" said Kinoshita with a smile. "Well, that's probably as honest a pair of answers as I'm likely to hear."

"I could lie and say you're a physically lovely race," said Blue Eyes. "If it would make you happier, that is."

"Not at all," said Kinoshita. "But somehow, I get the distinct impression that lying would make *you* happier."

"Truth is a greatly overrated virtue, to quote your Jane Austen," agreed the dragon.

"If you say she said it, I'm sure she did—but somehow I don't think she was encouraging blue dragons to lie from morning till night for the sheer joy of it."

Blue Eyes shrugged. "It's all a matter of interpretation."

"Go strap yourselves in," interrupted Nighthawk. "We're about to land."

They touched down a few moments later, and emerged from the ship onto a slidewalk that took them to Customs. Given their appearance and the lack of any records of a current Jefferson Nighthawk, they passed through with a minimum of hassle.

"What now?" asked Melisande as they emerged from the spaceport into the warm Cellestra sunlight and took a broad, rapid-moving slidewalk toward the city center.

"Now we go into town and see what we can learn."

"I can already tell you that your presence is making most of the men we've passed very apprehensive."

"They don't know who I am," said Nighthawk.

"One look at you and they know generically," answered Melisande.

"That's encouraging," said Kinoshita.

"That I scare people?" said Nighthawk.

Kinoshita nodded. "They're not criminals. They're just spaceport employees and businessmen. They have no reason to be afraid of a man who might be a killer or a bounty hunter . . . "

". . . Unless they're afraid I've come for someone they don't want to see killed," concluded Nighthawk. He considered the notion. "It's a possibility."

"So, to repeat, what do we do now?" asked Melisande.

"We find a hotel. We've all been cooped up in that ship too long. We could use a little time away from each other, and a little room to stretch in. This isn't the Oligarchy, so there shouldn't be any trouble finding a place that will take all five of us." He paused. "Then, after dark, we'll go out looking for some sign that Ibn ben Khalid's here, or at least that someone can direct us to wherever he is."

"We'll look kind of strange, all five of us together," said Blue Eyes.

"That's why we'll split up." He faced Blue Eyes and Friday. "You two go to wherever the aliens hang out—even here on the Frontier, I can't believe they're rubbing shoulders with Men. Ito and I will hit the human gathering places. Melisande will come with me."

"Why not with Kinoshita?" she asked.

"Because if there's any trouble, I can protect you better—and until we learn where Ibn ben Khalid is, you're the most valuable member of the team. We'll arrange a meeting place later."

Nighthawk stepped onto a slower local slidewalk

as they approached a small hotel, and his companions followed suit. The hostelry had seen better days, but it was clean enough, and it possessed a restaurant that catered to both humans and aliens. The five took a quintet of rooms at the far end of the fourth level, relaxed until dinnertime, and then descended to the main lobby.

"Friday, if they've got anything you can eat, I think it would be best for all parties concerned if you sat as far from us as possible," announced Nighthawk, and Kinoshita nodded approvingly.

"I have no more taste for dead flesh than you have for my form of nutrition," responded Friday. He stared directly at Kinoshita. "I just have better manners."

The alien walked off to the far end of the restaurant and seated himself.

Nighthawk and the rest of his party found an unoccupied table near the door, punched out their orders from the menu, and ate in relative silence.

Melisande kept shifting uncomfortably during the meal.

"Either you ate something that's making you sick, or you're getting a lot of bad vibrations," noted Nighthawk.

"It's very uncomfortable when so many people are so frightened," she admitted.

"Can't you turn it off?" he asked. "Like closing your eyes or plugging your ears?"

"How do you turn off your mind?" she shot back.

"There must be some way, or you'd have gone crazy years ago," he continued. "You can't be aware of every vicious, perverted emotion on the planet."

"Distance helps," she replied.

"How about walls?"

"Not really. Just distance."

"You must really have suffered on the ship."

"You find ways to cope," she said. "Friday hates all Men, but most of that hatred is beneath the surface. It comes out from time to time, but not often. And Kinoshita's emotions only flare up when he confronts Friday."

"What about me?" asked Blue Eyes.

"I can't read you at all," answered Melisande. "We're too different."

"And the boss?" asked Blue Eyes, gesturing toward Nighthawk.

She stared at Nighthawk for a long moment. "I've never met anyone quite like him. There's almost no emotional radiation at all. No apprehension, no fear, no hatred. This is all just a job to him. Nothing upsets him, and nothing seems to excite him."

"I suppose that's what makes him the Widowmaker," said Blue Eyes. "Probably the most you'll ever get from him is a sense of satisfaction at a job well done after he wipes out fifty or sixty bad guys."

"That's a terrible way to be" was her answer.

"It's the only way to survive when you put your life on the line so often," said Nighthawk.

"Life is more than surviving," she said.

"Not for everyone," he answered.

"What would you do if you weren't the Widowmaker?" asked Blue Eyes. "If you could do or be anything you want?"

"It's a silly question. I am what I am."

"But *if*," persisted the alien.

Nighthawk shrugged. "Grow things, I guess."

"Things?"

"Flowers, plants, animals," he answered vaguely.

"I've killed enough things in my life. It might be interesting to try growing them for a change."

"What's stopping you?" asked Blue Eyes. "Your creators are half a galaxy away. You could vanish on the Frontier and they'd never find you."

"I have an obligation."

"To *them*?" said Blue Eyes contemptuously.

"To me."

"To yourself?"

"To a version of me that's lying in a frozen chamber on Deluros VIII," answered Nighthawk. "Once his future is secure, I'll worry about my own."

"I know how Men feel about their parents and siblings," continued Blue Eyes. "But how does a clone feel about his—what would you call it?—his original self?"

"He's not a separate person. He's a part of me, just as I'm a part of him."

"I don't understand."

"I don't either," admitted Nighthawk. "But I know what I feel."

"I wonder why cloning humans carries such heavy penalties?" mused Blue Eyes.

"All the legal problems," answered Kinoshita. "Is a man responsible for his clone's criminal actions? If DNA is found at the scene of a violent crime, whose is it? For the purposes of inheritance, who is more closely related—a man's son or his clone?"

"You would think they could solve them."

"They probably can—but they'd rather not," said Melisande. "Each of us likes to think he's unique. Clones would change all that."

"I don't know," said Kinoshita. "I never met the original Widowmaker, but I spent some time with the first clone, and he was nothing like this one."

"How was he different?" she asked.

"He was very immature, very impetuous—and he fell passionately in love with the first woman he saw."

"He was also two months old," said Nighthawk. "Not physically, but in every other way." He paused. "The poor bastard never had a chance."

"You speak as if you knew him," said Blue Eyes.

"I did more than know him," answered Nighthawk. "I *was* him."

"There!" said Melisande. "That's the first really powerful emotional reaction I've read since I met you."

"Emotions get in the way of things," said Nighthawk, his expression halfway between annoyed and embarrassed.

"I disagree," said Kinoshita. "Without lust and greed, the race would still be Earthbound."

"Lust and greed and curiosity," Melisande corrected him.

"Well, let's start satisfying our curiosity," said Nighthawk. He left his thumbprint on the bill, got to his feet, waited for the others to rise, and walked to the door.

Friday joined them, and a moment later Nighthawk's team had gone out into the cool Cellestra night in search of information about his quarry.

# Chapter 13

"*So where do we begin?*" asked Melisande *nervously as she* and Nighthawk rode down the almost-empty slidewalk.

"Your choice," said Nighthawk. "Pick a tavern or a drug den or a coffee shop where the emotions aren't too painful. I want you to be able to read *new* emotions, passions I hope to raise; I assume its easier if you're not already overwhelmed."

"True," she said. "But why didn't you offer me the same choice back on Sylene IV?"

"Because my . . . ah . . . sponsors had tipped me that Ibn ben Khalid had been seen a couple of times in Blue Eyes' establishment. It wouldn't have made much sense to choose a barroom three blocks away, would it?"

"No," she admitted. Then: "How will you do it this time, without Kinoshita around to start an argument?"

Nighthawk shrugged. "I'm sure something will come to me." He paused. "I want you sitting in the light this time, where I can see your face without any difficulty. If anyone reacts to anything I say or do, just stare at him for a minute."

"I'll attract his attention," she said uneasily. "What if he tries to do something?"

"Then he'll find out what happens to people who bother the Widowmaker's friends."

"I'm comforted to hear that—but are you aware of how arrogant that sounds?"

"I've earned my arrogance," responded Nighthawk. "Would you rather I simpered and sucked my thumb and said 'Aw, shucks!' every time the subject of my abilities arose?"

"No," she said with a sigh. "I suppose not."

"How's this place?" asked Nighthawk, indicating an exotic-looking tavern.

She concentrated for a moment. "As good as any. They've got a very beautiful dancer."

"How can you tell?"

She smiled. "There's a lot of lust in the air. What would *you* credit it to?"

"Sounds logical. I think maybe we'd better go in as a couple."

"Why?"

"You're an attractive woman, and if you walk in alone, I imagine some of that lust is going to be directed toward you."

"That's thoughtful of you."

He shrugged. "Why make my job harder?"

She stared at him for a moment, then took his arm and entered the tavern with him.

It was a curious room, sixteen-sided, dark, with alien tapestries hanging on the walls. An almost-nude girl stood atop a huge transparent globe that rolled around a small stage in the middle of the room, and the girl's attempts to keep her balance bore such grace that Nighthawk decided she could have just as easily tapped or pirouetted on it had she so desired. The music seemed live, but he couldn't spot the band.

There were about thirty small tables circling the stage, about half of them occupied by Men, the rest empty. As far as Nighthawk could tell, the dancer and Melisande were the only two females in the place.

Nighthawk walked to a table very near the stage, pulled out a chair for Melisande, then sat down himself. He didn't see any sign of a waiter, either robotic or human, so he examined the table and found an almost invisible button which, when pressed, produced two drink menus. The selection was suitably exotic: Dust Whores, Blue Zebras, Green-and-Whites, Chiller Killers, even a wildly expensive bottle of seventy-five-year-old Alphard brandy. They each selected a drink, Nighthawk placed his thumb next to each on the menu, and a moment later two slots opened on the table and the drinks magically appeared.

"Anyone look likely?" asked Nighthawk, scanning the room.

"They *all* look dangerous," she replied.

"Looks can be deceiving."

"Don't you feel any fear or even apprehension?" she asked, staring at him.

He grinned. "If you don't know, we've got a serious problem."

"I can't detect any."

"This is my work. It doesn't pay to be nervous."

"There's a difference between controlling or ignoring your fear, and not feeling any at all."

"Maybe that's my edge, then."

"You're a very strange man, Jefferson Nighthawk."

"That's how you become a legend," he replied. The semi-nude girl finished her routine, and Nighthawk leaned over toward her. "We'd be happy to buy you a drink once you get your clothes back on," he said.

"I don't drink with the customers."

"Ah, but this is a drink in honor of Ibn ben Khalid," he said in a voice that was just loud enough to be overheard.

"You must not have heard me," replied the girl. "I don't drink with the customers."

"Next you'll be telling me you're a patriot," he said as she left the stage. Then he turned back to Melisande. "Well?"

"Nothing from her," she replied, "but when you mentioned Ibn ben Khalid I got a couple of rushes of emotion from somewhere in the room, and your comment about patriotism got one of them quite agitated."

"For us or against us?"

"I don't know," she said. "I read emotions, not thoughts—but given that we're two thousand light-years from the nearest Oligarchy world, I'd have to think it's *for* us."

"Let's find out," said Nighthawk.

He stood up, glass in hand.

"A toast to Ibn ben Khalid!" he said in a loud voice.

No one joined him.

"Bunch of goddamned cowards," he muttered,

downing his drink and sitting down again. He looked at Melisande and asked softly, "Anything?"

"Everything," she answered. "Loyalty, outrage, love, hatred, even fear."

"Directed at me or at Ibn ben Khalid?"

"I don't know."

"It could mean they know him, or simply that they know *of* him. And that they love him and fear me, or the other way around." He grinned ruefully. "Empathy isn't an exact science, is it?"

"You knew what it was when you hired me."

"Don't get angry," he said, and suddenly looked around the room. "Or maybe that's the best thing for you to do?"

"I beg your pardon."

"If I slap you and pull my punch, can you fall and make it look real?"

"I don't know. I'm not an actress."

"Don't worry about it then," he said.

"What's this about?"

"I can't wait all night for someone to approach. Maybe we can precipitate some action."

"By hitting me?" she said. "I'll never be able to convince them I was really hurt."

"Yes you will," he assured her.

"But I—"

His hand shot out and slapped her, hard. She fell off her chair and rolled onto the floor.

"Get up!" he bellowed. "Get up and say that again!"

She sat erect, her eyes refusing to focus. He yanked her to her feet, dragged her to the door, and pushed her out into the street. "Wait for me at the hotel," he whispered, then reentered the tavern.

"Promises me a night's entertainment and then

starts lecturing me about Cassius Hill's virtues," he announced, sitting down again at his table. "That bastard wouldn't know a virtue if it jumped up and spit in his face."

There was still no reaction, so he stood up.

"I've had my fill of this place," he said, walking back to the door and out into the street.

He had walked, swaying as if drunk, about forty feet when a voice called out from behind him.

"Hold on, friend!"

Nighthawk repressed a secret smile, then turned to see who was approaching him. It was one of the men from the tavern, a broad-shouldered beer-bellied man with a huge black beard and bold, glaring gray eyes.

"I couldn't help hearing what you had to say," said the man.

"And?"

"I happen to have fought under Cassius Hill's command in the war against the Borolites. He's a great man, and I take issue with what you said."

*Wonderful. There are probably fifty Ibn ben Khalid supporters in the tavern, and I get the one who hates his guts.*

"That's your privilege, brother," said Nighthawk at last. "I didn't mean any harm."

"Then you'd better apologize right here and now," said the man.

"Okay, I apologize."

The man seemed angrier than ever. "That's not good enough!"

Nighthawk noticed that a crowd had begun gathering.

*Well, maybe it's not so bothersome after all. If I stand up for Ibn ben Khalid, maybe someone here will finally decide I'm on their side.*

"It'll have to do," said Nighthawk. "It's all you're going to get."

"So you've found a little backbone after all," said the man with a dangerous smile.

"A little."

"Do you have anything to say before I rip you apart?"

"Yeah," said Nighthawk. "You and Cassius Hill can both go fuck yourselves."

The man bellowed a curse and charged, but Nighthawk was ready for him. He sidestepped, grabbed the man's arm, twisted it and put his weight into it, and the man somersaulted through the air, landing with a bone-jarring thud.

The man got to his feet slowly, brushed himself off, and stared at Nighthawk. He approached more slowly this time—and walked face-first into a spinning kick that sent him reeling.

"Who *are* you?" he demanded, wiping the blood from his face and approaching even more carefully this time.

"I'm the man you were going to rip apart," said Nighthawk.

The man approached him warily, feinting with his left. Nighthawk didn't wait for a second feint, but stepped inside and delivered six blows to the belly, so rapidly that most of the observers never saw the last four. His opponent collapsed, gasping for air.

Nighthawk looked around, hoping someone would approach to congratulate him or offer him a drink or show *some* form of solidity with a man who had just risked his life for Ibn ben Khalid. Instead, three men stepped forward, each with a drawn pistol—two sonic, one laser.

"I didn't know Cassius Hill was so popular," said Nighthawk wryly.

"We don't give a shit about politics," said one of the men. "But that was our friend you damned near killed."

"*He* attacked *me*."

"That doesn't make him any less our friend."

"Then take him home and tell him not to argue politics." *And don't make me kill you.*

"First we have to decide what to do about you."

"Just walk on," said Nighthawk. "I've got no argument with you."

"*We* have one with you," said the second man. "I saw the way you took him apart. You're no amateur. You should have warned him, or found some way to step aside."

"I apologized to him," said Nighthawk. "I'll apologize to you, too, if it'll make you feel any better." He paused. "But I'll only apologize once. Walk on."

"You're talking as if *you* have the drop on *us*," said the first man.

Nighthawk was about to reply when an ear-shattering explosion rang out. Bricks and debris rained down on him, and the ground shook beneath his feet. He threw himself to the ground, covering his head with his hands and wondering what the hell was happening. He could hear screams of agony nearby, and a moment later he felt a building collapse down the street.

Then an alien hand was on his shoulder, helping him to his feet.

"Are you all right?" asked Friday.

"Yes," said Nighthawk, looking around at a scene of total devastation. Wounded bodies littered the street, and a couple of men lay motionless, their bodies in such awkward positions that he knew instantly they were dead. "What the hell happened?"

"I saw three men with their weapons trained on you."

"You mean this was *your* doing?" demanded Nighthawk, wiping some blood from his left ear.

"It's my specialty."

"I didn't even know you had any explosives with you."

"I am never without them," said Friday.

Kinoshita came running up.

"What's going on?" he asked.

"This asshole wiped out half a city block," answered Nighthawk.

"I saved your life."

"My life was never in danger."

"You idiot!" snapped Kinoshita at Friday. "Look what you've done. How are we going to make contact with Ibn ben Khalid's people now?"

Men and women began regaining consciousness and staggered to their feet.

"That's the easy part," said Nighthawk. He turned to Friday. "All right, there's no undoing what happened. Get the hell back to the hotel—no, make that the ship—and stay there until you hear from me. Ito, find Blue Eyes and get him out of here. Take him to the ship and make him stay there. Melisande, too."

"Aren't you coming too?"

Nighthawk shook his head. "Not right away. I still have a job to do."

"Then at least let us help protect you."

"You too?" replied Nighthawk. "I don't need any protection. You can help me by getting the aliens to the ship and not letting them set foot outside it."

"All right," said Kinoshita. "But someone just killed and maimed a bunch of Ibn ben Khalid's supporters on your behalf. If I were you, I'd run like hell."

"You're not me."

"I don't see how you're going to get close to him now."

"By standing still," said Nighthawk. He looked up and down the street. "His people will find *me*."

# Chapter 14

*Nighthawk stood alone on the rubble, waiting patiently.*

He didn't have long to wait. Within minutes he was surrounded by bruised and bloody men, all pointing weapons at him. Ambulances sped by, floating above the street, coming from and returning to the city's only hospital.

There were no police, but a pair of bounty hunters showed up, only to leave when they found out there was no price on his head. Finally the confusion and noise abated somewhat, and Nighthawk turned to face a middle-aged man, one he recognized from the tavern.

"Why am I being held?" he asked.

"Look around you."

"I'm not responsible for that. I was in plain

view every second. I defended myself from one man, that's all."

"There's a red alien. We want him."

"What is that to me?" asked Nighthawk.

"We know he's your friend."

"I have no friends."

"He set off the explosives, and he was overheard saying he did it to save you. That's enough."

"What he did was *his* business. I didn't set off any bombs and I didn't kill any people. You have no right to keep me here."

"We want to know where the alien is. We think you can tell us." The man leaned forward. "I heard you in the tavern. I know you believe in Ibn ben Khalid's cause."

"So what?"

"So the alien killed six of Khalid's men."

"I'm sorry to hear that," said Nighthawk. "I may kill him myself."

"He works for you. Or with you. If we let you go, you'll just join him and leave Cellestra."

"How wise of you to know what I will or won't do," said Nighthawk. "If you're typical of the kind of men Ibn ben Khalid recruits, maybe I'd better reconsider who I support."

"Let's just kill him and be done with it!" snapped one of the men.

"I'm a supporter of Ibn ben Khalid, and you know that I didn't set off the bombs, and you want to kill me anyway? I wonder what Ibn ben Khalid would say if he were here."

"He'd probably say to kill you," said another man.

"If he would, then Cassius Hill's got nothing to

worry about," said Nighthawk. "I've got more faith in his judgment than you do."

"Then turn the alien over to us."

"Not a chance."

"Why the hell not, if you had nothing to do with the bombing?"

*Say it right, now, and put some fire in your eyes.*

"Because I know what you're going to do to him. It's the same thing Men have been doing to aliens since the first day we found out we aren't alone in the galaxy, and I don't plan to be a part of it."

"But he's a killer!"

"Even a killer deserves a trial," said Nighthawk. "But he only gets it if he's a Man. If I tell you where the alien is hiding, you'll shoot him or string him up."

"You bet your ass we will!" said the first man. "He killed six of us!"

"Okay, he overreacted, and he deserves to go to jail for it. But I'm not going to turn him over to a bunch of human bigots who want to lynch him!"

"Who the hell are you calling a bigot?"

"Who's threatening to kill me if I don't turn over the alien?" shot back Nighthawk.

*Are they actually buying this shit? I sure as hell can't tell by their faces—and I don't even know what Ibn ben Khalid feels about aliens. What if he's not a bleeding heart?*

"Look, fella, whoever you are," said the first man, "if we don't find him, all we have is you, and you're going to have to answer for the bombing."

"Fine," said Nighthawk. "String *me* up—but I'm not turning an alien over to you until I know he's going to be safe in his jail cell and get a fair trial."

"We don't *have* a goddamned jail!" exploded the man. "And what's all this fair trial crap? You know he couldn't get a trial of any kind back in the Oligarchy."

"That's one of the reasons why we came out to the Frontier, isn't it?" shot back Nighthawk. "To get away from a government that wouldn't give an alien a fair chance."

The man stared at him for a long moment.

"All right," he said at last. "What was the alien doing here in the first place?"

"He was here on business."

"What kind?"

"You'd have to ask him."

"Damn it, I'm trying to be reasonable. Your companion just destroyed the better part of a city block and killed some of my friends."

"I'm sorry, and I'm sure if he's had time to reflect on it, *he's* sorry. He thought he was saving my life."

"*Thought?*" echoed another man. "You were two seconds away from getting blown to kingdom come."

"If you say so."

"You don't think so?" continued the man. "Hell, even the Widowmaker in his prime couldn't have gotten out of that spot alive."

Nighthawk shrugged and made no reply.

"Let's get back to what happened," said the first man. "You walked out of the tavern. Rigby followed you. Then what?"

"He asked me to apologize. I did."

"He attacked you for that?"

Nighthawk looked at his antagonist's still-unconscious body. "I don't know why the hell he attacked me. Ask him when he wakes up."

"Let's keep going. He attacked you. Why?"

"He didn't like my opinion of Cassius Hill," answered Nighthawk. "Or maybe he didn't like what I think about Ibn ben Khalid. It comes to the same thing."

"And you knocked him out?"

Nighthawk gestured to the unconscious Rigby. "There he is."

"Then what?"

"Then three of his friends came up with their guns drawn. I don't think they were going to shoot me, I think we were on the verge of talking things out—but my friend saw them and assumed they were about to kill me, and he did what he felt he had to do to save me."

"So you might say that the six men who were killed died because you were defending their leader?"

"It's a little simplistic, but if you want to say it, I won't disagree with you."

"You present us with a problem," continued the man. "You got into a fight defending a man we respect, that some of us all but worship. You refuse to turn the alien over to us for fear he won't get a fair trial."

"*Any* trial," Nighthawk corrected him.

"Any trial," amended the man. "Those are both virtues that we should respect. Yet it won't bring the six men back."

"Ibn ben Khalid's at war with Cassius Hill," said Nighthawk. "Casualties happen in wartime."

"I know. That's what we have to consider."

"Consider it until hell freezes over, but I'm not turning the alien over to you. If I have to be a seventh casualty, so be it. If I told you where he is, I'd be no better than Cassius Hill."

"We're going to have to talk this over," said the

man. He turned to a couple of the younger men in the crowd. "Harry, Jason, keep him covered while we decide what to do."

The two men stepped forward, their guns trained on Nighthawk, while the rest of the men and women went into the tavern. Nighthawk stood motionless, seemingly oblivious of his two guards, for the better part of ten minutes. He still had three small concealed weapons, and felt confident that he could disable or kill the guards at any time, but it suited his purposes to wait for the judgment of the men and women who were currently deciding his fate.

Finally they emerged from the tavern, and the middle-aged man who seemed to be their leader walked up to Nighthawk.

"All right," he said. "You seem willing to die for your principles. We've decided that you deserve to live for them."

"I don't understand," said Nighthawk, who understood perfectly.

"We'd like you to join us, to fight for the cause."

"What about the alien?"

"He killed, he dies—but we'll find him ourselves."

"Fair enough," said Nighthawk. "How and where do I enlist?"

"You already have," said the man. "A statement of principle is as formal as it gets—and you've already made yours." He paused. "There are hundreds of thousands, maybe millions, of us all across the Frontier, waiting for the word."

"When will it come?"

"When Ibn ben Khalid decides we're ready."

"And when will that be?"

The man shrugged. "You'd have to ask him."

"I'd like to. Where is he?"

"Who knows?"

"Somebody must," said Nighthawk.

"If I knew, his enemies could torture it out of me, or drug me and make me reveal it. Much better that I don't know."

"I repeat: *some*body must know."

"There's a complex chain of command. You could follow it until you were a very old man and still never come to the end of it."

"Sounds inefficient to me," said Nighthawk. "If it takes that long to get to the top, it'll take as long for commands to come down."

"He's been one of us for less than three minutes and already he's criticizing the operation," said another man contemptuously.

"If I'm going to put my life on the line for Ibn ben Khalid, I'd like to meet him. If he's too busy to see me personally, and I can certainly understand that, I'd at least like to attend a speech or a rally. Everything I know about him is secondhand."

"Then why did you risk your life fighting Rigby?"

"First, I didn't risk my life, and second, everything I know about Cassius Hill is firsthand. I'll support anyone who's against him."

"Good answer," said the middle-aged man approvingly.

"Thanks," said Nighthawk. "*Now* will you tell me where I can find Ibn ben Khalid?"

"I don't know. None of us do."

"When's the last time he stopped off at Cellestra?"

"Never," said the man, surprised.

"Never?" repeated Nighthawk sharply.

The man shook his head. "Don't you think we'd know if he had? He's never been here."

Nighthawk stood motionless for a moment. He could almost hear a distinct *clink!* as another piece of the puzzle fell into place.

# Chapter 15

*Nighthawk entered the ship and ordered the hatch to close* behind him.

"We were getting worried," said Blue Eyes, rising to greet him.

"*Some* of us were getting worried," Kinoshita corrected him. "I kept telling him that you were the Widow-maker, that if he was going to worry about anyone, he should be worrying about the townspeople who thought you were their prisoner."

"So what happened?" persisted Blue Eyes.

"I put on a performance," said Nighthawk. "They bought it, hook, line, and sinker."

"What does that mean?" asked Friday.

"It's an old expression, from the time Men were

still Earthbound. In this instance, it means I've been welcomed into their organization, such as it is."

"Such as it is?" repeated Kinoshita, frowning.

"Ibn ben Khalid's not here."

"There *is* one other planet where I know he's been recently," said Blue Eyes.

"Oh?"

"Yes," continued the dragon. "A little world called Causeway. It's on the route from Jefferson II to Far London. The Oligarchy sent some agents in there, and from what I hear, he had them all tortured and killed."

"A resourceful man," remarked Nighthawk.

"Would an unresourceful man have survived this long?"

"Depends on the man and the situation," said Nighthawk.

"Do you want me to lay in a course for Causeway?" asked Blue Eyes. "I think its official name is Beta Dante IV."

"No, I'll do it," said Nighthawk. He turned to Kinoshita. "Take charge of getting our clearance to leave. Be polite and accommodating, but no one boards us or scans us. If you have to, take off without permission and get us up to light speed as fast as you can. I'd rather leave peacefully, but the main thing is to get the hell out of here. This world's a dead end." He paused. "Once we're a couple of dozen light-years out, let me know and I'll program the new destination."

"Why not now?"

"I want us to seem to be heading back to Sylene now, just in case anyone has any idea of following us. Once we're out of tracer range, we'll turn and head off for Causeway."

"I can do it."

"I know you can," said Nighthawk. "But if we make a mistake and allow someone to tail us, at least this way you won't bear the blame."

"Right," assented Kinoshita. "I can accept that."

Nighthawk allowed himself the luxury of a small smile. "I thought perhaps you could." He walked toward Melisande's cabin. "Is she in here?"

"Yes," said Kinoshita. "She didn't like what I was thinking about Friday."

"I can imagine," said Nighthawk. He stood beside the door. "I'll be out in a couple of minutes. Don't disturb us."

The door slid back, and he entered the cabin just before it closed again.

Melisande, who was sitting in the cabin's only chair, looked up from the book she was reading.

"What is it?" she asked.

"You tell me."

She stared at him. "There *is* something!" she said at last. "You're excited!"

"What else?"

She concentrated for a moment. "I don't know. Just that you're translating very powerful emotional radiation."

"But you don't know what it's about?"

"Not as an empath," she replied. "But I'd be awfully surprised if it doesn't concern Ibn ben Khalid."

"It does," said Nighthawk. "I don't want you leaving the cabin until we land."

"Why?"

"I don't want you to inadvertently reveal what you just discovered."

"Still why?"

"I have my reasons." Nighthawk paused. "Take your meals in here."

"How long will this trip last?"

"A couple of days."

"Who don't you trust?" asked Melisande. "Who am I not supposed to reveal this to?"

Nighthawk smiled. "Just stay in the cabin." He turned to the door, waited for it to open, and stepped back out into the corridor that led to the galley. A moment later he was in the control room.

"That was quick, even for a human," said Blue Eyes.

"That was vulgar, even for a dragon," Nighthawk shot back.

"Of course. Vulgarity is my charm."

Nighthawk walked over to Kinoshita, who was at the navigational computer.

"How's it going?"

"They're not happy about it, but they can't come up with a good reason to deny us permission to leave." He looked up at Nighthawk. "They've already requested permission to search the ship. I denied it."

"Have the sensors spotted any weaponry trained on us?"

Kinoshita shook his head. "No. They just haven't given us permission to take off."

"Scan deep space."

"Done."

"When's the next incoming ship due to hit the atmosphere?"

Kinoshita studied the holographic screen. "About forty Standard minutes."

"Okay, there's no likelihood of hitting it. Take off."

"You're sure?"

"They're not going to shoot until they *know*

Friday's on the ship. The longer we stay on the ground, the more likely they are to find out."

Kinoshita gave the order to the computer, and a moment later the ship was streaking through the upper atmosphere of Cellestra. When it entered space, it jumped to light speed.

"Any pursuit?" asked Nighthawk.

"Not that I can find."

"We'll stay on this course for an hour or two, just in case they're tracking us. Then we'll head back to Causeway."

"Sounds good to me," said Kinoshita, finally looking up from the control panel.

Nighthawk turned to Friday. "I haven't had a chance to speak to you since you blew up those buildings."

"I saved your life."

"First of all, my life was in no danger. And second, even if it was, we both know that you did it because you enjoy *killing* Men, not *saving* them." Nighthawk paused and stared at the red-skinned alien. "If you ever set off an explosive again without my permission, all bonds are broken, all agreements forgotten, and I will hunt you down and kill you like an animal. Do you understand?"

"Yes. The next time your life is threatened, you wish me to take no action at all."

"If that's the way you choose to interpret it."

"You should not alienate me, Widowmaker," said Friday. "I can be of enormous use to you."

"You can also be an enormous handicap," answered Nighthawk. "Actions have consequences. Yours came very close to getting me killed."

Friday stared at him, then turned his back and stared at a viewscreen.

"I would have liked to have heard your line of bullshit," said Blue Eyes. "You must have done some snappy talking to get those men to let you go."

"I told them what they wanted to hear."

"But you must have told them with sincerity," said the dragon. "No one can lie like a Man."

"You think not?" asked Nighthawk.

"Well, except maybe for blue dragons."

Blue Eyes threw back his head and hooted, and Nighthawk joined him. Kinoshita suddenly realized that it was the first time he'd heard the Widowmaker laugh in any of his incarnations. It wasn't a comforting sound.

After an hour Nighthawk sat down at the navigational computer, fed in the coordinates of the ship's destination, and walked to the galley, where he ordered a sandwich and a beer. Kinoshita and Blue Eyes joined him a few minutes later, while Friday continued staring at the viewscreen, back turned to the three of them.

"This is pretty awful stuff," offered Blue Eyes, indicating his drink.

"The galley wasn't programmed for your needs."

"An understatement," said Blue Eyes, tossing his cup in the atomizer and ordering a different concoction.

"Actually, the food's pretty good compared to some ships I've owned," said Kinoshita.

"I agree," said Nighthawk.

"I wonder how you managed to conquer the galaxy on such poor rations," said Blue Eyes.

"We only conquered a very small part of it," answered Kinoshita with a smile. "The rest we bought."

"You should have bought some good food synthesizers while you were at it."

"We did. It's hardly our fault that a human ship

isn't equipped to feed a blue dragon with fangs that would give any child nightmares."

"If you two are going to argue about the food, wait until I've finished eating," said Nighthawk.

"I thought you liked it," said Blue Eyes.

"I do. But when you start talking about it, I think about what it really is instead of what it tastes like, and then I lose my appetite."

"Talk about self-delusion!" said the dragon with a hoot of amusement.

"It has its uses," said Nighthawk, finishing his sandwich and downing his beer.

"I thought you were the ultimate realist."

"I am," replied Nighthawk. "Who but a realist would admit the benefits of self-delusion?"

"That is either the stupidest or most intelligent remark I've heard in years," said Blue Eyes. "Now I'll have to spend the next day or two figuring out which."

Nighthawk got to his feet. "I think I'd better check on Melisande."

"Is she ill?" asked Kinoshita.

"Just a bit under the weather. She should be fine by the time we land."

He left the galley and returned to Melisande's cabin.

"I didn't expect to see you again for the duration of the trip," said Melisande, still sitting in the same chair.

"I need to know something."

"What?"

"Can you tell if someone's lying?"

"Someone on the ship? Probably not, if it's one of the aliens."

"No, a human, not Kinoshita or me."

"It all depends."

"On what?"

"On what kind of pressure he's under. Point a gun at him and he might be so scared that his fear of the gun will mask all other emotions. I might even read it as fear of telling the truth, and interpret that as a lie."

"Too bad."

"Why?"

"That's the very situation I had in mind," said Nighthawk.

"Who is it?"

"Who is *what*?"

"I'm not a fool, Nighthawk," said Melisande. "You were asking about a scenario you've already devised in your mind. You think that Ibn ben Khalid is masquerading as someone else. You think you know who. You want to confront him with your suspicions, probably at gunpoint. And you want me to tell you if he's lying or not. Isn't that what this is all about?"

"In essence."

"I'm sorry, but I can't give you a definite answer."

"I'll just have to proceed without one, then," said Nighthawk. He walked to the door. "I won't bother you again."

"I'm happy to have your company," she replied. "You're the most fascinating man I've met in a long time."

"I thought I didn't project any emotions."

"I misspoke. You don't *react* emotionally, but you do have emotions. Most of them are buried so deep that one of Friday's bombs probably couldn't get them out. I find that curious in so successful a man."

"Possibly because you mistake me for a successful man."

"You're a legend all over the Frontier," said Melisande. "You have more self-confidence than any man I know. You have never been defeated. That is my definition of a successful man."

"I would think a woman with your gifts wouldn't dabble on the surface of things," said Nighthawk.

"I don't understand."

"I was created with *all* of Jefferson Nighthawk's memories. Not just those that he possessed at age thirty-eight."

"Ah!" she said. "I see now!"

"Each time I see my face in a mirror, I expect to see the white of my cheekbones piercing through my diseased flesh," said Nighthawk. "I look at my hands, and I'm surprised not to see the skin peeled back from my knuckles and my fingernails missing." He paused uncomfortably. "You wondered that I didn't lust after you in the whorehouse. I learned not to. After all, what kind of woman could possibly be attracted to a man in an advanced state of eplasia? I watched myself dying of a disfiguring disease for the better part of two years, before they finally accepted my application to go into the deep freeze and await a cure. You learn to sublimate a lot of emotions when you go through something like that."

She nodded her head. "Yes, it makes much more sense now. You must forgive me, but like everyone else, I assumed you were what you appeared to be. I'll have to adjust."

"So will I," replied Nighthawk. "I'm on a mission now, and every move I've made since I was created has been directed toward accomplishing it. But when I've finally killed Ibn ben Khalid and returned Cassandra Hill to her father, I'm going to have to come to grips with the fact that every human I know except for you and Kinoshita has been dead for over a century, that most of the buildings are distant memories, that my knowledge of everything except weaponry and spaceships is a hundred years out of date."

"Frankly, I'm surprised that you're not even more repressed than you are," said Melisande.

"I haven't got time to be an emotional basket case," said Nighthawk. "I've got work to do."

"You don't take much pleasure in it."

"I did once. I will again."

He walked out of the room and let the door slide shut behind him, leaving Melisande to wonder how much longer he could remain simmering before the explosion came.

# Chapter 16

"We're ready to land," announced Nighthawk as he instructed the autopilot to turn the controls over to the spaceport's computer.

"They didn't ask us to identify ourselves," noted Kinoshita. "That's very strange."

"They know who we are," said Nighthawk.

"You radioed ahead?"

"I didn't have to."

"I didn't know you've been to Causeway," said Blue Eyes.

"I haven't."

"I meant your ship."

"I know what you meant," said Nighthawk.

They fell silent then as the ship burst into the

atmosphere and activated its heat shields. Another five minutes and it gently touched down on the reinforced concrete of the spaceport.

"That's it," said Nighthawk. "Let's go to work."

"Do you want to divide the place up, the way we did on Cellestra?" asked Kinoshita.

"No need to."

"I disagree," said Blue Eyes. "We can cover four times the ground if we go off on our own."

"But we don't have to," said Nighthawk, walking to the hatch and opening it. "I know where we're going."

Blue Eyes followed him to the hatch, then froze.

"What the hell's going on here?" he demanded.

"We're going after Ibn ben Khalid," answered Nighthawk.

"But this isn't Causeway!" snapped the dragon. "It's Sylene IV!"

"That's right," said Nighthawk. "This is where he is."

"Is this some kind of joke?" said Blue Eyes.

"No, it's not," said Nighthawk, drawing a pistol and aiming it at the dragon. "You slipped up."

"I don't know what you're talking about!"

"You told me that Ibn ben Khalid had been seen on Cellestra. His own followers, who had accepted me as one of them, told me that he'd never been there." Nighthawk paused. "Cellestra is two days closer to the Core than Sylene. Causeway is a couple of days closer than Cellestra. How far away from Sylene did you think you could lead me before I got tired of chasing ghosts?"

Blue Eyes glared at him. "If you're going to shoot, shoot. I don't have to listen to you too."

"I haven't decided if I'm going to shoot you," replied Nighthawk. "I admire loyalty, even if it's misdirected."

"Then what happens next?"

"You leave the ship and we go find Ibn ben Khalid. Melisande, you and Kinoshita come along. Friday, wait here; I don't need you blowing up anything else."

"If the adventure is to end here, I insist on coming along," said Friday.

Nighthawk stared at him for a long moment, then turned to Kinoshita. "Frisk him. Make sure he's not carrying anything that can go *bang!*"

Kinoshita slid his hands over the red alien with obvious distaste, then turned back to Nighthawk. "He's clean."

"Okay, you can come with us," said Nighthawk. "And don't forget what I told you on the ship about blowing things up without my approval."

"I will not forget," said Friday, joining them on the ground.

Nighthawk turned and began walking toward Customs, followed by his motley little crew. A few moments later they were cleared to leave the spaceport. He flagged down a vehicle and directed its computer to take them to The Blue Dragon.

"Why are we going there?" asked Blue Eyes.

"Nostalgia," replied Nighthawk, so ominously that the dragon fell silent, afraid to ask any more questions. Kinoshita never took his eyes off Friday, and every time the alien moved the little man's hand snaked down toward his weapon.

Melisande looked acutely uncomfortable, as indeed she was, with powerful and unpleasant emotions emanating from both Kinoshita and Friday. From Nighthawk all she could read was eagerness, an urge to confront whatever he thought was waiting at The Blue Dragon.

"You know, we don't have to do this," said Blue Eyes at last.

"Do what?" asked Nighthawk.

"Kill him."

"Yes, we do. That's why I was created."

"You don't even know him. He's a good man, Widowmaker."

"I'm not political. This is just business."

"It's *more* than business! You're killing an important man!"

"The fate of someone who's closer to me than a father or a brother depends on my killing him," said Nighthawk.

"You could *say* he was dead," urged Blue Eyes. "Your employers are half a galaxy away. They'd never know."

"I can't take the chance. The Widowmaker has got to survive."

"You *are* the Widowmaker."

Nighthawk shook his head. "I'm his shadow. He's depending on me. I can't let him down."

"Ibn ben Khalid might kill you instead."

"He might," admitted Nighthawk.

"What then?"

"Then Friday will blow up the whole damned city before he has a chance to get out of it," said Nighthawk.

The vehicle came to a stop in front of The Blue Dragon and hovered a few inches above the ground. Nighthawk paid the driver while his companions were getting out, then joined them in front of the entrance.

"I beg you," said Blue Eyes. "Let him live!"

Nighthawk stared at him emotionlessly, offered

no reply, and finally entered the tavern, followed by the rest of his team.

As usual, The Blue Dragon was filled with a motley assortment of Men and aliens. There were two Canphorites, a Lodinite, four Gengi, a huge Bortai sitting alone in one corner, two other races that Nighthawk couldn't identify, and perhaps a dozen Men scattered at tables around the room.

Nighthawk and his companions sat down at a table near the entrance.

"Is he here?" asked Kinoshita, scanning the room.

"If he isn't, he will be soon," answered Nighthawk. "Order your drinks. I'm paying."

And then, just as the drinks were delivered to the table, a slender young man, carelessly dressed, his hair poorly combed, walked in and approached the bar.

"Stay here," said Nighthawk softly, as he got to his feet and walked across the tavern to confront the young man.

"You're back early," observed Nicholas Jory. "Did you find your man?"

"Eventually," said Nighthawk.

"Kill him?"

"Soon."

Blue Eyes got to his feet and approached the bar. "I'm sorry, Ibn ben Khalid. I tried to lead him away from you!"

Nicholas looked at Blue Eyes, then back to Nighthawk.

"So you've figured it out, have you?"

"It wasn't that difficult."

"And now you're going to kill me?"

"That's the general idea."

"What did I ever do to you?"

"It's what you did to Cassandra Hill," answered Nighthawk.

"You've never even met her," said Nicholas. "Why do you want to kill me over a woman you don't know?"

"I have my reasons."

"Why don't you use that brain of yours to come up with a reason to join my cause instead?"

"Not interested."

"I may kill *you*, you know."

"Anything's possible," replied Nighthawk.

"You don't believe it for a second, do you?" said Nicholas with a slight smile. "Maybe you should consider the fact that every man who wears a weapon out here is undefeated, just like you."

"That's why I never take anyone lightly," said Nighthawk.

"Well, I can see your mind's made up," said Nicholas, stepping away from the bar and positioning his hand over his sonic pistol. "Let's get on with it."

"Let's."

Nighthawk was a microsecond from going for his own weapon when suddenly the silence of the room was broken by the shout of a familiar voice.

"*STOP!*" yelled Melisande.

# Chapter 17

*Nighthawk froze, never taking his eyes off Nicholas Jory.*

"You're making a terrible mistake!" said Melisande, getting to her feet and approaching the two men at the bar.

"Move and you're a dead man," said Nighthawk to Nicholas. Then, to Melisande: "What the hell's going on?"

"He's not Ibn ben Khalid!" she said.

"Just because he's seen to it that the Oligarchy has holographs of the wrong man?" demanded Nighthawk. "It's one of the oldest tricks in the book. You heard Blue Eyes. You heard Jory. They both admitted that he's Ibn ben Khalid!"

"You hired me for my ability," said Melisande urgently. "Make use of it, don't ignore it!"

Nighthawk drew his weapon before Nicholas quite realized what was happening, and pointed it at the young man.

"Put your hands on the bar," he ordered.

Nicholas complied.

Nighthawk frisked him briefly, disarmed him, and then stepped back.

"All right," he said to Melisande. "Talk to me. I thought you couldn't read Blue Eyes' emotions."

"I can't."

"And you're not a telepath."

"I'm not."

"Then how can you know for certain that this man's not Ibn ben Khalid?" persisted Nighthawk.

"I know from his emotions," answered Melisande. "When Blue Eyes addressed him as if he was Ibn ben Khalid, his reaction was shock and surprise. As he realized what Blue Eyes was doing, that was replaced by feelings of exultation and loyalty. He was willing to sacrifice his life to preserve Ibn ben Khalid's true identity. Finally, when you refused to be dissuaded, his only emotional reactions were sorrow and fear."

"Was there anything else?" asked Nighthawk. "Any other emotion at all?"

Melisande frowned for a moment, then looked up at Nighthawk. "Just one thing—a rush of conflicting emotions, too forceful and too contradictory for me to separate them, when you mentioned Cassandra Hill."

"Do you think he knows where she is?"

"I read feelings, not thoughts," replied Melisande. "I have no idea if he knows where she is."

"Thanks," said Nighthawk. "Go sit down. I'll take it from here."

She walked back to the table. As she passed Blue Eyes, who was still standing near the bar, he fell into step beside her.

"Not you," said Nighthawk.

Blue Eyes looked at him questioningly. "Are you talking to *me*?"

"Get your blue ass over here. You've got some explaining to do."

The dragon approached Nighthawk. "I was protecting my leader," he said with no show of fear. "I have no regrets. I did what I thought was best, and I'd do it again."

"You may not live long enough to do it again," said Nighthawk. "You've been lying to me ever since we met, and you almost got an innocent man killed by lying to me a couple of minutes ago."

"Nicholas Jory was willing to die for the cause. I commend him for his courage."

"I couldn't care less about your cause. I want to know where Ibn ben Khalid is."

"I'm sure you do," said Blue eyes defiantly. "And after you kill me, you'll *still* want to know."

"Maybe I'll kill *him* instead," said Nighthawk, indicating Nicholas.

"He was willing to die two minutes ago to protect Ibn ben Khalid," responded the dragon. "I'm sure he still is. Do your worst."

"Or maybe I'll just find the girl and take her away until he's willing to talk."

Neither Nicholas nor Blue Eyes made any response, but Nighthawk was concentrating on Melisande, who had seated herself at the table some fifty feet away. She jumped like she'd been hit by a flying brick.

"She's here on Sylene, isn't she?" continued Nighthawk, staring intently at Nicholas.

"That's none of your damned business!"

"For the time being, it's my *only* business," Nighthawk replied. "Have you got Cassandra Hill stashed away at your place?"

"Go look. I'm not telling you anything."

*You just did. If you're willing to have your rooms searched, she's not there. But she's got to be close. You're too nervous for her not to be.*

He turned to face Blue Eyes. "You know where she is, don't you?"

"Why don't you just return to Deluros and leave us in peace?" answered the dragon. "You don't belong here. You don't belong anywhere. You should have died a century ago. Stop meddling in our business."

Nighthawk stared at the man and the dragon for a long moment, then turned to the tavern at large.

"All right," he said in a loud voice. "Everybody out. The bar's closed."

A few patrons looked at him curiously. He waved his gun in their direction.

"Now," he said.

Most of the Men and aliens got up and left. The Canphorites and a trio of Men remained.

"Ito, count to thirty and shoot any customers who are still in the tavern."

Kinoshita got to his feet, guns drawn, and faced the remaining patrons. The Canphorites made it out the door in ten seconds, the Men in twelve.

"All right," said Kinoshita to Nighthawk after the last of them had left. "What's going on?"

"I didn't want them to distract Melisande."

"Distract me from what?" she asked.

"You told me that proximity makes a difference in your ability to read emotions."

"Yes, but—"

"I want you to concentrate—hard," said Nighthawk. "Can you read anything that isn't coming from me, Kinoshita, Friday, or Jory?"

"You think that she's *here*?"

As Melisande uttered the words, she reeled as if she'd been hit.

"She's not at his place. And he just reacted at the suggestion, didn't he?"

"*Some*one did," she confirmed.

"All right. Tell me if you can read anyone else."

"I'll try."

"Don't bother," said a female voice from behind them, and they turned to see a slim, dark-haired woman in her late twenties stepping out through a sliding panel in the wall.

"Cassandra Hill, I presume?" said Nighthawk.

"Yes," she said.

"Are you all right?"

"Perfectly."

"I'm here to—"

"I know why you're here," said Cassandra Hill. "I'm sorry you've wasted your time, but I was not kidnapped by Ibn ben Khalid. I'm here of my own free will."

"What about the ransom demand?"

"Ibn ben Khalid saw a way to extort two million credits from my father. When you're in the revolution business, you do what you have to do."

"And you didn't object?"

"There is no love lost between my father and me. He's a vile, corrupt man, and I hope Ibn ben Khalid brings him to justice."

Nighthawk frowned. "That's too bad."

"Why?"

"I'm going to have to return you to him."

"But I've already told you—I wasn't kidnapped!" she said. "I'm here because I want to be here." She paused. "And if I know my father, I'll bet he's more interested in killing Ibn ben Khalid than in having me returned."

"True enough," admitted Nighthawk.

"Well, then?"

"I sympathize—but I don't have any choice."

"You can choose to walk away and forget you ever saw me," said Cassandra.

"It's not that simple," said Nighthawk. "The life of someone very important to me depends on my returning you to your father."

"I don't want to go back." She nodded her head toward Melisande. "Ask your Balatai woman."

Nighthawk turned to Melisande. "She's telling the truth, of course?"

"No."

"That's a lie!" snapped Cassandra.

"She doesn't want to go back," continued Melisande. "And she seems to genuinely hate her father. But there was a lot of insincerity in her answers—I would characterize it as misdirection."

"Once we find Ibn ben Khalid, we'll find out how much of what she said is the truth," said Kinoshita.

Melisande reeled again, like a boxer absorbing a blow to the head.

*Well, I'll be damned*, thought Nighthawk. *Suddenly the pieces fit together*.

"I think that would be a waste of time, don't you, Miss Hill?" said Nighthawk.

She stared coldly at him. "I don't think he could tell you anything I couldn't tell you myself."

"That remains to be seen," said Kinoshita.

"No it doesn't," said Nighthawk.

"What the hell are you talking about?"

Nighthawk looked at Cassandra Hill. "Do you want to tell him, or should I?"

"You do it," she replied.

"Tell me *what*?" demanded Kinoshita.

"Cassandra Hill is only one of her names," said Nighthawk. He paused for effect. "Say hello to Ibn ben Khalid."

# Chapter 18

*"You're crazy!" exclaimed Kinoshita.*

"Am I?" responded Nighthawk. He gestured to Melisande. "Ask *her*."

"He's right," said the empath.

"But it doesn't make any sense!"

"It makes all the sense in the world," said Nighthawk. "We know she hates her father. We can assume he's as corrupt as most politicians, since he paid my law firm to oversee the performance of a highly illegal act—and, of course, he's also commissioned an illegal hit." Nighthawk paused. "I submit to you that that kind of corruption doesn't occur overnight. If Cassandra was appalled by it as an adolescent, she probably had access to enough information to start thwarting him. And since she didn't want to do it openly, for any number of reasons ranging from preserving her sources of information to preserving her life, she needed another identity."

"But Ibn ben Khalid is a *man's* name!"

"It just means she's better at misdirection than most of us," answered Nighthawk.

"Ibn ben Khalid has been operating out here for a decade," continued Kinoshita, not yet willing to admit he was wrong. "She'd have been a teenager then. Who would follow a teenaged girl into battle?"

"You still don't understand, do you?" said Nighthawk. "Think back, Ito. We've been all over the Frontier. How many of Ibn ben Khalid's followers have actually seen him? *That's* why there's such a complex chain of command. There are probably less than a dozen people out here who know Ibn ben Khalid is actually Cassandra Hill."

"Nineteen, to be exact," interjected Cassandra.

"Well, I'll be damned!" muttered Kinoshita.

"Probably you will be," she agreed. Suddenly she turned to Nighthawk. "Now that you know, what do you propose to do about it?"

"Nothing, for the moment."

"It is our mission to kill her," said Friday.

"Don't be a fool," shot back Nighthawk. "You don't think she'd have shown herself if we weren't covered, do you?" He looked at Cassandra. "How many guns are pointing at us right now?"

"Eight," she said. Then, "I know how good you are, Widowmaker. But they're well hidden; even *you* can't kill all of them before one of them gets in a fatal shot."

Nighthawk looked carefully around the tavern. "All right," he said. "You're calling the shots. What next?"

"Next? Next we talk."

"What about?"

"What are your intentions if you survive this meeting?" she said. "You're being paid to return Cassandra Hill and kill Ibn ben Khalid. You can't do both."

Nighthawk poured himself a drink. "I'll have to think about it."

"There's another alternative," said Cassandra.

"There usually is."

She looked at his team. "The rest of you go outside and wait for us. I want to talk to the Widowmaker alone."

They arose and began moving to the door.

"Just a minute!" she said firmly. "You—the red one!"

Friday turned back to her.

"Leave your weapons here on the table."

"Why just me?" demanded the alien.

"Because I don't trust you. Do what I say."

Friday shrugged, unstrapped his various pistols and knives, and placed them gently on the table, then walked out to join the others.

"You look approving," noted Cassandra, sitting down across from Nighthawk.

"You picked the right one. He'd just as soon kill the two of us as look at us."

"Then why is he working for you?"

"If he wasn't working for me, he'd be following me," answered Nighthawk. "At least this way I can keep an eye on him. And . . ." He paused.

"Yes?"

"We weren't going on a picnic," he continued. "He's good at his job."

"I heard about his 'job' on Cellestra."

"He thought he was coming to my rescue," said Nighthawk. "I can't fault him for that."

"You can fault his judgment."

Nighthawk shook his head. "It had nothing to do with judgment. He'll use any excuse he can find for killing Men. That excuse was better than most."

"What about the others?" asked Cassandra. "Do you trust them?"

"I don't trust anyone. But I'm willing to turn my back on them."

"They say that Kinoshita used to be a lawman out here on the Frontier."

"So I've been told," replied Nighthawk.

"Is he good at his work?"

"Relatively."

"But he's no Widowmaker?"

"No," answered Nighthawk. "He's no Widowmaker." He stared at her. "Are you going to make your offer pretty soon? I'm starting to get hungry."

"What offer?"

"It's pretty obvious," he said. "You want me to join you, and you're wondering whether to make the offer just to me, or to my whole team."

"Well, you're not stupid, I'll give you that."

"I never said I was."

"When you virtually accused poor Nicholas of being me, I had my doubts."

"I didn't have sufficient information," he replied. "He was dead drunk the first time Melisande encountered him. Once I realized Blue Eyes was leading me *away* from Ibn ben Khalid, I assumed the drunkenness was Jory's way of disguising his thoughts." Suddenly Nighthawk smiled. "How could I know he didn't have any?"

"He's a lot brighter than you think."

"He's willing to die for you, and you don't care a fig about him. I wouldn't call that bright."

"Not for *me*," she corrected him. "For the cause."

"Most tax dodgers are in favor of overthrowing the government," commented Nighthawk.

"He's more than that."

"If you say so."

She stared at him again. "I'll ask you once more: if I let you live, what do you plan to do?"

"I haven't decided."

"You will concede that I can have you killed before you reach the door?"

"I concede it," answered Nighthawk. "But I don't concede you can kill me before I can kill you."

"Why should either of us die? Especially for the benefit of someone as evil as my father?"

"I told you: I don't have a choice."

"Since when don't clones have free will?"

He stared at her.

"Oh, yes," Cassandra continued. "I know all about you, Jefferson Nighthawk. You're the second clone of the original Widowmaker. You were created for the sole purpose of returning me to my father."

"And killing Ibn ben Khalid."

"And killing Ibn ben Khalid," she agreed. "But you're out here, hundreds of thousands of light-years from Deluros VIII. What power do they hold over you? Why can't you just say no?"

"If I don't bring you back, I don't get paid," answered Nighthawk. "And if I don't get paid, the first Jefferson Nighthawk gets evicted from his cryonic chamber before they've completed the cure for his disease." He paused. "I kill *other* people. I'm not suicidal."

"And you feel it would be suicide?"

"He and I are one and the same."

"How much money does he need?"

Nighthawk shrugged. "Three million, four million, five million credits. Who knows? They're close to a cure, but they haven't got it yet."

She stared at him intently, then sipped the drink that Melisande had left behind. "What would you say to ten million credits?"

"Explain."

"Would you help me bring my father down if I paid you ten million credits?" she asked. "That could keep the original Nighthawk alive for a long time—and you'd be fighting on the right side."

"Which side I fight on makes no difference to me," said Nighthawk. "But I don't have any desire to kill you. If your offer is legitimate, I'd certainly have to consider it."

"Which side you fought on made a difference to you once," she continued. "I've studied your career. The Widowmaker killed an awful lot of Men and aliens, but he was always a lawman or a bounty hunter, never an outlaw."

"I was only feeding one of me then," he replied with an ironic smile.

"You can't convince me that you're not still an ethical man," she said adamantly.

"It's not my job to convince you of anything," said Nighthawk. "*You* have to convince *me* not to kill you or return you."

"I can offer you ten million reasons."

"Okay, where are they?"

"In my father's safe."

Nighthawk leaned back in his chair and considered it. "You're saying that there's no money unless we're successful, right?"

"In essence."

"And it could take months to assemble and prepare your forces for an attack on your father, and even then they'll probably be outnumbered."

"You can't take him by force, only by stealth and surprise," she said. "We'll have to go in with a carefully assembled team." She paused. "That's one of the reasons I need you. Like I said, I've studied your career. You've done this kind of thing more than once. I need your expertise."

"But you're not prepared to pay until we succeed?"

"That's right."

"I have to consider it," he said. "If we fail, you've killed two Widowmakers."

"If I kill you right now, I've done the same thing," she noted.

"True," he acknowledged.

"Consider something else," she continued. "If you succeed and return to Deluros, they're almost certain to terminate you. It would be very awkward to have a clone walking around, one who could identify the people who created him."

"I've known that from the moment I woke up on a lab table," he replied. "That's why I'm never going back to the Oligarchy."

"There's enough in my father's safe to keep the original Widowmaker alive *and* give you a stake for a new life."

He stared at her without replying.

"You're weakening, aren't you?" she said with a smile.

"I'm *considering*."

He fell silent again.

"Well?" she demanded after another moment had passed. "Are you still considering?"

"No—I'm counting."

"Millions?"

"Men."

"I don't understand."

"If we're going to become partners, we have to trust each other," said Nighthawk. "Until you know I could have killed all eight of your gunmen and chose not to, you'll never be sure that I won't turn on you when the opportunity presents itself." He looked around the room. "Three behind the see-through mirror in back of the bar. Another one behind the door to the dressing room. One behind the picture that's hanging askew on the south wall. Two in the attic"—he pointed to the ceiling—"there and there. I haven't spotted the eighth yet."

"You're *good*," she said, impressed. "I made the right choice."

"Not yet," he said, still scanning the room. Suddenly he smiled. "Oh, hell, I'm an asshole. The eighth one is *you*."

She returned his smile, withdrew a tiny pistol that was attached to her wrist just inside her sleeve, and placed it on the table.

"So do we have a deal?"

"Yeah, I think we do."

"Good," she said. "I'll tell my people that your team can come and go freely."

"Tell them to keep an eye on the red alien," said Nighthawk. "He doesn't much care about sides, as long as he gets to kill Men."

She nodded and extended her hand. "Welcome to the cause, Widowmaker."

"Keep your cause," he said, taking her small hand in his own. "You'd just better be right about how much is in the safe."

# Chapter 19

*It was evening. Nighthawk's team had returned to the* hotel, and he had remained behind at The Blue Dragon. There was an apartment above the bar, and Cassandra Hill had invited him upstairs to join her for dinner.

"This place is too tastefully decorated for it to belong to Blue Eyes," commented Nighthawk as he entered the place. "You've a good eye for art."

"You recognize some of the artists?" she asked.

"A few. The Morita sculpture is exquisite."

"I'm genuinely surprised," she said. "I never expected a man in your profession to have any knowledge of art."

"I've been sent out to retrieve it often enough."

"There's a difference between retrieving it and studying it."

"You think a man who kills for a living can't appreciate art?" he asked wryly.

"Well . . . I . . ."

"Let me tell you something," he said. "When you put your life on the line all the time, it heightens *all* your perceptions." He paused, staring at the sculpture. "Also, since you become aware of your mortality, you tend to appreciate those things that will outlive you. Morita died more than a millennia ago, and people still flock to see his work."

"I meant no offense," she said.

"None taken. I was just explaining."

"Well," she said, "you like artwork, so maybe my pride and joy won't be wasted on you. Follow me."

She led the way to a large room, paneled with imported hardwood. Three walls were covered with shelves, and the shelves themselves were covered with books. There were thousands of them, beautifully bound, many with gilt pages, a few with engraved covers, all with bent or broken spines that proved they were for reading rather than for decoration.

Nighthawk walked to the middle of the room, stood with his hands on his hips for a long moment, and then began examining the shelves.

"What do you think?" she asked.

"I've never seen so many books in one place," he replied.

"There used to be lots of libraries like this, I'm told, before you could fit an entire encyclopedia on a chip a tenth the size of my fingernail." She picked a volume up from the shelf. "I like the heft and smell of a book. The reading experience seems inadequate and lacking when you read from a holoscreen."

"I see you even have one by Tanblixt," noted Nighthawk.

"The greatest of the alien poets."

"I know. I've read him."

"Recently?"

He smiled. "About a century and a half ago."

She stared at him for a moment. "If there are any books you'd like to borrow . . ."

Nighthawk paused, then shook his head. "I'd be afraid something might happen to them," he said. "But if we're on Sylene for any length of time, I'd like to be able to read some right here in your library."

"You're welcome to." She paused. "You're a most unusual man, Widowmaker. It's very rare to find a cultured, educated man in your line of work."

"You find all kinds of men in my line of work," he replied. "There are as many reasons as there are practitioners."

"I would have thought most of you had an overdeveloped sense of justice, or perhaps a death wish," she said with a smile.

"Take a look at Friday," responded Nighthawk. "All he wants is the opportunity to kill Men. Justice means nothing to him, and I doubt that he ever considers his own mortality."

"He's an alien."

"Don't aliens count?"

"They have different motivations."

"Do they?" said Nighthawk. "An alien named Blue Eyes did his damnedest to lead me away from you, and when I came back he was willing to sacrifice both his life and Jory's to keep your identity a secret."

"That's Blue Eyes. He's one of us."

"I thought he was an alien."

She sighed. "You're right. Here I was, sounding like exactly what I'm fighting against."

"Suppose you tell me a little more about what you're fighting against?" suggested Nighthawk.

"I'll be happy to," she said. "Just let me serve our dinner first."

"You cook, too?"

"Not when I can help it," said Cassandra. "Actually, Nicholas cooked dinner tonight."

"You live with him?" asked Nighthawk.

"I live with *me*," she answered firmly. "Nicholas likes to cook."

"I always thought I'd take it up someday."

"Cooking?"

He nodded. "You visit a couple of hundred alien worlds and suddenly nice bland digestable food becomes very important to you." He smiled. "Especially when your life may depend upon not being sick."

"I never considered that."

"Stay in the revolution business long enough and you will," he assured her.

"Perhaps."

"Now suppose you tell me just how you got into the business," said Nighthawk.

"My father," she replied. "He's the most corrupt man alive."

"I think every girl believes that at one point or another. Most of them outgrow it. How come you didn't?"

"Because in my case it wasn't a fantasy. I've heard my father give orders to kill political rivals or ambitious subordinates. He's getting kickbacks from every contractor who ever worked for the planetary government, from every spaceship company that wants docking space at our orbiting hangars, from every interest group that wants a favor."

She paused for breath, and Nighthawk noticed that her cheeks were flushed. After a moment she brought their food to the table, and they both sat down.

"He's especially vicious toward our alien population. It's his policy to hold them without trial and without bail. Any alien who kills a Man is summarily executed without a trial. The penalty for a Man who kills any alien is two hundred credits." She grimaced at the memory. "So I decided that he had to be overthrown. I created the myth of Ibn ben Khalid to misdirect his attention, and began building an organization of Men and aliens who want to see Cassius Hill overthrown."

"They say you number over a million now," commented Nighthawk. "That's an impressive force."

"It's an inflated figure, just to scare him. Hell, if I had a million men, I'd have attacked already."

"You'd have lost."

"What are you talking about?" she demanded heatedly.

"He's got a standing army of close to four million men, and he's got—what?—something like thirty thousand ships. You're not going to overthrow him with a million men, or three million, or ten million."

"We will, if right is on our side."

"I'm no historian," said Nighthawk, "but it's my observation that God tends to favor the side with the best weapons and the most manpower."

"Are you saying he can't be overthrown?" she said. "Tyrants are overthrown every year."

"Not at all," he replied. "I said he can't be success-

fully attacked by a force ten times the size of the one
that's at your disposal."

"Then what do you suggest?"

He stared at her for a long moment. "I don't know
that I'm in a position to suggest anything. Remember:
he's my employer."

"What if I showed you proof that he's every bit as
evil and corrupt as I claim he is?" she asked.

"I believe you."

"But you insist that you owe him your loyalty?"

"I don't judge the men I hunt, and I don't judge
the men I work for."

"Maybe it's time you started."

He shrugged. "Maybe it is," he agreed. "Let's discuss it while we eat."

"What's to discuss?" she said. "Either you're for
me or you're against me. Or, in your case, either you're
going to join me or you're going to try to take me back."

"Nothing's ever that simple."

"This is."

"*Nothing* is," he repeated. "I like you. I'm predisposed to like people who take moral stands, and I'm
predisposed to like people who still read books. You're
smart, and you're tough, and you've managed to convince a hell of a lot of people to join your cause. I
believe everything you said about your father, and I
have no admiration for those who take advantage of the
weak."

"Well, then?"

"Half a galaxy away, on Deluros VIII, there's a
cryonics chamber almost a mile beneath the surface of
the planet. A few thousand men and women are frozen
there. Most of them have diseases and are awaiting
cures. A few committed crimes and are waiting for the

statue of limitations to run out. A handful simply don't like the government or the economy, and are waiting for better times to live out the rest of their lives. There's even one, I'm told, a botanist who found a flower that only blooms once every three centuries, and wants to be alive to see it." Nighthawk took a bite of his meal, chewed it thoughtfully, and nodded approvingly.

"The one thing all these men and women have in common is that they're extremely wealthy," he went on. "Wealthy enough to be able to afford the enormous expense of remaining frozen. There's only one man there who *doesn't* have the financial wherewithal to remain frozen until his disease can be cured. His name is Jefferson Nighthawk. He's not my father, he's not my twin brother. He's *me*, and I can't let him down."

"I see."

"I told you: nothing is ever as simple as it seems," he said with a rueful smile. "If I don't deliver you to your father, I won't get paid—and if I don't get paid, the original version of me, the man who *is* the Widowmaker, who gave me his body and his memory so that I could protect his existence, is going to die. I won't allow that."

"So no matter what you feel about me or about my father, you're going to try to return me?"

" 'Try to' is a misstatement. If I decide to return you, I'll do it."

"Not without a fight," she promised.

"I'd expect one."

"Even the Widowmaker can die."

"I'm living proof of that," answered Nighthawk. "Or, rather, the original is dying proof of it."

"Then I guess the battle lines are drawn," said Cassandra. "Do you just plan to eat dinner, read a good book, and then carry me off?"

"There are always alternatives," said Nighthawk. "I thought we might explore some of them."

"I'm willing," she said. "What do you have in mind?"

"How liquid is your father?"

"I beg your pardon?"

"You said he has ten million credits in his safe. Are you guessing, or do you *know*?"

"Why?"

"Because ten million is enough to keep the original Nighthawk alive, and pay for my cure as well, once a cure is developed."

"He's got it, and more," she said decisively.

"If I helped overthrow him, I'd want that money as payment for my services."

"You've already said that Pericles V is impregnable. How will my agreeing to pay you make a difference?"

"What I said was an army of a million men couldn't overthrow your father," he said. "I didn't say there weren't other ways to accomplish it."

"Such as?"

"Well, most obviously, we try to lure him out here, where he's vulnerable, and kill him," said Nighthawk. He took a deep breath and let it out slowly. "And if that doesn't work, we'll do it the hard way."

"All right, Mr. Nighthawk," she said. "What's the hard way?"

"We take my team to Pericles V," he answered. "I assembled them for the purpose of killing one man, and that's still our purpose. Only now the man will be Cassius Hill instead of Ibn ben Khalid."

She stared at him. "I admire your confidence."

"I handpicked that team for a reason. They're not much to look at, and they don't get along very well—but they're goddamned good at what they do." He finished his food and shoved the plate aside. "Still, it'll be much easier if we can draw him out here, where he's not protected by so many men and devices."

"How will you do that?"

"It shouldn't be too hard," said Nighthawk. "After all, I've got something he wants."

"What is that?"

"You."

# Chapter 20

Cassandra looked up from the book she was reading. "You're back again."

"Not much to do on this little dirtball," replied Nighthawk, as he entered her apartment. "At least you've got books I can read."

She put her book on a table and stared at him. "I've also got an army you can use."

He shook his head. "Too disorganized. And too outnumbered." He paused. "I keep telling you: you can't storm a well-armed fortress with a ragtag mob. Your father's probably got a ton of spies in your army, ready to tell him every order you give. And there's something else, too."

"Oh?"

"Only Blue Eyes and Jory and maybe a handful of others know you're Cassandra Hill. When the rest find out, your life won't be worth ten credits. At least half of them will think the creation of Ibn ben Khalid was a trick created by your father to pinpoint who was disloyal to him."

"Not after I explain it to them."

"This is the Frontier. There's going to be at least one man in each audience who doesn't feel like waiting for an explanation."

"You're wrong," she said adamantly. "These are *my* men. They're committed to my cause."

"Let's hope we don't have to find out. Much better to present them with a fait accompli."

"So when are you going to do it?" she asked.

"It's too soon," said Nighthawk.

She looked annoyed. "He's not getting any weaker, you know."

"I know. But I haven't been out here long enough. If I find Cassandra Hill and Ibn ben Khalid too easily, he'll think something's wrong."

"How can you be sure of that?" she demanded. "You don't even know him."

"I know that he's suspicious of just about everyone. It's not as if he hasn't got his share of enemies."

Cassandra nodded. "His share and more."

Nighthawk walked over to a bookcase and started scanning the titles. He pulled a couple out, thumbed through them, and put them back.

"Too much fiction," he announced at last.

"I beg your pardon?"

"You want to be a leader," he said. "You should be reading books about politics and leadership. Even Machiavelli. Ninety percent of your library is fiction." He grimaced in contempt. "Totally useless."

"It teaches you about people."

"It's filled with lies."

"Its plots are lies—but it's filled with truth. The good stuff, anyway."

"You want to be a leader," he noted. "How does a made-up story about people who never existed teach you anything about how real people think?"

"That's very strange," she said.

"What is?"

"It seems to me that you, the cold-blooded killer, should be the one who wants to escape into fiction."

"Me? Why?"

"As an alternative to the horrors and grimness of your occupation."

"I've been a lawman and a bounty hunter," answered Nighthawk. "I've never been a criminal."

"Meaning what?"

"There's nothing horrible about my work," he explained. "I bring felons to justice. There are times when it can be very satisfying."

"You take satisfaction in killing people?"

"Not as much, I suspect, as you'll take in the death of your father."

"That's different," she said. "It's personal."

"Are you saying you've assembled an army just to help you settle a personal grudge?" he asked.

"No, of course not. They're the dispossessed and disenfranchised."

"And you're their spokesman?"

"In a way."

"Then, in a way," he said, "I'm the ombudsman

for all those people who have been swindled or killed by men with prices on their heads."

He half expected a furious outburst. Instead she threw back her head and laughed.

"You're a very intelligent man."

"Thank you."

"You're wasted in your current profession."

"I don't think so," he replied. "There are lots of bright men. There's only one Widowmaker."

"Perhaps."

"Perhaps?" he repeated.

"What about the original—the man you were cloned from?"

"As I told you, he's frozen until they come up with a cure for eplasia."

She made a face. "You hadn't said it was eplasia. Is there a chance you could catch it too?"

"There's considerably more than a chance," he said. "I've already got it."

She studied him, looking for some sign of it.

"It's in the very early stages," he continued. "You won't see any sign of it for another year or two."

"It's a horrible way to die!" she said with a shudder. "The skin just rots away until the body is exposed to so many infections that it finally can't fight them off any longer."

"I don't plan to die."

"No one ever plans to die. But we all do."

"Let me amend that, then. I don't plan to die from *eplasia*. They'll have a cure before much longer. That's why I'm here—to earn enough to keep the original Widowmaker alive and eventually cure him." He paused. "And I'll need some extra money for me."

"We'll get it," said Cassandra. She paused thoughtfully. "You should get quite a thrill when you meet him after you're both cured."

"I don't think I will."

"Get a thrill?"

"Meet him."

"Why not?"

"I don't know," he admitted. "I just have a feeling that the two of us should never meet, that it would somehow be like a time paradox where you meet yourself. I'm sure it won't destroy the universe or bring time to a stop, but I think it would be better if it never happens."

"Will he at least be able to thank you?"

"It's not necessary," said Nighthawk, and when she looked dubious, he added: "You don't thank yourself for brushing your teeth, or sterilizing a cut, do you? He's me, I'm him. This is just self-preservation."

"You must have some interesting nightmares," she said.

"A few," he admitted.

"Then why be something that disturbs you?"

"That's the kind of question men are supposed to ask of women who are in Melisande's line of work," he replied with a smile.

"I'm serious."

He shrugged. "I don't know," he replied. "It's one of those things you don't think about much. I guess I've just got a talent for it."

"How do you *know* you have a talent for it?" she persisted. "Did you kill the butler when you were three years old?"

"I suppose I might have, if we'd had one," he said with a amused smile.

"You're not very forthcoming."

"That's because it's *his* life, and I don't know if he'd want me to answer you or not."

"But you told me you had all of the original's memories," she said. "So it's your life as well."

"They're his memories, not mine," answered Nighthawk. "He's got a proprietary claim on them."

"I've never met anyone quite like you."

"I'll assume that's a compliment."

She fell silent, and he continued looking at the spines of her books, considering first one title, then another, and finally withdrawing one.

"What have you decided on?" she asked.

"Tanblixt," he replied.

"That's a collector's item," she noted. "It's in the original Canphorian."

"I can read it a bit."

"You continue to surprise me," said Cassandra.

"I've had to work with Canphorites in the past," he said. "They're easier to get along with if you try to learn their language."

"Even though the law demands that all aliens must learn Terran or equip themselves with T-packs?"

"Especially because of the law."

"Good," she said. "I approve."

"Of course you approve. You're Ibn ben Khalid."

"When I'm not being Cassandra Hill."

He smiled. "At least I'm always Jefferson Nighthawk, even if I don't always know *which* Jefferson Nighthawk I am."

She laughed again. "You're just not what I expected the Widowmaker to be like."

"You haven't seen the Widowmaker yet. Just Nighthawk."

"Aren't you one and the same?"

"No," he said. "I'm always Nighthawk. I'm only the Widowmaker when I have to be."

"With all our identities, I'm surprised the room doesn't feel more crowded," said Cassandra.

He smiled at her. "You're all right, Hill. I'm glad we're going after your father instead."

"I'm pleased you should think so."

He uttered a statement that was totally incomprehensible to her.

"Would you repeat that, please?" she asked.

He did so.

"What was that?"

"A compliment," said Nighthawk.

"In Canphorian?"

"Lodinese."

"You speak Lodinese too?"

"A little."

"You're a man of many accomplishments."

"I've tried to be," he said. "It's ironic that I'll only be remembered for one of them."

"It's the one that topples empires," she noted.

He shook his head emphatically. "Empires don't fall because the emperor dies. There's always another one eager to take his place. They fall, when they fall, because they're too corrupt *not* to fall."

"So you don't think my father's little empire will come tumbling down?"

"Maybe so, maybe not," answered Nighthawk. "It depends on the nature of the empire. Personally, I'll be satisfied if he has enough money to keep my progenitor alive."

"He has that, and more."

"We'll see."

"You don't believe me?"

"It's nothing personal. I don't believe anyone. Ever. That's how I lived to be sixty-one."

"You don't look sixty-one."

He smiled ruefully. "One of me does."

"That one's not getting any younger or any healthier," she said. "How soon do you think you can contact my father?"

"A few weeks, maybe a month."

"That's too long. I can have my army assembled here in less than two weeks."

"I told you before: I don't want your army."

"I know what you told me. But they're loyal and motivated. Surely you can find some way to use them."

"They'd just be cannon fodder," responded Nighthawk. "I'm a killer, not a general. I don't need them."

"But—"

"You really want to make them useful to us?" he interrupted her. "Have them assemble, publicly and noisily, on some world halfway across the Frontier. Maybe we can draw a few of your father's divisions out there to keep an eye on them. It might make our escape—assuming we live long enough to *attempt* an escape—easier." He paused. "But first, let's see if your father is dumb enough to come out here, before we do it the hard way."

"He'll come," she said firmly.

"Don't bet your last credit on it," said Nighthawk. "He didn't get where he is by being stupid."

"He paid whatever it cost to create you, just to rescue me," she said. "Of course he'll come. All this waiting is useless."

"You've waited this long to get to him," said Nighthawk. "Wait a few weeks more."

"No," she said. "It's time."

"You're sure?"

"I know him."

*Personally, maybe. But I know him generically. And I've got a bad feeling about this.*

"Okay," said Nighthawk aloud. "I'll contact him this afternoon."

"Good!" she said. "Now you can do me another favor."

"I'm not in the favor business."

"You won't mind this one," she said.

"Oh?"

"Pour us each a drink, and then translate some of Tanblixt's poems for me."

"You have a translation right there on the shelf," said Nighthawk, walking across the room to the bar, selecting a thirty-year-old Cygnian cognac, filling a pair of glasses, and handing one to her.

"I'd like to hear how *you* translate it."

"You're sure?"

She nodded. "And I like the way your voice sounds—possibly because I've yet to hear you threaten my life."

He stared at her and made no reply. Finally he took a sip of his drink, and a moment later he was reciting an intricate rhyming triplet about the incredible light refraction at sunset on Canphor VII.

# Chapter 21

*Nighthawk was sitting at a table in the bar, nursing a* drink before making his transmission to Cassius Hill, when Ito Kinoshita entered and sat down next to him.

"What's up?" asked Nighthawk.

"I thought maybe *you* might tell *me*," replied Kinoshita. "We've been sitting around for days, waiting for action." He signaled for a beer, and took a long swallow when it arrived. "I think Friday may blow up the town this week, just to keep his hand in."

"I'll have work for him soon."

"And the rest of us?" asked Kinoshita.

"Are you that anxious to go out and shoot people?" asked Nighthawk.

"I'm anxious to stop feeling useless. We all are.

We know why you originally assembled us ... but we've *found* Ibn ben Khalid, so do we serve any further purpose?"

"A bigger one."

"Would you care to enlighten me?"

"Soon," said Nighthawk. "I have to speak to Cassandra's father first."

"Cassius Hill?" said Kinoshita sharply.

"That's right."

"Are you going to turn her over to him?"

Nighthawk shook his head. "If things were that simple, I wouldn't need you and the others."

"But he's your employer!"

"I'm sure it pleases him to think so," answered Nighthawk. "I don't plan to do anything to spoil the illusion."

Kinoshita stared at him for a long moment. "You've thrown in with her, haven't you?"

"In a way."

"In what way?" demanded Kinoshita, lighting a smokeless Altairian cigar. "Either you're with her or you're against her. It's as simple as that."

"Nothing's ever as simple as that," said Nighthawk.

"Just what have you got in mind?"

"I'm going to try to draw him out here to Sylene, hopefully with a huge cash box," said Nighthawk calmly. "If he comes, I'll kill him."

"You're kidding, right?"

"I never kid about business."

"You think he'll come alone, or with just one or two bodyguards?" scoffed Kinoshita. "Hell, he'll come with a whole division, and he won't get out of his ship until they've searched every inch of the landing field and secured his route to wherever you plan to meet him."

"I'd expect no less of a man who's been in power as long as Cassius Hill," agreed Nighthawk.

"Well, then?"

"I'll ask if he has the money with him, and Melisande will know if he's lying or not. If he's brought it along and left it in the ship, I'm sure Friday can rig something that will wipe out most of his landing party and maybe his ship's motive power while leaving the interior of the ship intact."

"And if he's got it with him?"

"Then you and I and Blue Eyes will figure out how to separate him from it."

Kinoshita snapped his fingers. "Just like that?"

"Just like that."

"You don't believe in long, intricate plans, do you?"

"The more intricate a plan is, the more likely it is to go wrong," answered Nighthawk. "Just like a machine. The more moving parts, the more likelihood of failure." Suddenly he sighed heavily. "Unfortunately, Hill himself is one more moving part than we need. That's why I'm uneasy."

"I don't follow you."

"If I'm attacking his headquarters, even with just my handpicked crew of five, *I'm* in control of things. I decide when we approach, how we get in, when we use force, when we retreat, whether we complete our mission or abort it. But if he comes here with his men, however many or few, *he* can disrupt the most carefully laid of plans."

"Seems to me we'll save a lot of lives if he comes here."

"Maybe."

"Did anyone ever tell you that you are not the most loquacious fellow in the world?"

"You did," answered Nighthawk. "Every time we were alone together on the ship."

"Well, I was right."

"Probably. Now I want you to do me a favor."

"What is it?"

"Tell Friday to get ready to travel."

"Just Friday?"

"Melisande, too."

"Now I'm confused," said Kinoshita. "I thought Hill was coming here, to Sylene."

"He's being invited. If he comes, fine. If not, I want them ready to go to Pericles V."

"Just them?" asked Kinoshita, trying to keep the resentment out of his voice.

"Just to talk," said Nighthawk. "I'm not going to war. Yet."

"Why not Blue Eyes or me?"

"She can tell me if he's lying, and Friday can blow up the whole goddamned planet if they kill me. I need you and Blue Eyes for other things."

"You're sure?"

"I'm sure." Nighthawk gestured toward the door. "You might as well start hunting them down."

Kinoshita downed his drink and walked to the door. Once there, he turned to face Nighthawk again.

"I hope to hell you know what you're doing," he said. "We've got the girl and Ibn ben Khalid in one package. That *is* what we came out here for, isn't it?"

"We came out here to secure the Widowmaker's future," said Nighthawk. "Since I'm his shadow, I'm best qualified to decide how to do it."

"I just keep wondering if you have your priorities straight. That's a very attractive woman, and you're just a couple of months old."

Nighthawk tapped his left temple with a forefinger. "I'm sixty-one up here," he said, and then slapped his chest. "And I'm thirty-eight everywhere else. If I was going to lose my head over the first woman I saw, like the previous clone did, I'd be sneaking into Melisande's bed every night."

Kinoshita stared at him for a long moment, then turned and left, muttering to himself. Nighthawk watched him walk away, then finished his drink, got to his feet, and headed off to Cassandra's subspace transmitter.

# Chapter 22

"You'd better scram," said Nighthawk as he seated himself before the video transmission camera. "If he sees you, I'm going to have a hard time explaining why he's got to come out here with ransom money."

Cassandra nodded. "All right. And Jefferson?"

"Yes?"

"Be *very* careful. I don't think you can imagine how dangerous he is."

"I've faced dangerous men before," said Nighthawk.

"They were dangerous because they had guns. *He's* more dangerous because he's the man who pays for the bullets."

"Noted. Now leave."

She walked out the door, and a moment later he had contacted the governor's mansion on Pericles V.

"Name?" asked the bearded secretary at the other end.

"Jefferson Nighthawk."

"Where is your message originating from?"

"Sylene IV."

"And the purpose of this transmission?"

"I want to speak to Cassius Hill."

"That's quite impossible."

"You just tell him who's calling, sonny," said Nighthawk. "I guarantee he'll want to speak to me."

"I have instructions not to interrupt him, Mr. Nighthawk," said the secretary.

"That's up to you," said Nighthawk with a shrug. "But when he fires you for not putting my call through, remember that you were warned."

The secretary stared nervously at Nighthawk's hologram. "What, exactly, do you wish to speak to Governor Hill about?"

"That's none of your business," said Nighthawk. "Just get him."

"I have to tell him *something* besides your name!" said the secretary.

"It's your funeral," said Nighthawk, reaching out to deactivate the subspace tightbeam.

*"Wait!"* shouted the secretary suddenly.

Nighthawk froze.

"I'll see what I can do. Please stay where you are."

The screen went blank for a full minute, and then the secretary's image was replaced by that of a man in his mid-fifties, gray-haired and gray-eyed, with hard lines running down his face and jaw.

"Mr. Nighthawk," he said. "We meet at last." He

puffed on a New Kentucky cigar, filling the air with clouds of white smoke. "Please forgive my fool of a secretary."

"It wasn't his fault," replied Nighthawk. "He has no idea who I am."

"I fired him anyway."

Nighthawk shrugged. "You do what you have to do. It's no skin off my ass."

"Good."

"What's good about it?"

"I don't tell you how to do your job," said Hill. "I don't want you telling me how to do mine."

"No problem," said Nighthawk. "Your job couldn't interest me less."

"Fine," said Hill. "Now let's talk about *your* job. I assume that's why you contacted me?"

"That's right."

"Well? Have you found him?"

Nighthawk nodded. "And her."

"Well, of course if you found *him* you'd find *her* too," said Hill. He puffed thoughtfully on his cigar for a long moment. "Is he dead?"

"No."

"Shit." Another puff. "I thought you were under orders to kill him. What went wrong?"

"I was under orders to bring your daughter back alive and well," answered Nighthawk. "I assumed that took precedence."

"Never assume a damned thing, Mr. Nighthawk," said Hill angrily. "All right. Where are they?"

"Not far."

"*How* far?"

"I don't think you really want me to say, just in case this is being monitored."

"What the fuck do *I* care if it's being monitored?" demanded Hill. "Where the hell are they?"

"Are you going to listen to me, or are you going to bluster?" asked Nighthawk.

Hill glared at him, then nodded his head. "Okay, Mr. Nighthawk, you have the floor. Make use of it."

"He wants to deal."

"Ibn ben Khalid?" asked Hill sharply.

"That's who we're talking about, isn't it?"

"Continue."

*What do I need? Five million for the cryonics lab back on Deluros VIII, another million for my own medical treatment, more to live on . . .*

"He'll turn her over to you for eight million credits, or its equivalent in Maria Theresa dollars."

"Eight million credits!" exploded Hill. "What does he think I'm made of—money?"

"He thinks you're a loving father who will pay to have his daughter returned unharmed."

"He wants small unmarked bills, no doubt," said Hill sardonically.

"He didn't say. But there's a condition."

"There always is. Out with it."

"He wants you to deliver the money in person."

"So he can blow me away the second I get off my ship," said Hill. "I know he's a bastard, but I never thought he was such a transparent bastard."

"That's where I come in," said Nighthawk.

"Explain."

"I'm the guarantor of the transaction. I guarantee your safety, I guarantee your daughter's safety, and I guarantee that you're not paying him off in bogus bills."

"Not good enough," said Hill. "He's got a million men."

"Not on Sylene IV, he doesn't," said Nighthawk.

"Is that where they are—him and my daughter?"

"No," said Nighthawk. "You come here. I make sure the money's real, and that you're not dragging an army or navy behind you, and then I take you to them."

"What's to stop him from killing both of us?" demanded Hill.

"Me."

"Still not good enough," said Hill, noting that his cigar had gone out and relighting it. "You may be the best, but when all is said and done, you're just one man. He's got a million of them."

Nighthawk caught himself just as he was about to say, in reassuring tones, "Spread all across the Frontier." *No sense letting him think there are so few men here he can march right in with his own forces.* Instead he said, "I've arranged for you to meet him with no one else present. If he reneges, we won't go in. Believe me, he wants his ransom money as much as you want your daughter."

"I don't doubt it," said Hill. "But I don't like the feel of this. Too many things can go wrong."

"Nothing will. That's what you created *me* for."

"I created you to kill Ibn ben Khalid and bring my daughter back to me!" snapped Hill. "And from where I'm sitting, you've failed."

"I can kill him tomorrow and bring you back a corpse, if that's what it takes to make you happy," said Nighthawk.

Hill glared at Nighthawk's image again, then lowered his head in thought. He looked up a moment later. "What does he need eight million credits for?"

"What does anyone need eight million credits for?"

"Is he buying guns for his army?"

"I've seen them," said Nighthawk. "And believe me, they've *got* guns."

"Payroll, then?"

"This is a revolution, Governor Hill. His army doesn't want money, just blood—yours."

Hill puffed away at his cigar without saying anything, and finally Nighthawk spoke again:

"It's up to you, Governor Hill. What do you want to do?"

There was still no answer.

"Do you want me to set up a meet with Ibn ben Khalid or not?" continued Nighthawk.

"There are too many intangibles," said Hill at last.

This time it was Nighthawk's turn to stare silently at the governor's image, waiting for him to clarify his meaning.

"Too many ways to walk into a trap. Too many ways to lose the money without getting what I want."

"You won't turn over the money until he turns over your daughter," Nighthawk explained patiently.

"That's *part* of what I want," said Hill. "I also want that wild-eyed radical scum dead, remember?"

"First one, then the other," said Nighthawk agreeably.

"It won't be that simple. We'll be walking onto *his* world, under *his* conditions. He'll have five hundred guns pointed at me the second I show up."

"What makes you think so?"

"Because that's what *I'd* do!" snapped Hill. "He's not stupid, you know."

"I know. In fact, he's remarkably well read."

"Most of these revolutionary fools are."

"I need to know your decision, Governor Hill. Are you coming out here?"

"Not yet. There's too much to be considered, too many preparations to make." He paused. "I want *you* to come to Pericles."

"I think you're making a mistake."

"I told you before: I don't like people telling me how to do my job."

"Your job is being a governor. Mine is getting your daughter back and killing Ibn ben Khalid."

"And since you haven't done it, I want you here to discuss strategy."

"All right. When?"

"Immediately."

"I can be there in about twenty Standard hours."

"Fine. And come alone."

"I have a friend who goes where I go," said Nighthawk.

"Human or alien?"

"Human."

"Male or female?"

"Female."

Hill considered it for a moment, then nodded. "All right. But no one else."

"Agreed."

"I'll see you tomorrow," said Nighthawk, deactivating the machine.

Cassandra returned a few minutes later.

"Well?" she said. "What do you think of him?"

"I'm very grateful to him."

"You're grateful?" she repeated with a frown.

"That's right."

"Why?"

"Because every now and then, I wonder about the moral and philosophical implications of my business. Then I meet someone like your father, and I realize that

I was put here to kill men like that." He paused. "I find the thought of killing him very satisfying."

She stared at him. "You puzzle me. You love literature, and you have excellent manners, and you're considerate of my wishes, and you *seem* to have a well-developed sense of right and wrong—and every time I think I'm growing fond of you, you say something like that."

"And now you're not fond of me?" he asked.

"I wish I knew," she said in troubled tones.

# Chapter 23

*The ship settled down gently on the Pericles V landing strip.*

"Are you certain that you don't want me to accompany you?" asked Friday, getting to his feet and stretching his legs, one at a time, as a dog might.

"You take one step outside the ship and they'll either blow you away or cancel the meeting," answered Nighthawk.

"Then I still don't see why you brought me."

"You like to blow things up, don't you?"

"Yes."

"If Melisande and I aren't back in twenty-four Standard hours, blow the whole fucking planet to kingdom come."

Friday smiled an alien smile. "I knew I would enjoy working with you, Widowmaker."

"Don't jump the gun," cautioned Nighthawk. "I have every expectation of being back here long before the deadline."

"Deadline," repeated Friday. "I like that word."

"Somehow I'm not surprised," muttered Nighthawk. He turned to Melisande. "Are you ready?"

She nodded her head.

"Okay," continued Nighthawk. "Remember, you don't have to say a word *during* the meeting. I just want to know afterward when he was lying and when he was telling the truth."

"I understand."

"I hope so."

"I'm not a fool, Nighthawk."

"Nobody's a fool," he replied. "But you'd be surprised how many people can pass for fools when things go wrong."

He ordered the hatch to open and escorted her out onto the tarmac. A vehicle with a built-in robotic chauffeur was waiting for them.

"Jefferson Nighthawk?" asked the mechanical driver.

"Yes."

"May I ask the name of your companion?"

"Her name's Melisande."

"That's a lovely name."

Melisande smiled, and Nighthawk suddenly winked at her.

"I was mistaken," he said. "Her name's Fungus."

"What an absolutely beautiful name!" said the driver enthusiastically.

Nighthawk grinned. "But everyone calls her Melisande."

"I see."

"You know," said Melisande, "I think that might be the first time I ever saw you smile."

"Stick around a decade and maybe I'll do it again," said Nighthawk. He looked ahead and leaned forward. "Driver, where are we going? The spaceport's off to your left."

"We are going to the governor's mansion, friend Nighthawk," replied the driver.

"Don't we have to clear Customs?"

"You already have."

"We have?"

"I have transmitted your retinagram, fingerprint, and bone structure to Security at the governor's mansion, and they have identified you as the clone of Jefferson Nighthawk, born 4933 G.E., still living." It paused. "I regret to inform you that we have not yet identified the woman Fungus, who prefers to be called Melisande."

"I was mistaken," said Nighthawk. "Her true name is . . ." He frowned and looked at Melisande. "What the hell *is* your real name?"

"Private."

"Whatever you wish."

"Am I to understand that the woman's name is Private?" asked the driver.

"No," said Nighthawk. "You are to understand that she does not choose to divulge her name, but that you may call her Melisande."

"It's a lovely name."

"We're delighted that you think so."

They took a sharp left turn and began speeding along a paved road that cut through some farm fields.

"To your left," announced the driver, "we are growing the mutated soybeans that form the staple of the

Periclean diet. To your right, the hybrid cattle, imported from Earth itself, that yield 99.2 percent meat and only .8 percent fat. The tall plants just past the cattle pasture are native to this world, and closely resemble the nutritious Calaban fruit of Pollux IV. Have you any questions, friends Nighthawk and Melisande?"

"How long until we reach the governor's mansion?" asked Nighthawk.

"In terms of distance or time?"

"Whichever makes you happy."

"I am incapable of emotion," answered the driver. "I feel a certain mathematical satisfaction by answering a question completely and accurately. The answer to *your* question is 3.27 miles and/or four Standard minutes and nineteen seconds."

"Thanks," said Nighthawk. "Are you programmed to answer all questions?"

"Yes."

"Good. How many Security personnel are at the governor's mansion?"

"Please withdraw your question, friend Nighthawk."

"Why?"

"You have created a conflict within me. I am programmed to answer all questions, but I have been specifically forbidden to answer any question relating to Security."

Nighthawk was silent for a moment, and the vehicle started veering crazily.

"I withdraw the question."

"Thank you," said the driver as the vehicle once again began moving straight and true.

Nighthawk had been studying the countryside during the trip, filing bits and pieces away for future use. If he had to hide in this sector, that tree was hollow and this hill could shield him from the road. If he needed to get to the spaceport, an airsled could shave two minutes off the time it was taking this vehicle to get to the mansion while keeping to the roads. If he had to approach under cover of night, which means of approach offered the least number of obstacles? Could a ship land in one of these fields, and if so, in which one? Was the grass too tall and too dry to chance using a laser pistol? Were there enough trees and rock outcroppings to deflect the almost solid sound of a sonic gun?

A large estate soon came into view, and the vehicle made a beeline toward it.

"I have a question, driver," said Nighthawk.

"Yes?"

"The city looks to be about eight miles to the north. Isn't this very far out for a governor's mansion?"

"There have been attempts on Governor Hill's life," answered the driver. "His Security staff felt that he could be better protected in this location. When his physical presence is required, he is only a short trip from the various government buildings."

"And what are all those long low buildings to the left?" continued Nighthawk, staring at a series of concrete structures. "They look like barracks."

"They are. That's where his Security forces reside."

"He's got a lot of them, doesn't he?"

"I couldn't say," replied the driver. "I have no basis for comparison."

They pulled up to a shimmering gate and stopped.

"Force field?" asked Nighthawk.

"That is correct."

"What do we do now?"

"We wait. I have been identified. They are now checking you." The driver paused. "I am sorry, friend

Nighthawk, but you will have to relinquish your sonic pistol, your projectile pistol, and the three knives you have secreted around your person. If you will place them here"—a hidden compartment opened up—"you may retrieve them when you leave."

Nighthawk did as he was requested, and the door to the compartment slid shut.

"What about my laser gun?" he asked out of curiosity. "Surely your Security system didn't miss it."

"Once inside the gate your laser pistol will be totally ineffective," answered the driver.

"How is that possible?"

"Our power plant projects a field that instantly drains the charge from your pistol, while simultaneously rendering your power pack impotent."

*Good thing to remember. Someone ought to program you to be a little less forthcoming.*

"The force field is still up," noted Nighthawk. "Maybe you should tell them to shut it off now that I'm disarmed."

"That will not be necessary," answered the driver as the vehicle slowly began moving forward. "Please do not stick your head or any limbs out beyond the limits of my body. I can neutralize the field, but only within the parameters of my physical structure."

Nighthawk watched as the vehicle went right through the force field. There was no bump, no jolt, no buzzing; one moment they were outside the property, the next they were inside, and the same force field that kept intruders out would now serve to keep Nighthawk in.

There was a long winding driveway leading to the front doorway of the mansion, where three men and a pair of robots stood guard. The vehicle slowed to a stop, and Nighthawk and Melisande got out.

"I will be waiting for you, friends Nighthawk and Melisande," said the driver. "I don't want to block traffic, so I will pull some forty meters ahead and then stop. Enjoy your visit."

"Friendliest damned car I ever met," said Nighthawk wryly to one of the guards, who ignored his comment.

"Please follow me," he said. "You are expected."

"I've been scanned, sonogrammed, and X-rayed," said Nighthawk. "I'd damned well better be expected."

He waited for Melisande to take his arm, then followed the guard into the mansion's enormous hexagonal foyer. The walls were a phosphorescent alien marble, with streaks of some shimmering metal running through them. Nighthawk noted them, but was more intent upon the number and placement of the doors.

They were led through the foyer to a grand circular stairway. The guard stopped at the foot of the stairs and signaled to a pair of robots.

"You will accompany Mr. Nighthawk and his companion up to the governor's office," he ordered.

"Yes, sir," answered the robot in a more grating monotone than the robotic driver had possessed. "Please follow me."

They ascended the stairs, then turned down a long corridor. At the end of it was a large outer office containing a number of comfortable chairs and sofas, as well as a selection of tasteful alien paintings, and another robot immediately approached and offered them their choice of drinks.

"Nothing for us," said Nighthawk. "We're here to see Cassius Hill."

"You are expected," said both robots almost in unison.

"Well?"

The robots exchanged mechanical glances.

"We do not understand the question, sir."

"If he's waiting for us, why don't you take us to him?" asked Nighthawk.

"There is a difference between the governor's expecting you and being ready to meet with you," explained the robots that had offered them the drinks. "He will signal me when he is ready to meet with you."

"You tell him he's got five minutes or I'm leaving," said Nighthawk. "Tell him that the Widowmaker doesn't like to be kept waiting."

"I will deliver your message immediately, sir," said the robot.

The robot stood at attention, and Nighthawk stared at it for a long moment, then said, "Well?"

"We do not understand the question, sir."

"I thought you were going to deliver my message to Cassius Hill."

"I already have, sir. He is aware that you will leave in"—slight pause—"two hundred and seven Standard seconds if he has not invited you into his office by that time." A longer pause. "Will there be anything else, sir?"

Nighthawk looked from one robot to the other. "Yes," he said at last.

"What can I do for you, sir?"

"Send this other robot away."

"I cannot do that, sir."

"Why not?"

"He is a Security robot, programmed to protect the governor. I am merely an office robot, unqualified to analyze the potential risk to the governor in any real or hypothetical situation. Therefore, I cannot order a Security robot to leave the governor's office."

"Who do you think might harm the governor?" asked Nighthawk.

"No one, sir."

"Then why can't you order him to leave?"

"Because I may be wrong, sir."

"You," said Nighthawk, turning to the Security robot. "Do you think he's wrong?"

"No, sir," answered the robot. "I think there is only a seventeen percent probability that he is wrong."

"That's rather a high probability, isn't it, given that we're unarmed?"

"If you were any human other than Jefferson Nighthawk, I would rate the probability at four percent."

"I'm flattered."

"I am pleased that you are flattered."

"Are you really?" asked Nighthawk.

"No, sir, but I have been programmed to respond with those or similar words."

"I thought robots couldn't lie."

The robot was silent for a moment, as if it were internally scanning some data. "You have been asleep for more than a century. During that time, the directive against lying has been eliminated from most robots."

Nighthawk considered the robot carefully. "What makes you think I've been asleep for a century?"

"You are Jefferson Nighthawk," said the robot, as if that was the only answer required.

*Well, you're not infallible*, thought Nighthawk. *That's a comfort of sorts.*

The other robot took a step forward. "The governor will see you now."

"I will accompany you," said the Security robot,

walking toward a door that dilated to let the three of them pass through. They found themselves in a small office, manned by three more robots, all busy doing secretarial work. The Security robot led them to still another door, and this time when they passed through there was no doubt that they were in Cassius Hill's opulent office.

The governor, cigar in hand, sat behind a large desk made of an alien hardwood. The wall behind him was covered with holographs showing him in the company of the rich and the famous and, occasionally, the notorious. A Security robot was stationed in each of the four corners of the office. Nighthawk suddenly realized that Hill's desk and chair were on a small platform, so that seated visitors would have to look up to him.

"Mr. Nighthawk," acknowledged Hill, getting out of his chair and walking around the desk to shake Nighthawk's hand. "I'm glad to finally meet you in person."

"This is Melisande," said Nighthawk.

Hill glanced briefly at her. "She goes."

"I beg your pardon?"

"What kind of fool do you take me for?" demanded Hill. "Do you think I don't know a Balatai woman when I see one? We don't talk until she leaves."

"What have you got against Balatai women?" asked Nighthawk.

"Come on, Widowmaker," said Hill contemptuously. "If I was stupid enough to let her stay here, we wouldn't have anything to discuss." He turned to the Security robot that had escorted them to the office. "You! Take the woman back downstairs to wait for Nighthawk."

The robot took Melisande gently by the arm.

"Please come with me," it said.

She looked at Nighthawk, who nodded his acquiescence, then accompanied the robot out of the room.

"I'm disappointed in you," said Hill, sitting back down and puffing on his cigar. "Imagine thinking that I couldn't spot a Balatai woman!"

"They're very rare," said Nighthawk.

"Maybe they were a century ago, but not these days."

"Perhaps I was misinformed."

"You can't depend on your memories, you know," said Hill. "They're all a hundred years out of date. They'll betray you when you least expect it." Suddenly he leaned forward, his chin jutting out. "I'm the man who's responsible for your being alive, and I'm the man who's paying you. Why did you think you *needed* a Balatai woman in the first place?"

"I don't know you," said Nighthawk. "And therefore I don't trust you."

Hill considered Nighthawk's statement, and finally nodded his head. "I approve."

"I see you're not the most trusting man in the galaxy either," noted Nighthawk. "Four security robots in your office, and no Men."

"Robots are quicker to react and harder to kill," answered Hill promptly. "Also, their loyalty is programmed into them and can't be bought."

"They're a lot rarer where I come from."

"No," Hill corrected him. "Only *when* you come from." His cigar went out. He considered relighting it, finally tossed it into a tiny atomizer built into a corner of his desk, and lit another. "All right, Widowmaker. Talk to me. What's going on out there?"

"I found Ibn ben Khalid and your daughter."

"So you told me."

"He says that he wants eight million credits for her safe return."

"I know."

"Do you want the details?"

"No."

"No?" asked Nighthawk.

Hill snorted. "I wouldn't give him eight credits for that bitch! When I'm dead, she'll be first in line to dance on my grave." He stared across the desk at Nighthawk. "Sit down, Widowmaker. I don't like it when people stand. It makes me uneasy."

"I don't like looking up to people," replied Nighthawk. "I'll stand."

"I could have the robots make you sit."

"I wouldn't advise it," said Nighthawk so calmly that Hill decided not to force the issue.

"Sit, stand, do what you want," he muttered. "Just tell me about Ibn ben Khalid."

"He hasn't harmed her in any way."

"I don't give a shit about her!" snapped Hill. "She's hated me from the day she was born, and I hate her right back!"

"I thought you hired me to get her back," said Nighthawk.

"I hired you to find Ibn ben Khalid and kill him! I couldn't care less what happens to her!"

"That's not what I was told."

"Of course not," said Hill. "They wouldn't clone the Widowmaker just to eliminate a political upstart. I had to give them a reason that those weak-kneed bleeding-heart bastards back on Deluros could subscribe to." He paused. "You should be pleased. If I hadn't lied to them, you wouldn't exist."

"Why didn't you just send your navy out to kill him?" asked Nighthawk.

"You tell me where he is and I'll do just that," said

Hill. "But in the meantime, there's no way I'm going to send them thousands of light-years away after some will-o'-the-wisp while he invades Pericles with his army."

"Or decimates your fleet."

Hill shrugged. "To be perfectly blunt, they're just cannon fodder. I'd happily see three million of them blown to hell in exchange for Ibn ben Khalid." He stared hard at Nighthawk. "In fact, if you will tell me where he's keeping my daughter, where he himself is . . ."

"Not a chance," said Nighthawk. "You're paying *me* to kill him, remember?"

"I'll pay you to tell me where he is."

"How much?"

"A million credits."

"Good-bye, Mr. Hill," said Nighthawk. "We have nothing further to discuss."

"Two million!"

"Go to hell, Mr. Hill. That won't keep the Widowmaker alive, and we both know it."

"*You're* the Widowmaker now!" retorted Hill. "We're alike, you and I. We both use force to get what we want, and we both know that life is the cheapest commodity on the Frontier. So don't pretend that you care any more about the first Widowmaker than I care about my soldiers or my daughter."

"I'm not here to argue motivations with you. I need money, and if you want my help, you're going to have to pay for it."

"All right," said Hill. "Sit down and we'll talk some business."

"I'll stand."

"I said sit."

"I heard what you said."

"You're going to have to learn who's in charge here," said Hill. "Number Three, help Mr. Nighthawk sit down."

One of the robots approached him, arms outstretched. Nighthawk ducked, grabbed a metallic arm, twisted it, and jerked suddenly—and the robot did an awkward somersault in the air and clanged heavily to the ground.

"Human or robot, leverage is leverage," said Nighthawk, never taking his eyes off the robot as it clambered awkwardly to its feet. "Now call it off before one of us gets hurt. You don't want the cost of replacing a robot, and like it or not you *can't* replace me."

Hill looked from Nighthawk to the robot. "At ease, Number Three," he said, and the robot walked back to its position in a corner of the room. "If I hadn't said that, he'd have killed you eventually."

"Perhaps."

"And if he couldn't, there are three more in this office who would have helped on my command."

"Proving what?"

"That when I give an order, I want it obeyed."

"I don't take orders," replied Nighthawk. "Not from you, not from anyone." He paused. "Why don't you *ask* me to sit down?"

"What?"

"You heard me: ask me to sit."

Hill frowned but complied. "Won't you please sit down, Mr. Nighthawk?"

"Thanks, I think I will," said Nighthawk, finally seating himself on a chair.

Some of the tension left Hill's face. "Now let's talk business."

"I'm listening."

"I want Ibn ben Khalid dead. If you can kill him

this week, within seven Standard days, I'll pay you ten million credits."

"What about your daughter?"

"If she gets in the way of a laser beam or a bullet, well,"—Hill shrugged eloquently—"that's too bad, but she's very young and very foolish and unfortunately these things happen."

"And if she survives?"

Hill shook his head. "She doesn't."

Nighthawk stared at him. "I can see why you prefer surrounding yourself with robots."

"The life expectancy of men who were privy to my secrets was getting to be embarrassingly short," said Hill with a smile. "At least I know I can trust my robots. Each of them will burn out all its neural circuits before divulging anything that gets said in this room." Hill puffed on his cigar again, and the smoke almost obscured his face for a few seconds. "Well, Widowmaker, have we got a deal?"

"Can you pay in cash?"

"I thought you'd want it credited to your attorney's account."

"I don't trust lawyers."

Hill chuckled. "I agree. That's one thing that hasn't changed in a century." Suddenly the smile vanished. "Yes, I can pay you in cash."

"Then you've got a deal."

"Remember: I want him dead in one Standard week, or we're back to our original agreement and our original price." He paused. "Pull this off and you can walk away a rich man. Deluros never even has to know. Think about it."

"I've been thinking about it since yesterday," said Nighthawk.

"You're a man after my own heart, Widowmaker."

"Maybe I'll just cut it out right now."

"I don't find that very funny."

"Probably it isn't," said Nighthawk. "I don't have much of a sense of humor."

Suddenly Hill tensed. "Or was it a joke at all?" he demanded. "How much did Ibn ben Khalid offer you to kill *me*?"

"Not as much as you're offering me to kill him," answered Nighthawk. "He's only a poor corrupt man of the people; you're a rich one."

"A rich, well-protected one," said Hill pointedly. "You kill me, and you'll never make it out of the mansion alive. And even if you did, my Security forces would hunt you down long before you reached the spaceport. I assume you saw all the checkpoints as you drove up."

"I did."

"Good. Don't forget them."

"I don't plan to."

"That sounds like a threat," said Hill.

Nighthawk smiled. "Everything sounds like a threat to you. You're a very insecure man."

"I can live with my insecurities," said Hill. "Easier, I suspect, than you can live with being the ephemeral shadow of a real man."

"I may be a shadow," admitted Nighthawk. "I don't plan on being an ephemeral one."

"Then don't ever try to cross me," replied Hill. "And now, if we've no further business to discuss, get out. I may need you, but I find that I don't like you very much."

"No law says you have to," replied Nighthawk. "Just make sure the money's ready."

He turned and walked to the door, which remained

closed until one of the robots stepped forward and escorted him out of the office. A few moments later he and Melisande were driving back to the spaceport, hoping that Friday wouldn't get overeager and blow the whole planet to smithereens before they reached the ship.

# Chapter 24

· · · · · · ·

*"How did it go?" asked Cassandra when Nighthawk* entered The Blue Dragon, accompanied by Melisande and Friday.

He looked around. The place still wasn't open for business, but Kinoshita and Blue Eyes were sitting at one table, and Jory was at another.

"That's some father you've got," he said at last.

"I know."

"I think he's as eager to see *you* dead as you are to see *him* dead."

"You told him I was Ibn ben Khalid?" she said angrily.

Nighthawk shook his head. "He hates you for yourself."

"Good," said Cassandra emphatically. "I'd hate to be something he admired."

"You're in no serious danger of that."

"So is he coming to Sylene?"

"Not a prayer," said Nighthawk. "Your father isn't a trusting man."

"Damn!"

"You didn't really think he'd come, did you?"

"No, but I'd hoped . . ."

"He *did* offer me ten million credits if I kill Ibn ben Khalid within the week."

Suddenly Cassandra tensed. "What did you tell him?"

"I told him I'd need it in cash."

"And he said?"

"No problem."

She stared at him. "And what are you going to do?"

"Kill him and take the money."

She relaxed visibly. "Good."

"Why didn't you kill him while you were there?" asked Blue Eyes.

"Because I'd like to live long enough to enjoy the money," answered Nighthawk.

"He's that well protected?" continued the dragon.

"He'd have been easy to kill. It would have been impossible to escape."

"So what do we do?" asked Kinoshita. "He won't come here, and you can't escape if you kill him there."

"We work out a way to kill him and escape."

"But you just said—"

"I was alone and expected. They knew when I was coming, with whom, who I was, what I could do." Nighthawk paused. "Next time I won't be alone, and they won't be expecting me."

"How many men are stationed on Pericles?" asked Blue Eyes.

"A few million."

"Against five of us?"

"Six," said Cassandra.

"Seven," chimed in Jory.

"That's still not the kind of odds to give one a sunny sense of confidence," said Blue Eyes wryly.

"You won't have to worry about more than a few hundred of them," said Nighthawk. "The rest will be stationed around Pericles V."

"Only a few hundred?" said the dragon unhappily. "I feel better already."

"Just a minute," said Kinoshita.

Everyone turned to him.

"He doesn't know that Cassandra is Ibn ben Khalid?"

"No," answered Nighthawk.

"That means he has no idea what Ibn ben Khalid looks like, right?"

"Right," said Nighthawk with a smile, as he saw where Kinoshita was leading him.

"So why not kill some outlaw out here, cut off his head, and present it to Hill as Ibn ben Khalid? Then take the money and run like hell before he figures out he's been had."

"By God, I *like* it!" bellowed Blue Eyes, slamming a fist down on the table.

"You know," said Jory, "it's not bad."

"It's out of the question!" said Cassandra furiously.

"Yes, it is," agreed Nighthawk. "Though two days ago I think I might have agreed to do it."

"What's happened in the past two days?" asked Blue Eyes.

"I've met Cassius Hill." Nighthawk paused and

looked from one member of his band to the next. "He's got to die."

"You bet your ass he's got to!" snapped Cassandra.

"Hold on a minute," said Kinoshita. "If you think killing one corrupt politician will make the galaxy a better place for all Mankind or anything noble like that . . ."

"I know it won't," said Nighthawk.

"Then what makes you so suddenly noble?"

"It's not a matter of nobility, but of brainpower."

"I don't follow you."

"I met Cassius Hill. I spoke to him. He may be an evil man, but he's not a stupid one. He'll know in a matter of days, or weeks at most, that I didn't kill Ibn ben Khalid."

"So what?" said Kinoshita. "We'll be out on the Rim, or deep into the Spiral Arm, enjoying our money."

"You don't understand," said Nighthawk. "Once he figures out he's been duped, the first thing he's going to do is freeze the money in my attorneys' account, and see to it that the original Widowmaker is thrown out of the cryonics lab to die. I can't allow that."

"To hell with the original Widowmaker!" said Cassandra. "Cassius Hill has got to die as punishment for all the criminal acts he's performed. He's betrayed his people a hundred times over!"

"All right," said Kinoshita. "There's no sense shooting each other because we differ about *why* he has to die. The question now is how do we go about it?"

"We don't do anything for the next Standard week," said Nighthawk.

"Why not?" asked Friday, who was still unhappy about not being permitted to blow up the planet.

"Because he thinks I'm going to kill Ibn ben Khalid this week. That means he thinks Ibn ben Khalid is relatively close to Pericles V. As long as he believes that, his navy isn't going anywhere—and we don't want them around if we have to land there."

"So he's a coward in addition to everything else?" asked Blue Eyes.

"Not at all," answered Nighthawk. "It's just sound tactics not to disperse your forces when the enemy might be lurking nearby." He paused. "Still," he added, "maybe we can convince him to do just that."

"Oh?" said Cassandra. "How?"

"He's got to have followed me here—not Hill himself, but some of his men—or else he's managed to put some kind of trace on my ship."

"No one landed while I was in the spaceport," said Friday adamantly.

"It wouldn't have had to be a *person*," said Nighthawk. "This guy depends on machines more than most people do. It could have been anything that passed for a Service Mech. Anyway, I'm sure he's keeping tabs on the ship." He turned to Cassandra. "Based on your knowledge of him, is that a logical conclusion?"

"Absolutely."

"Good. Then all we have to do is have one of your men fly my ship halfway across the Inner Frontier. He'll think I'm after Ibn ben Khalid . . ."

". . . and once he thinks he knows where I am, he'll send half his navy there to be in on the kill and wipe out any of my forces that happen to be on the scene!" concluded Cassandra.

"Well, it *sounds* logical, anyway," said Nighthawk. "But will he do it? I mean, he didn't strike me as the most gullible man I've ever encountered."

"I really don't know," she said, frowning. Suddenly she looked up and smiled. "Unless he's convinced

beyond any shadow of a doubt that Ibn ben Khalid is
really there!"

"How do we convince him of that?" asked
Kinoshita.

"We put *her* on the Widowmaker's ship," said
Friday.

"Not a chance," said Cassandra. "I'm going to be in
on the kill. But I can make a holographic recording,
pleading for his help."

"Will he listen?" asked Kinoshita dubiously.

"Not sympathetically," said Cassandra. "But yes,
he'll listen, because he'll have no reason to think it's
phony."

All eyes turned to Nighthawk, who considered the
suggestion for another minute, then nodded his head.

"Yeah, I think it'll work. And anything that might
lower the odds is worth trying."

"Right," said Blue Eyes unhappily. "Send half his
forces out after her, and it's only two million to seven."

"Oh, we'll have more than seven," said Nighthawk.
"And half of his two million will be sound asleep."

"Well, that's wonderful," said the dragon. "You
don't hang around casinos much, do you?"

"No. Why?"

"You've still got the shirt on your back. The
way you compute fair odds, that's the only logical
conclusion."

"Hey," said Nighthawk. "This is *your* cause. I'm
just in it for the money."

"Thanks," said Blue Eyes. "I feel so much better
now."

"Shut up!" said Cassandra.

"I was just teasing him," said Blue Eyes petulantly.

"Enough," she said. "This is serious business. You may be joking, but the odds *are* two million to seven."

"We'll start lowering them before we strike," said Nighthawk.

"Good," said Blue Eyes. "How?"

"As soon as I come up with an answer to that, you'll be among the first to know."

He got up and walked to the airlift behind the bar.

"Where are you going?" demanded Blue Eyes.

"I've had a long day," answered Nighthawk. "I'm going to go relax with a good book."

"That's *it*?" demanded the dragon. "That's all you're going to say about the overthrow of Cassius Hill?"

"For the moment."

Nighthawk floated gently upward to Cassandra's apartment. She joined him a few minutes later.

"He's a monster, isn't he?" she asked as the door slid shut behind her.

Nighthawk looked up from his book. "Blue Eyes?"

"My father!"

"I've seen better."

"I'll wager you've never seen worse."

"You're young yet," said Nighthawk. "I hope *you* never meet worse."

"He really wants me dead?"

"He insists on it."

She stood silent and motionless for a moment. "It's strange."

"What is?"

"He may be a monster, but he's still my father. The thought that he could want me dead . . ." She shook her head and shuddered.

"You want *him* dead," Nighthawk noted mildly.

"That's different. I've hated him my whole life."

"Maybe it's mutual."

"It couldn't be. How do you hate an infant? A little girl? He hardly knows me. How could he hate me so much?"

"I don't think he hates you," said Nighthawk. "I think you just annoy him."

"That's even worse!" she said. "To kill someone because she *annoys* you!"

"There are worse reasons," said Nighthawk. "Besides, it's just a guess."

"Probably an accurate one," replied Cassandra. "He doesn't know me well enough to hate me. In fact, when he finds out who Ibn ben Khalid really is, you may not have to kill him; the shock may do it for you."

"Try not to think about it."

"How can I stop thinking about it?" she demanded. "He's my *father*!"

"Just a toss of a coin. He could be anyone's father, you could be anyone's daughter."

"I don't believe that for a moment. Do you?"

"Not really. You've got some of his steel, a touch of his arrogance."

"I do?"

Nighthawk nodded. "I find them admirable qualities when they're not carried to excess."

"Thank you, I suppose."

"You've got his eyes, too."

"His are gray, mine are blue."

"Neither of you ever look away or blink. You're not afraid of what you see."

"Why should I be?"

"I'm the Widowmaker. I came here to kill you. And *he* has to know I've considered killing him."

"I'd rather you pointed out the differences between us," said Cassandra. "I hate the man."

"Well, you're a lot prettier."

She grimaced. "That's not what I meant."

"So much for romance," said Nighthawk wryly.

"I never expected a killer to be a romantic."

"Nonsense," answered Nighthawk. "Killers make the best romantics."

"Sure."

"We do," he insisted. "Sooner or later we have to convince ourselves that what we're doing is necessary, and ultimately good. What's more romantic than that?"

"Then why don't you stop this incessant talking and take me to bed?"

He stared at her, surprised. "Are you sure that's what you want? You don't know me."

"You're an attractive man. I'm an attractive woman. And we're both going to be dead in less than two weeks." She paused. "Blue Eyes isn't the only one who can compute the odds, you know. So we might as well make the most of it while we can."

Nighthawk got to his feet. "Sounds good to me."

He followed her to the bedroom.

"I plan to enjoy this," she said firmly.

"I'll do my best."

"How long has it been for you?"

He grinned at her as he began talking off his clothes. "Oh, a century, maybe a little longer."

"I hope you haven't forgotten how."

He hadn't.

# Chapter 25

*Nighthawk was sitting in The Blue Dragon three days later* when Kinoshita entered and walked over to him.

"Mind if I sit down?" he asked.

"Be my guest."

"I saw your ship take off yesterday." Pause. "I guess you weren't on it."

"Not much gets past you, does it?" remarked Nighthawk dryly.

"I thought you might want to tell me about it."

"Not especially," said Nighthawk, sipping his drink.

"You refuse to?"

"I didn't say that."

"Well?"

"It's a decoy."

"Part of the plan you worked out with Cassandra Hill?" said Kinoshita.

"Do I detect a note of disapproval?" asked Nighthawk.

"Damn it, we're part of your team, me and Melisande and the aliens!" said Kinoshita angrily. "We all know you're sleeping with her, and nobody minds it, but we *do* mind being left out in the cold. If something's going on, if we're expected to risk our lives for her cause—*her* cause, not ours—then we think you should let us know just what's going on. We had no idea you'd even started!"

Nighthawk stared at him. Kinoshita looked at his expressionless face and cold eyes, and for just a moment he had an impulse to race for the door and consider himself lucky if he made it.

"All right," said Nighthawk at last. "Fair is fair. You've got a point." He paused long enough to finish his drink and signal the bartender for another. "We're going to invade Pericles and take out Cassius Hill."

"We?" repeated Kinoshita. "You mean her army?"

Nighthawk shook his head. "Her army, such as it is, is ragtag, undisciplined, poorly armed, and spread all the hell over the Inner Frontier. More to the point, it's outnumbered four to one. If we approached the planet with it, we'd be blown out of the sky before our first ship could land."

"Then who's invading Pericles?"

"Us."

"Us?" repeated Kinoshita with a sick feeling in the pit of his stomach.

"You, me, her, Melisande, Friday, Blue Eyes, Jory, and maybe twenty of her most trusted men and women."

"Just a minute," said Kinoshita. "You're going to

invade Cassius Hill's heavily guarded home world with an attack force of thirty men?"

"And women," said Nighthawk.

"You're good, Widowmaker," said Kinoshita. "Better than I thought, better than anyone I've ever seen. But you're nowhere near *that* good."

"I appreciate your confidence."

"It's not a matter of confidence," insisted Kinoshita. "It's a matter of numbers."

"Actually, it's a matter of planning."

"Cassius Hill has four million men on that planet. I don't care how widely dispersed they are. I don't care if half of them will be asleep. I don't care if he's isolated in his mansion with only ten thousand crack soldiers guarding him." Kinoshita paused and tried to regain his composure. "Look, even if you kill him, we've still got to get away from there. What'll we have—one ship? Three? Five? Against his entire fleet and his planetary defense system?"

"I've worked out some of the problems," said Nighthawk. "We won't move until I work out the rest."

"What about Cassandra?" continued Kinoshita.

"What about her?"

"I got the impression you cared about her."

"I do—not that it's any of your business."

"You can't," said Kinoshita, "or you wouldn't let her risk her life like this."

"You're a fool, Ito," said Nighthawk slowly. "It's not up to me to stop her. More to the point, I care about her precisely *because* she's willing to come along and risk her life for a cause she believes in."

"Can you trust her to do the right thing under pressure?"

"More than I trust anyone else. She's Ibn ben Khalid, isn't she?"

"You sound like you find that attractive," suggested Kinoshita.

"Out here on the Frontier the two things that count are courage and competence," said Nighthawk, "and she has them both. I'm glad that she's a good-looking woman, but I'd be just as attracted to her if she were three hundred pounds and pockmarked."

"Curious."

"What is?"

"I'd have thought that a man who lives for the moment would be more concerned with style than substance."

"What makes you think I live for the moment?" asked Nighthawk.

"Your profession."

"Never planning more than a moment at a time would be an admission of defeat," replied Nighthawk. "The first Widowmaker made it to his sixties, and if they come up with a cure for eplasia, he could make it to a hundred. He never once thought that he might die in the course of earning his living. I know: his memories are mine." He paused. "I want a woman with those same virtues—courage and competence. I found one." Another pause. "I'll tell you something else: it's more important to me that she reads books than that she's good in bed."

"Sure it is," said Kinoshita sardonically.

"Sooner or later you have to stop fucking and start talking," said Nighthawk. "I want someone who won't bore me to tears, someone to exchange ideas with."

"You are a constant source of amazement to me," admitted Kinoshita.

"That's because you bought into the myth. You think I live for killing—whereas what I really cherish are the hours and days *between* killings."

"Point taken."

"Is there anything else you want to ask?" said Nighthawk. "Let's get it over with now, because I don't plan to discuss my personal business with you again."

"Just that it seems a waste," said Kinoshita. "The rest of us have our reasons for following you, but if you care for Cassandra, why send her up against heavily armed soldiers?"

"You keep forgetting that this is *her* cause. I'm just in it for the money." He paused. "Besides, whether she weighs a hundred and ten pounds or three hundred and ten pounds, a gun is a hell of an equalizer."

"Okay, then I've got another question for you."

"I'm listening."

"What am *I* in it for?" asked Kinoshita. "*She's* in it to overthrow her father, and so are Jory and Blue Eyes. You're in it for the money. Melisande is here because you're paying her. Friday's here because he can't wait to blow up a few thousand Men. But what am *I* here for?"

"I thought you came along to watch me in action," remarked Nighthawk dryly.

"I know why I came this far," said Kinoshita irritably. "But why do *you* want me to come the rest of the way? I know you, Widowmaker—you never leave anything to chance. If you want me along, there's got to be a reason. I think I deserve to know what it is."

"Fair question," answered Nighthawk. "Your job is to stay alive."

Kinoshita frowned. "I don't understand."

"If only one person survives this operation, it has to be you."

*"Me?"* said Kinoshita, surprised. "Why?"

"Because you're the only one who's both trustworthy and knowledgeable enough to transfer the money I plan to appropriate into the Widowmaker's account at Hubbs, Wilkinson, Raith and Jiminez, and to make sure that Marcus Dinnisen and none of the others try to divert it for their own use."

"You don't trust them?"

"They're lawyers, aren't they?" replied Nighthawk, making no attempt to hide his contempt.

"How much money are we talking about?"

"At least five million, hopefully more. Your fee for seeing that it gets where it belongs will be ten percent."

Kinoshita grinned. "Suddenly I'm less opposed to attacking Pericles."

"Somehow I thought you might be."

"But I still don't understand someone who'd let the woman he loves go in there with guns blazing."

"No one's going anywhere with guns blazing," said Nighthawk. "This is not an enemy we can overpower."

"You know what I mean."

"I know exactly what you mean. Some men put women on a pedestal. I prefer to work side by side with them. My work just happens to be more dangerous than most."

Kinoshita shrugged. "Okay, I'm all through arguing. Do what you want with her. I can hardly object to your plans when I'm the designated survivor."

"I plan on all of us living through this," said Nighthawk. "You're just the one we're going to make absolutely sure survives."

"I appreciate it. When do we attack?"

"Not for a while. First, I want to make sure that a sizable number of Hill's ships are following mine."

"Where is it headed?"

"Socrates VII."

"That's clear across the Inner Frontier!"

"Right. And second, as I said, I have to work out the rest of the details." Nighthawk paused. "We should be ready in six or seven Standard days."

"I hate to say this . . ."

"Yes?"

"Quite seriously," said Kinoshita with obvious reluctance, "if you're going to protect someone's ass, make it Melisande's. You won't need an empath in a pitched battle. You might need *me*."

"That's a generous offer," said Nighthawk. "But I'll definitely need an empath."

"You're sure?"

"I'm sure."

"Then I guess I'll just have to live," said Kinoshita with a smile. "How much of this can I tell the others?"

"I'll be speaking to each of them myself in the next day or two," said Nighthawk. "We have a lot of details to sort out."

Kinoshita observed him thoughtfully. "You don't seem overly nervous."

"Should I be?"

"Well, you're about to take on four million soldiers with a handful of untrained men, and to try to assassinate the best-protected politician on the Inner Frontier," replied Kinoshita. "That would make most men a little nervous."

"Most men," agreed Nighthawk.

"But not you?"

"Not the Widowmaker" was the calm reply.

# Chapter 26

Melisande walked up to Nighthawk, who was standing in the street outside The Blue Dragon.

"You sent for me?" she said.

"Yes, I did," replied Nighthawk. "I need to know more about your power."

"Being a Balatai woman isn't so much a power as a curse," she replied. "You don't know what it's like to be bombarded by emotions every day of your life."

"Do you?"

She frowned. "What are you driving at?"

"Can you get away from them?"

"Sometimes."

"What's the closest someone can get before you can't avoid his emotions?"

"It depends on what he's feeling as well as his proximity," answered Melisande.

"That's not good enough."

"Why don't you tell me what you want, and I'll try to answer you."

"All right," said Nighthawk. "Pretend you're in the middle of a desert or a farm field, and there's a man a mile away, walking toward you. You can't see him. He's not mad at anyone. He's not frightened. He's not thinking lustful thoughts about his woman. He's not bursting with joy. He's just walking, his mind's kind of drifting, he's not noticing much of anything. How close would he have to be before you knew he was there?"

"I don't know," she said. "I might see him before I sensed him."

"It's midnight and this world doesn't have any moons."

"I assume there's a purpose to all this?" said Melisande.

"I wouldn't ask if there wasn't," replied Nighthawk. "Could you sense him at five hundred yards?"

"I don't know."

"Three hundred?"

"Damn it, *I don't know!*"

"Well, we're going to have to find out." He gestured toward The Blue Dragon. "How many men are in there right now?"

She closed her eyes, and the muscles in her face tightened as she concentrated.

"Seven."

"Six," said Nighthawk.

"I sense emotional radiations from seven."

"There's a bartender and five men."

"You're wrong."

"Oh—right. I forgot Cassandra. She's upstairs. Can you differentiate?"

"Can I tell that one of the seven is on the second floor? Not from out here, but when I'm inside I can."

Nighthawk took her by the arm and walked her one hundred yards down the street.

"Can you still read their radiations?" he asked.

"Of course."

"How many are there?"

She concentrated again, then looked at him, surprised. "Four."

"That's right. I told three of them to leave when they saw me walking you over here. Let's go a little farther."

He stopped two hundred yards from the tavern, and she stared at it.

"Six?"

"Are you asking me or telling me?"

She lowered her head for a moment, then looked up at him. "Six," she said firmly.

"Once more," he said, walking her another hundred yards away.

"Two," she said when they had stopped.

"You're sure?"

"Yes."

Nighthawk made a gesture, and Kinoshita walked out of the tavern and jabbed the air three times with a thumb.

"You missed one," said Nighthawk.

"Have I failed some kind of test?"

"Not at all," he replied. "We just had to know where your limit was. It seems to be somewhere between two and three hundred yards, at least when no one's pitching any powerful emotions."

"All right," said Melisande. "Now that we know that, what are we supposed to do about it?"

"Ito will help you try to narrow it down even farther over the next few days," answered Nighthawk.

"And then?"

"And then, when we infiltrate Pericles V, you are going to be Friday's alarm system."

"I beg your pardon?"

"He's going to have to create a number of distractions. While he's planting his explosives, he's not going to be able to concentrate on anything else. *You're* going to let him know if anyone's coming."

"But why this experiment?" she asked. "If an armed guard thinks he hears something, or that he's spotted something, he'll radiate much stronger emotions, and . . ."

"We'll try to adjust for that," interrupted Nighthawk. "In the next couple of days, Ito will try to dope out your limits for men who are angry, or lustful, or frightened. But the most likely scenario, assuming we plan this properly, is that someone will be much more likely to stumble onto you by accident. So now we know if he's just patrolling an area that he patrols every night, and he has no reason to believe anyone's there, and you can spot his emotional radiation, he's probably within two hundred yards of you. That means you'll have to dope out some kind of signal with Friday that will either get him to freeze until the man passes, or kill him before he sees you."

"Now I see." She paused. "But if he's armed, how can you be sure Friday will be able to kill him? If there's any kind of commotion his friends might hear it."

"You'll have the advantage. You'll know he's there before he knows you are."

"*I'm* no killer. My question remains."

"When I hired you, you were in the business of making men think only about you. If need be, I'm sure you can do it long enough for Friday to sneak up and bludgeon him." Suddenly he smiled. "Trust me, if the first thing a man sees is *you*, he won't immediately start looking for an alien explosives expert."

"Just how many explosives is Friday going to plant?"

"As many as necessary."

"And how many Men will we be responsible for killing?" she continued.

"Less than you think."

"What if I say no?" asked Melisande.

Nighthawk sighed. "*Are* you saying no?"

"I'm considering it."

"Then you'll book passage back to Barrios II and that'll be the end of it."

"No repercussions, no threats at gunpoint from the Widowmaker?"

He shook his head. "This isn't what I hired you for. The rules of the game have changed, and so have the players. If you want to leave, I'll pay you what I owe you and see you safely to the spaceport."

She stared at him for a long moment. "You're telling the truth."

"Of course I'm telling the truth," said Nighthawk. "I know better than to lie to a Balatai woman."

"Everyone else knows you as a killer called the Widowmaker," said Melisande. "I know you as a man named Jefferson Nighthawk who has never lied to me. So I want to ask Jefferson Nighthawk one last question."

"Ask away."

"Is Cassius Hill really such a terrible man that

you're willing to betray your creators, pervert your mission, and possibly sacrifice your life, just to bring him down?"

He looked into her eyes. "He is."

"And your feelings for Cassandra Hill haven't influenced you?"

"Possibly they have," he replied. "But not as much as meeting him did."

"All right, Jefferson Nighthawk," she said after a long pause, as she analyzed his emotions and found him to be telling the truth, at least as he knew it. "I'll do what you ask. And God have mercy on both our souls, as He'll be receiving them soon enough."

# Chapter 27

*Nighthawk stood at the bar of The Blue Dragon, waiting for Blue Eyes to bring him a drink.*

"Are we *ever* leaving Sylene again?" asked the dragon as he approached Nighthawk, carrying a blue concoction in a uniquely shaped glass.

"You worked here for years. What's your hurry?"

"I know what's at the other end of the rainbow."

"It hasn't rained on Sylene for close to a century. All the water's underground. You wouldn't know a rainbow if it spit in your eye."

"It's an expression I picked up."

"Well, in answer to your question, what's at the other end of this particular rainbow is a lot of bloodshed, probably including yours. So I repeat: what's the rush?"

"For the first time I think we can take that bastard," answered Blue Eyes. "I'm anxious to do it."

"There's a handful of us and millions of them," noted Nighthawk.

"But you're the Widowmaker. You'll find a way. Besides . . ."

"Yes?"

"You wouldn't go there if you thought you wouldn't come out alive," said the dragon. "I've been watching you for weeks. You're the most cautious man I ever met." He paused. "Seems a strange characteristic in a man who was known all over the Frontier as a killer."

"I was a lawman, not an assassin," replied Nighthawk.

"Same thing. You killed people."

"I killed killers. It's not the same thing at all, though you'd never know it from a couple of biographies of the Widowmaker that I read in Cassandra's apartment."

"Six of one, half a dozen of the other," said Blue Eyes with a shrug. "The main thing is, I figure the closer to you I stay, the more likely I am to come out of this with my beautiful skin unblemished."

"You're not standing anywhere near me," said Nighthawk.

"Why not?"

"First, because you're mistaken about standing next to me being the safest place, and second, because I don't trust you."

"You've spent all this time with me and you don't trust me?" bellowed Blue Eyes. "Have I ever lied to you? Betrayed you? Tried to do you any harm?"

"Not to my knowledge."

"Well, then?"

"You're an alien, and—"

"So now you hate aliens, do you?" demanded the dragon.

"Let me finish," said Nighthawk calmly. "You're an alien, and Melisande can't read your emotions. That means until we're in a life-threatening situation, I can't be one hundred percent sure where you really stand, and that's too late."

"What about Friday? He's an alien too."

"She can read him."

"And what about Melisande herself?" continued Blue Eyes. "She's no more human than I am. She can read your emotions, but you can't read hers. How do you know *she* isn't manipulating you for her own ends? Why do you trust her, and not me—because she's got pink skin and I've got blue scales? She's a Balatai woman!"

"You say it like it's a separate species," replied Nighthawk. "Balatai is just a colony world. It was cut off from the Oligarchy, and before that the Democracy, for maybe fifteen or twenty generations, and when we finally made contact again, they had mutated and became empaths. But that doesn't mean they aren't human. They're human with an extra ability, that's all."

"And you trust any human over any alien, right?" persisted Blue Eyes.

"I'm a creature of my times," answered Nighthawk. "Humans don't betray their own. They did once, and I'm sure they will again, but not when we're outnumbered hundreds to one in the galaxy and trying to maintain our primacy."

"If they don't betray their own, why are we trying to overthrow Cassius Hill?"

"There's a difference between a crooked politician

robbing his constituency, and that same man selling them out to some alien race. Cassius Hill's as poor an excuse for a man and a governor as you'll ever find, but even *he* wouldn't sell his people out to an alien power."

"I thought we were friends," said Blue Eyes.

"We are. I just define it differently."

"You're as bad as the rest of them," muttered the dragon. "Just the thought of touching one of us must make your skin crawl."

Nighthawk stared at him for a long moment. Finally he noticed the drink Blue Eyes had brought, took a swallow, and replaced it on the bar. "The closest friend I ever had was an alien."

"Sure."

"It's the truth. He was a Silverhorn."

"A Silverhorn? What's that?"

"A native of Bonara II. Mildly humanoid, covered with white fleece, and sporting a big silver horn on the top of his head. We were partners for three years."

"Let me guess," said Blue Eyes sardonically. "He took a laser blast or a bullet meant for you."

"No, it was meant for him; we had enough enemies to go around. But he *would* have taken one meant for me if he could have, and I'd have done the same."

"Then why can't you afford me the same trust?"

"He earned it; you haven't." Nighthawk paused. "You'll get your chance."

"So we come back to my initial question: when are we leaving Sylene?"

"Soon."

"How soon?"

"I'll let you know."

"You know already, don't you?" said Blue Eyes. "And you don't want to tell me."

"That's right."

"Have you told *anyone*?"

"No."

"Not even Cassandra?"

"No."

"Well, I suppose I can take some small comfort from the fact that you don't even trust the woman you're sleeping with."

"You take comfort from strange things," remarked Nighthawk.

"I don't suppose you're willing to tell me who else is coming with us—I mean, besides our original team and Cassandra?"

"I don't know yet."

"When *will* you know?"

"Soon."

"How will you choose them?"

"There are ways," answered Nighthawk.

# Chapter 28

*Nighthawk leaned up against a purple-boled tree in the* small yard behind The Blue Dragon. He didn't have long to wait. A very young man, dressed in colorful silks and satins, and wearing shoes made from the sleek glistening skin of some alien reptile, approached him.

"I heard you were looking for men," announced the young man, throwing his coat open to reveal a truly stunning arsenal of weapons.

"That's right," said Nighthawk.

"You won't find anyone faster," said the young man confidently.

"If you say so," replied Nighthawk with a shrug. "Have you got a name?"

"Johnny Colt."

"That's a little old-fashioned, isn't it? Why not Johnny Laser?"

The young man's poise vanished momentarily. "There are already two Johnny Lasers on the Frontier, and there's a Johnny Blood out on the Rim," he replied unhappily. He pulled a pistol out of his belt and offered it, butt first, to Nighthawk. "But this is a genuine Colt, from the days when we were still Earthbound. Take a look at it. It's a museum piece. You wouldn't believe what it's worth on the market today."

Nighthawk didn't reach for the pistol. "I'm not a connoisseur."

"I thought you were the Widowmaker."

"I am," replied Nighthawk. "And take the Widowmaker's word for it: a hell of a lot more men are killed with weapons costing less than one hundred credits than with weapons costing over a thousand."

Johnny Colt returned the gun to its holster, looking somewhat perplexed.

"Well, am I in or out?" he asked.

"I plan to find out," said Nighthawk. He picked up three stones from the ground, walked to a fence some ten yards away, and lined them up at two-foot intervals. "Let's see what you can do with them."

"That's no challenge," said Johnny Colt contemptuously. "Let me stand a couple of hundred yards away."

"Forget it," said Nighthawk. "You hit anything with a pistol from two hundred yards and it's dumb luck. I don't want anyone shooting until they're as close to the enemy as you are to those rocks."

"Whatever you say." Johnny Colt faced the rocks, his fingers just above his pistol.

"Hold on," said Nighthawk.

"What now?"

"We're not having a fast-draw contest, and I'm not giving points for speed or form. I want your weapon to be in your hand before you confront the enemy." Nighthawk paused. "And one other thing."

"What?"

"Use your laser pistol."

"But my Colt is my trademark."

"It's a trademark that'll wake everyone for five miles in each direction," said Nighthawk. "This is supposed to be a covert operation."

Johnny Colt pulled out his laser pistol, held it steady with both hands, took aim at the three stones, and fired three short blasts. The first and third missed their targets; the second hit the middle stone.

"Kid, you're pissing away your advantage," commented Nighthawk.

"I don't know what you're talking about."

"One of the nice things about laser pistols, aside from the fact that they don't make a bang, is that you don't have to be all that accurate. You're shooting it just as if you were shooting bullets. Try keeping your finger on the trigger and spraying the target area."

Johnny Colt tried again, and this time he melted the other two stones.

"Not very sporting, is it?" said Nighthawk wryly.

"Not at all."

"Then it's lucky for you we're not going to a sporting contest, isn't it?"

Johnny Colt just grinned.

"Do you think you can remember to do that when people are shooting at you?" asked Nighthawk.

"Sure," said the young man. "Will I get a chance at Cassius Hill?"

"Probably not."

"You're saving him for yourself?"

"He's not a trophy; he's a target. I don't care who kills him, as long as he's dead."

"Then why not me?"

"Because if you're close enough to kill him, it means you've disobeyed my orders."

"I just want to leave my mark," explained Johnny Colt. "People will be talking about this for years. I want them to know I was there."

"We're not out for glory and we're not out for fame," said Nighthawk. "If we do our jobs right, no one will ever know we were responsible. If you can't live with that, then you're going to have to stay behind."

Johnny Colt frowned, then shrugged. "Whatever you say. Am I in or out?"

"I'll get back to you."

Johnny Colt wandered off, and Ito Kinoshita walked out into the yard.

"Very young and very eager."

"So were most of the men in most of the graveyards on the Frontier," replied Nighthawk dryly.

"Are you going to take him along?"

"I don't think so."

"Why not?"

"He's in love with that gun of his, and it'll alert every soldier in the area the first time he fires it."

"So tell him not to use it."

"It's his trademark," said Nighthawk sarcastically. "Imagine a seventeen-year-old kid having a trademark."

"Didn't you?"

"I still don't. It makes you too easy to identify."

"You don't think he's killed anyone, do you?" asked Kinoshita.

"Maybe a couple of old men who were looking the

other way. But this kid never faced anyone who wasn't afraid to look into his eyes."

"How can you tell?"

"Instinct. Experience. Gut feeling."

"What if you're wrong?"

"Then he'll live to fight another day, and maybe write a folk song or two about how we died on Pericles V."

"You think we might die?"

"If everyone does their job, we might get in and out before they know what's happened," answered Nighthawk. "But there are an awful lot of them and just a handful of us. Getting killed is certainly a possibility."

"Then why risk it?"

"I've told you why: for the Nighthawk who's frozen beneath Deluros VIII."

"I know you can't turn Cassandra over to her father," said Kinoshita, "but can't you bring in some killers with prices on their heads? I mean, there must be *some* other way to raise the money."

"I don't know how quickly he'll need it," said Nighthawk. "I can't risk being late with it and having him thrown out onto the street." He paused. "So I'll plan as carefully as I can, and try to cover all the possibilities, and hope that someone in our little group was born lucky."

"You're about as lucky as anyone I know," offered Kinoshita. "Look how long you survived in such a dangerous profession."

"I'm good, not lucky."

"What's the difference?"

"Lucky people aren't walking around with eplasia," replied Nighthawk with an ironic smile.

"Point taken," admitted Kinoshita. He looked off

and saw a slender woman approaching them. "I think you've got another volunteer."

The woman walked up to Nighthawk, totally ignoring Kinoshita. "They say you're looking for volunteers."

"That's right."

"Here I am."

"Name?"

"Pallas Athene."

"Strange name."

"It's for the Greek goddess," she replied. "People take any name they want out here. That's the one I wanted."

"Whatever makes you happy."

"Killing Cassius Hill will make me happy."

"Have you got a personal grudge, or are you just interested in making the Frontier a better place?"

"Do I ask you *your* motives?" she demanded. Before he could answer her, she whipped a knife out of her belt and hurled it at a low-flying avian. It caught the creature in the neck, killing it instantly. "*That's* all you have to know about me."

"That's enough to know," admitted Nighthawk. "You're in. I'll be in touch."

"Do you know where to find me?"

"You found me. I'll find you."

She walked away without another word.

"Give me two dozen like her and we just might pull this off," said Nighthawk.

"Take two thousand like her and you might conquer the whole goddamned Oligarchy," agreed Kinoshita.

"It's a thought."

"So, how soon are we ready?"

"I just told you: when I find two dozen more like her."

"That could take months."

"Or hours," said Nighthawk. "Or weeks. They'll show up when they show up. We're not offering any financial inducements, and besides, everyone I would offer it to has been dead for the better part of a century."

"Nicholas Jory was asking me why you haven't recruited *him*," said Kinoshita.

"I don't want him."

"He was willing to die to protect Cassandra's identity," noted Kinoshita.

"That's one of the reasons I don't want him," answered Nighthawk.

"I don't understand."

"It's undoubtedly noble that he was willing to die for her," said Nighthawk, "but I'd rather he'd tried to find some way to kill me instead. I don't want people who are willing to die. I want men and women who want to live, people like Pallas Athene who probably can't even conceive of their own deaths. Don't give me any noble sacrifices, just people who have every intention of returning to Sylene in one piece."

"It's an attitude that makes sense in you," said Kinoshita. "After all, you're the Widowmaker. But if *they* hold it, they're out of touch with reality."

"Haven't you figured it out yet?" said Nighthawk. "Nobody who is willing to face these odds without a reason is in touch with reality—and Cassandra and I are the only ones who've got a reason."

*Well, at least it pleases you to think you have one*, concluded Kinoshita.

Nighthawk looked up and saw a tall man approaching him. "Here comes another loser."

"That's a bit of a snap judgment, don't you think?"

"Look at his power pack," said Nighthawk. "It's flashing on empty."

"I never noticed."

"It's not your business to notice."

Kinoshita stared at Nighthawk for a long moment. *On the other hand, we're probably a hell of a lot better off taking three dozen madmen to Pericles than three dozen losers. I wish there were a third alternative . . . but the madmen and the losers constitute all the pieces. The sane ones own the game.*

# Chapter 29

◆ ◆ ◆ ◆ ◆ ◆ ◆

*Kinoshita broke the silence aboard the ship.*

"Pallas Athene reports that she and her team have landed," he announced.

"No problems?" asked Nighthawk.

"There don't seem to be any."

"What about the others?"

"No word from Friday and Melisande yet."

"How about Big Johann?"

Kinoshita shook his head. "Not a word. Do you want me to land?"

"No. Not until everyone else is down."

"I still don't see why we didn't all go in one ship," complained Blue Eyes.

"Why not just wave a flag and tell them we've come to assassinate the governor?" said Nighthawk wryly.

"We could have come as tourists on a spaceliner," said Blue Eyes defensively.

"Three dozen tourists from Sylene?"

"If we all had our passports and visas in order . . ." began the dragon without much conviction.

"I assume computers haven't gotten any stupider during the past century, and the ones I knew would have flashed every alarm they had if they'd been confronted by half as many tourists from a planet that is known to be sympathetic to Ibn ben Khalid," said Nighthawk. "Add to that that there probably haven't been ten tourists from Sylene in the past century, and—"

"Okay, okay," said Blue Eyes. "I get the picture."

Kinoshita looked up. "I just heard from Friday. He's on the ground. No problems."

"Good," said Nighthawk. "That leaves Big Johann's and Tuesday Eddie's groups." He checked his timepiece. "They should report any minute."

Nighthawk walked to the galley and poured himself a soft drink.

"Some ship!" muttered Blue Eyes, joining him. "Not a drop of booze on it."

"Liquor and action don't mix."

"Maybe they don't mix for *your* metabolism, but I find that a good Alphard brandy puts a fine edge on me."

"Then you'll have to make do without your edge," said Nighthawk.

"Your sympathy is appreciated" was the dragon's sardonic reply.

Nighthawk ignored him, finished his drink, tossed the container in an atomizer, and then returned to the control room.

"How are you holding up?" he asked of the girl sitting silently in a corner.

"I'm fine," said Cassandra. "Just anxious."

"You've waited this long," said Nighthawk. "You can wait another hour or two."

"I know."

"Well, *I* don't know," said Blue Eyes, joining them. "Why can't we land now?"

"Because I say so," replied Nighthawk.

"Look, you're the Widowmaker. You're the boss, and you're probably the only advantage we have—but so far you haven't told us what the hell is going on."

"Everyone knows what they have to do."

"But they don't know *why*," said the dragon. "If there's a master plan, and there'd damned well better be, no one knows it but you."

"Then no one can tell Cassius Hill what it is, can they?" said Nighthawk.

"You still think I'd tell him, just because I'm not human?" demanded Blue Eyes. "That I'd betray you because you *are*? Take a good look at Hill, Widowmaker—he's human too! Why would I betray one of you to the other?"

"I never said you would."

"You sure act like it," grumbled Blue Eyes.

"I haven't told anyone except Cassandra, and I only told her because someone has to coordinate things if I go down."

"But if you don't think there's a traitor . . . ?" began Blue Eyes.

"I don't think so," Nighthawk confirmed. "But I could be wrong. If I don't tell any of you my plans, then it doesn't matter, does it?"

"Except that you could still be shot in the back."

"You tell me a surefire way to prevent that, and I'll listen."

Kinoshita stood up. "Big Johann has landed. But he's almost three miles off target."

Nighthawk sat down in the captain's chair. "All right. We'll give him an extra forty minutes. Get in touch with Pallas Athene and tell her to adjust her schedule."

"Will do," said Kinoshita. "There's no word from Tuesday Eddie yet."

"Let's assume he's being cautious rather than stupid."

"How will you know the difference?" asked Blue Eyes.

"If he's being cautious, he'll report in eventually. If he's been stupid, then he's dead already and we're not going to hear from him."

"How long are we willing to wait for Tuesday Eddie?" asked Kinoshita.

Nighthawk considered the question. "Ordinarily I'd say ten more minutes and then we move without him. But since we're giving Big Johann forty minutes, we might as well give the same to Tuesday Eddie." He paused. "Stupid name."

"He was born on a Tuesday, got married on a Tuesday, had his first son on a Tuesday, got divorced on a Tuesday, and killed his first man on a Tuesday," said Blue Eyes. "So he finally took it as his name."

"What's today?" asked Nighthawk.

"Monday."

"For another hour or so. Let's hope he doesn't hit for the cycle and die on a Tuesday."

"I thought you were supposed to be the optimist."

"I'm a realist. Sometimes it's the same thing; sometime's it's not. Tonight it's not."

"He's checking in . . ." said Kinoshita.

"He made it?"

Kinoshita shook his head. "He's been denied landing clearance."

"Why?"

"No reason."

"Can he get low enough to dump a shuttle before he cuts out?" asked Nighthawk.

Kinoshita put the question to Tuesday Eddie.

"He says he doesn't think so. Too many sensors covering him. Do you want him to open fire?"

"Hell no!" snapped Nighthawk. "They'd blow him out of the sky in five seconds."

"He wants to know what to do."

"Tell him to break out of orbit, then try about four hundred miles south. If he gets through, have him try to fly under the sensors and get back to his rendezvous point."

"It can't be done," said Kinoshita.

"Sure it can, if he's a good enough pilot. They can't spot anything flying less than eighty feet above the ground."

"Who the hell told you that?" asked Blue Eyes.

"Nobody had to tell me. I *know*—oh, shit!" Nighthawk grimaced. "Let me guess: they've perfected them during the past century, right?"

Kinoshita nodded.

"All right. Tell him to fake engine trouble and make an emergency landing. They'll never buy it, but if he thinks he can take them out, have him do it. Otherwise, fuck around with the engine for half an hour and take off for Sylene."

Kinoshita transmitted the message. "We probably won't hear from them again. Even if they pull it off, they're not going to break radio silence to announce that they've just taken out a squad of Hill's men."

"Right," said Nighthawk. "Okay, let me know when Big Johann's in place, and then we'll get this show on the road."

"Message incoming from Melisande."

"What does she want?"

"Friday's planted his bombs and wants to know when he can set them off."

"Not until I say so."

"She says he doesn't want to wait."

Nighthawk walked over to the console. "Put him on." He leaned over it. "Listen to me—this is Nighthawk." A moment later Friday's voice muttered an acknowledgment. "I didn't create this plan so you could go off and do what you want. If a single explosive is detonated before I give the word, I'll personally hunt you down and kill you before I leave this planet. Do you understand?"

Friday muttered a protest.

"They'll be just as dead if you wait another hour. The only difference is, you might live through this so you can kill more Men. Think about it."

He broke the connection and returned to his seat.

"Can you trust him?" asked Cassandra.

"Probably."

"He's afraid of you, right?" said Blue Eyes. "He knows you can kill him."

"He doesn't know any such thing," replied Nighthawk. "But if he kills me, there will be no one to lead him against more Men—and he favors quantity over quality."

"And he's out there with an empathic prostitute," said Cassandra. "And you're here with an alien bartender and a woman who's been masquerading as a man." She smiled wryly at him. "You put together some crew, Widowmaker."

He shrugged. "You work with what you've got."

And then, to the surprise of everyone, even those who knew him best, he settled back in his chair, closed his eyes, and fell asleep.

It was Kinoshita who gently touched his shoulder half an hour later.

"What is it?" asked Nighthawk, as alert as if he'd been awake the entire time.

"Big Johann's in position."

"Then it's time. Get landing coordinates from the spaceport."

"Got 'em," said Kinoshita a moment later. "But they're asking questions."

"I'll take it from here," said Nighthawk, walking over to the console.

"I require your name and the name and registration number of your ship," said a mechanical voice.

"This is Jefferson Nighthawk. My ship has no name. Its registration number is BD711507JH, and we're two days out from Sylene."

"Purpose of visit?"

"I was commissioned by Governor Cassius Hill to find and return his daughter, Cassandra. I've accomplished my mission. She's onboard with me."

"I must check this out."

"Let me land while you're checking it," said Nighthawk. "I'm very low on fuel."

Pause.

"You may land if you will first transmit a live image of Cassandra Hill."

"No problem. Cassandra, step over here near the holo transmitter." It was Nighthawk's turn to pause. "Got it?"

"Image received. You have permission to land. I have loaded the coordinates into your navigational computer."

"Thanks." Nighthawk cut the transmission. "Well, that's that."

"They'll be waiting for us with half the army!" protested Blue Eyes. "How long do you think it'll take them to find out that Hill wants her dead, not returned?"

"All night," said Nighthawk. "Why do you think we waited for Big Johann to get into position? He's jamming all transmissions to and from the governor's mansion."

Suddenly Blue Eyes grinned. "You mean they can't contact him to tell him we're here?"

"That's the general idea."

"And I thought you were sending Big Johann out to wipe out some enemy squad."

"I know you did," said Nighthawk. "That's why I'm running this operation and you're not." He turned to Kinoshita. "How long before we touch down?"

"Maybe five minutes, maybe six."

"Are you packed?"

"Sonic pistol and laser pistol," said Kinoshita, touching the butt of each.

"Fully charged?"

"They'd better be."

"Double-check before we land." Nighthawk walked over to Blue Eyes. "Are your weapons in order?"

"Yes."

"I hope you know how to use them."

"Put me to the test," said the dragon.

"I don't have to. Cassius Hill will."

Nighthawk walked to a bulkhead, softly uttered its lock's combination, and waited while it slid back to reveal a very odd-looking weapon, half-pistol, half-rifle, with a large power pack and an unfamiliar configuration.

"What the hell is that?" asked Blue Eyes.

"A molecular imploder."

"I thought they were illegal everywhere in the galaxy!"

Nighthawk merely stared at him.

"Where did you get it?" continued the dragon.

"I had Pallas Athene pick it up for me." He paused. "She's a resourceful lady."

"Can these babies really do what I've heard?"

"Depends on what you've heard."

"That they turn everything they hit—people, buildings, vehicles—into jelly."

"You've heard right—deadly but localized."

"You'll *slaughter* them."

"This isn't a gentleman's contest, and it's not my intention to give the enemy an even chance," said Nighthawk. "Does that answer your next couple of questions?"

"You don't have to bite my head off," said Blue Eyes.

"Look," replied Nighthawk irritably, "I'm about to go into action against overwhelming odds. The likeliest outcome is that we'll all be killed. Even if we aren't, I'm going to blow away a lot of innocent men to get to one guilty one. So forgive me if I'm not in a friendly mood, okay?"

"All right, all right," said Blue Eyes, backing away. "Just remember who the enemy is."

Nighthawk turned to Cassandra. "You set?"

She patted each of her weapons.

"All right, Ito," he said. "Land the ship and let's get this show on the road."

# Chapter 30

◆ ◆ ◆ ◆ ◆ ◆ ◆

*Nighthawk emerged from the ship and surveyed his surroundings, the molecular imploder held carefully in his hands. A moment later he was joined by Cassandra, Kinoshita, and Blue Eyes.*

"Well?" asked the dragon.

"There probably aren't more than a dozen people here at this hour," replied Nighthawk. "See the west-facing section of the building?"

"Yes."

"It's yours."

"Mine?" asked Blue Eyes.

"Kill everyone in it."

"What about just taking them prisoner?"

"If you'd rather."

"*They're* not my enemies," said the dragon.

"Tell me that after one of them identifies you," said Nighthawk.

"I'll play it by ear."

"Do whatever you want," said Nighthawk. "But if any of them gets a message out, I won't wait for Hill's men to kill you. I'll do it myself."

"You could be a little more pleasant, you know," complained Blue Eyes.

"You could be a little more competent. We all have our shortcomings."

Blue Eyes glared at him, then pulled his laser pistol out of its holster and headed off in the direction Nighthawk had indicated.

"Well," said Nighthawk, "maybe he'll kill them and maybe he won't, but just to be on the safe side . . ."

He aimed the molecular imploder at the radio-transmitting tower. The metal turned to liquid and formed a large puddle on the roof of the spaceport. Inside the building a handful of men and women started moving rapidly, scurrying from desk to desk, trying to determine the cause of the problem, but as yet no one had looked out on the landing strip.

"Okay," said Nighthawk. "Ito, you've got the cargo area. Cassandra, go around to the exit and kill anyone who tries to get out."

They both acknowledged his orders with terse nods and went about their business, while Nighthawk approached the building. When he was some ten yards away he slung the imploder over a shoulder, withdrew a pair of pistols, and boldly entered the spaceport.

"Who the hell are—?" began a uniformed guard. He was dead before he could complete the sentence.

Nighthawk heard a slight noise behind him, spun

around, and dropped two more guards with bursts of solid light. He heard agonized screams from the west end of the building, and assumed Blue Eyes was either a lousy marksman or a bit of a sadist, or perhaps both.

He carefully searched the Customs area. It seemed empty. He then began walking toward the cargo area to see how Kinoshita was doing when a laser beam whizzed by him, burning the lobe of his left ear. He threw himself to the floor, shattered the one dim light with his sonic pistol, and then tried to pinpoint the source of the laser fire.

For a long moment all was stillness and silence. He knew that all he had to do was entice his unseen opponent into firing once, and he'd know his position . . . but the opponent knew it too, and seemed content to outwait him. Nighthawk threw one of his knives noisily across the room, hoping to draw laser fire, but there was no response. Suddenly a brass cartridge rolled across the floor in his direction, and he resisted the urge to pull a weapon and blow it away.

Finally he began crawling across the room on his belly, hoping he could come across some sign—heavy breathing, the rubbing of a leather holster against a crisp military tunic, *something*—that would pinpoint his opponent's location. After a couple of minutes he half expected to wind up in his enemy's lap, and finally he stopped, convinced that that strategy could be suicidal.

He examined his weapons: laser pistols, sonic pistols, bullet pistol, knives, looking for a tactic, an edge. Finally he found one.

He placed a laser pistol on the floor, and silently removed its power pack. He pressed the "charge" button, but because the pistol was fully charged, the button immediately popped back out. He pressed the button again, withdrew a knife, and used it to hold the button in place, then carefully crawled about twenty feet away and waited.

It took exactly two minutes and twenty-six seconds for the pistol to overload. Then it exploded with a bright flash of light, and Nighthawk's opponent instantly fired at the light. Nighthawk pinpointed the source of the firepower and shot at it with his sonic pistol. There was a scream, then silence.

"Light," muttered Nighthawk, and instantly two dim bulbs came to life.

His antagonist was stretched out on the floor, pistol in hand. He walked over, rolled the body on its back with the toe of his boot, and thoughtfully studied the youthful face.

There was a sudden noise, and he noticed that Cassandra had entered the area.

"I saw all the lights go out, and I kept waiting for some signal that you were all right," she said. "I didn't want to walk into any gunfire."

"You did right."

She indicated the weapon that was still slung over his shoulder. "Why didn't you simply spray the room with the imploder?"

"Look around you."

"I don't understand," she said, surveying her surroundings.

"I'd have hit a weight-bearing wall." She looked puzzled. "These walls hold up the building," he explained. "It would probably have collapsed on me—and even if it hadn't, I don't need the Oligarchy coming after me."

"Why would they care?"

"I can get away with melting an antenna, but if I turn an entire spaceport into silly putty, I'm going to

have the Navy on my tail for the rest of what figures to
be a very brief life." He paused. "I assume the spaceport
is secure?"

"No one tried to get out," she said.

"Yet."

"Ito and Blue Eyes are waiting out front. They
didn't take any prisoners."

"Check the west wing; I don't trust that dragon."

"Has he ever lied to you?"

"No more than most men," answered Nighthawk.

She shrugged. "Where will you be?"

"Trying to locate the computer that talked to our
ship—the one that has my name and the ship's registration number in it."

He found it before she returned, and used the
imploder so that it was totally destroyed and there was
no chance of experts later reconstructing the machine's
memory.

"Two dead women, and nothing is stirring," announced Cassandra a moment later. "I suppose there
could be some people hiding somewhere, but . . ."

"We can't spend all night looking for them, so
we'll have to assume they don't exist," said Nighthawk.
He looked around. "Okay, we're done with Phase One.
We've landed, we've made it past Customs, and no one
can identify us. Let's go."

They walked outside and joined Kinoshita and
Blue Eyes.

"So far so good," said Nighthawk. "Now we pay a
visit to the governor."

"There's a hell of a military vehicle sitting empty
just across the road," noted Blue Eyes. "That baby could
run through anything Hill's men throw at us."

"Forget it," replied Nighthawk. "We want a nice, simple, private vehicle."

"Why, when we could approach him safely in something like *that*?" persisted the dragon.

"Because something like that has probably got half a dozen communication devices, and since we don't know any of the codes or passwords, we'd be giving ourselves away before we went a mile." He paused. "Try to remember: if it comes to firepower, we're totally outgunned. We're trying to *sneak* in, not cut a swath through Hill's army."

Kinoshita stared at another vehicle. "By the same token, I assume we don't want a taxi?"

"I'd prefer not to use one," said Nighthawk. He looked around. "You see anything else?"

"No."

"Then we'll have to steal it. The second we get it moving, melt the radio."

Kinoshita frowned. "With the imploder?"

"One blast and you'd melt the whole car," said Nighthawk. "Use your laser."

"Uh . . . I think we're going to have a little problem here," said Kinoshita as they approached the vehicle.

"What is it?"

"This isn't like anything I've ever driven," said Kinoshita. "I mean, it *looks* like most of the vehicles I'm used to, but the panel is configured differently, and it sure doesn't seem to run on fusion." He peeked in through the window. "Hell, I don't even know how to start the damned thing." He turned to Blue Eyes. "You ever drive anything quite like this on any of the worlds you've been to?"

The dragon shook his head. "It shouldn't be too hard, though. How different can it be?"

"Different enough," said Kinoshita. "Unlike the other one, this *isn't* armored. You make any kind of mistake, however slight, and you've given us away. I mean, hell, the closer we get to Hill's mansion, the less leeway the guards will give us before they decide to shoot first and ask questions later."

"Enough talk," said Nighthawk, opening a door. "Get in. *I'm* driving."

"You?" repeated Kinoshita. "But you haven't driven a vehicle in a century! You have no idea how this works."

"I was in one just like it the last time I was on this world. I watched what the driver did."

He sat behind the panel, carefully touched the right screens in the right order, and the vehicle suddenly hummed with life.

"Well, I'll be damned!" said Kinoshita.

"I wouldn't be at all surprised," replied Nighthawk as the vehicle took off through the murky Periclean night.

# Chapter 31

• • • • • • • •

*They'd gone a little more than nine miles when Nighthawk* pulled the vehicle off the road and parked it behind a row of thick bushes.

"What now?" asked Blue Eyes.

"Now we walk."

"How far?"

"Maybe a mile, maybe a bit less."

"And you don't want to attract attention by driving the rest of the way, right?" continued the dragon.

"That's right."

"You don't think they're going to notice the four of us walking up to the front door?"

"First," answered Nighthawk, "we're not walking

up to the front door, and second, I think they're going to have other things on their minds."

"Such as?"

Nighthawk activated his communicator and set it to Friday's channel.

"You still there, Friday?"

"Yes," replied the alien's voice.

"Any problems yet?"

"No."

"Okay. Count to twenty and give 'em hell—and then get your asses out of there."

Nighthawk didn't wait for a response. He deactivated the device and recommenced walking in the direction of the governor's mansion.

Twenty seconds later the horizon was lit up by a series of explosions. They circled to the east, each brighter and louder than the last.

"Where did he get his hands on so many explosives?" asked Blue Eyes.

"He's very creative," replied Nighthawk dryly. "Come on. Stop staring—it's not a fireworks display. We've got serious work to do."

"Shouldn't we wait until they empty out the mansion?"

"Everyone who's going has left already," answered Nighthawk. "Cassius Hill's not going to leave himself totally defenseless."

"Look!" said Kinoshita, pointing to the northeast. "That looks like laser fire! There are snipers out there!"

"That means Tuesday Eddie got through," said Nighthawk, increasing his pace.

"So that accounts for Tuesday Eddie and Friday," said Blue Eyes. "And I know Big Johann was jamming their transmissions. But where is Pallas Athene and her group?"

"Around," said Nighthawk.

"You *still* don't trust me?" demanded the dragon.

"It's not a matter of trust. If you're captured, you can't tell what you don't know."

"And what if *you're* captured?"

"I won't be," replied Nighthawk with such absolute calm and certainty that Blue Eyes was suddenly afraid of him.

"Is that it?" asked Kinoshita as the huge mansion came into view.

"That's it," said Cassandra coldly. "I've waited a long time for this day."

Blue Eyes started walking, prepared to use the extensive landscaping for cover, but Nighthawk laid a heavy hand on his shoulder. "Wait," he said.

"What for?" responded the dragon. "We're sitting ducks out here."

"This whole place is honeycombed with security devices," said Nighthawk.

"Then how—?"

"Shut up and listen."

Cassandra stared at the ground ahead of her, and finally looked up. "There's a web of sensors throughout the yard. They're about a foot off the ground so animals won't set them off. I'm wearing infrared lenses, so I can see them. Walk exactly where I walk, and you should be all right. When we get to where they're too closely aligned to walk between them, I'll crawl beneath them until I get to the power source and deactivate them."

She began walking in a complex route, turning every few steps, showing them how to avoid the unseen sensor beams, every now and then warning one of them that he was getting too near a beam. Finally, when they were perhaps two hundred yards from the house, she gestured them all to kneel down and wait for her signal.

She got onto her belly and slithered beneath the beams that only she could see. In a moment she was one with the darkness, and even Nighthawk, who possessed excellent night vision, couldn't spot her.

He made himself as comfortable as he could on the cool, damp lawn and contented himself with watching the now-sporadic explosions and increasing laser fire. After what seemed an hour, but was probably closer to ten minutes, Cassandra walked back and joined them.

"It's safe now," she whispered. "At least until we're inside the house."

"Then what?" asked Kinoshita.

"Guards, alarms, robots," she said. "You name it, he's got it."

"I assume you have a plan?" said Blue Eyes to Nighthawk. "Other than sending me up to the roof, I mean?"

"You know what you have to know," said Nighthawk.

"Damn it, I have a right to know what's going on!" persisted the dragon. "*Why* do I have to climb up to the roof? Cassandra says there are alarms in the house. The house is all lit up, so infrared lenses won't help. How are you going to get around them?"

"I'm not," responded Nighthawk.

"You're just going to blithely walk through the house setting them all off?"

"That's right."

"You're crazy!" snapped the dragon.

"You're welcome to think so," said Nighthawk,

"but keep your voice down or you'll get us all shot before we even enter the mansion."

Blue Eyes glared at him, but didn't say anything more, and Nighthawk led his little party toward the house. When he was some eighty yards distant, he saw a number of troops on the driveway leading to the front entrance, and he changed directions, circling around to the back.

There were two uniformed men standing guard at the back of the mansion. Nighthawk put his finger to his lips, then gestured his group to stay put. He began sneaking up on the men, patient as Job, silent as death. When he was some twenty feet away, he pulled out a knife and hurled it into the throat of one man while leaping from the shadows onto the back of the other. A quick twist of the head, a loud *snap!*, and then all was still again.

Nighthawk signaled his party to join him, and a moment later they were all huddled in the shadows just outside the rear entrance.

"Blue Eyes, Ito, get these men out of sight."

They dragged the two guards off behind a row of thick, neatly trimmed shrubbery, then returned.

"You still plan to just walk right into the house?" demanded Blue Eyes.

"Yeah," said Nighthawk. "After Cassandra reconnects the outside alarm system."

"*Re*connects it?" exclaimed the dragon. "Why?"

"So I can set it off."

"What the hell are you talking about?"

"As you've pointed out, there's no way to get into the house without setting off dozens of alarms. So, since we can't avoid setting them off, the only thing to do is make the guards ignore them."

"How?"

"By setting off every outside alarm as well. Then these will just be one more set of alarms on the blink."

"You think he'll buy that while there are bombs going off and sniper fire, and his radio transmissions are being jammed?"

"Not initially," replied Nighthawk. "But eventually he'll have to, when his men check the grounds and can't find anyone setting off the alarms."

"And how are you going to accomplish that?"

"I'm not," said Nighthawk. "*You* are."

"Me?" demanded the dragon. "I want to be in on the kill!"

"You're going to make the kill possible," replied Nighthawk. He pointed to a staircase. "There's a set of stairs leading to one of the bedroom balconies. Once you're up there, you shouldn't have any trouble reaching the roof."

"You've been telling me since we left Sylene that I have to be able to get on the roof. I assumed there was some secret entrance up there."

"I wish there were."

"So I get onto the roof. What then?"

"Then you fire *this*"—Nighthawk handed him one of his sonic pistols—"randomly in every direction."

"A Screecher? I'll be spotted in three seconds!"

"No, you won't," said Nighthawk. "There's no light, and no explosion. The guards will be too far away to hear the hum . . . but the sensors are sensitive enough to react to it." He paused. "I want you to hit every area with that thing, to set off every system they've got. Don't hit any guards, just alarms. Especially toward the front of the mansion; that's where I want most of them congregated."

"And then you just walk in the back door and set off more alarms—and nobody pays attention?"

"That's the general idea."

"You know, it might work," admitted the dragon. Suddenly he tensed. "How do I get down after the place is teeming with guards?"

"Just be patient," said Nighthawk.

"For how long?"

"Ten minutes, twenty minutes, an hour," said Nighthawk with a shrug. "It depends on conditions inside. But either I'm going to kill Cassius Hill, in which case the whole planet will be after me and you can probably climb down and walk to the spaceport in broad daylight; or else he's going to kill me, and then you can testify that I forced you to do all this and swear everlasting fealty to him."

"He'll never believe me."

"Then you'd better hope I kill him, hadn't you?" responded Nighthawk with a smile. "Now get your ass up there, and don't start shooting until you see my signal."

Blue Eyes began cautiously climbing the stairs, muttering to himself. When he reached the balcony, he balanced precariously on the railing for a moment, then laboriously pulled himself onto the roof. He felt a surge of vertigo, lay as flat as he could, and waited until it passed. Finally he withdrew the sonic pistol, got carefully to his feet, and located Nighthawk, who was standing in the shadows just past the rear entrance.

Nighthawk waited for Cassandra to join him. He asked her something, she nodded her head, and he looked up at Blue Eyes, raised his hand above his head, and dropped it.

Wondering how he had gotten himself into such a situation, Blue Eyes trained the sonic pistol on a point some two hundred yards from the front door and pulled the trigger.

The response was deafening.

# Chapter 32

*As the guards streamed out of the house, looking for the* intruders, Nighthawk motioned Cassandra and Kinoshita to keep to the shadows. Then, when Blue Eyes had set off at least a dozen different alarms, he walked in through a side door, spotted a security camera, and blew it away.

"Not you," he said, as Kinoshita followed him.

"Why not?"

"I told you before. You're the one who has to survive and get the money back to Deluros VIII. I can't take a chance on you getting killed inside the mansion."

"So where do you want me?"

"See that room on the second floor, the one with all the lights on?"

"Yes. Looks like he's got bars on the windows and the balcony door."

"Those bars are to keep people out, not in. It's Hill's office. Stay within sight of it. When I get the money, I'll toss it down to you."

"And if the yard is swarming with guards?"

"Then I'll find some way to distract them while Cassandra gets the money to you." He handed the molecular imploder to Kinoshita. "And if it gets really hairy, use this."

"I'm still not happy about this," said Kinoshita. "You could use me inside."

Nighthawk shook his head. "You'd be one more person I'd have to protect." Nighthawk briefly noted Kinoshita's hurt expression. "I'm sorry. I don't have time to be diplomatic."

He stepped aside as Cassandra entered, then closed the door behind him.

"Can he keep clear of the guards?" she asked as they walked through the small room.

"He's a good man. He'll stay clear."

Nighthawk paused before the door.

"What's on the other side of this?" he asked.

"A corridor. It leads to a staircase on the left, and a library and eventually the summer kitchen on the right."

"Summer kitchen?" he repeated.

"Where the staff cooks for outdoor functions. It used to be outside, but the insects on Pericles are not only large, they can be incredibly aggressive, so my father had it enclosed a few years ago."

"Are we likely to run into any guards in the corridor?" asked Nighthawk.

"Ordinarily, I'd say no. But with alarms going off

all over, and the building's security board lit up like a Christmas tree, I can't be sure."

"All right," he said. "Stand back and let me go first."

"I'm armed too," she protested. "And don't forget— this is *my* battle."

"I'm going to be as blunt with you as I was with Kinoshita," said Nighthawk. "If there's more than one guard out there, you haven't got a chance. I'm the Widowmaker. This is what I do for a living. I guarantee it'll take more than two or three men to bring me down."

She seemed about to protest, realized that he was right, that his decision to go first was practical rather than noble or falsely heroic, and she stepped back.

"Open," muttered Nighthawk, and the door dilated. He stepped through, weapons in hand, and put a burst of laser fire through the security camera.

"Halt!" yelled a voice.

Nighthawk spun and fired, dropped a guard, then crouched down and shot two more as they raced down the stairs at the sound of the first one's voice.

He stood motionless, listening intently, for almost a full minute, then turned to Cassandra.

"All right, let's go," he said softly, heading toward the stairs.

"Not that way!" she whispered.

"They lead to your father's office, don't they?"

"And they're wired. The first step will read your weight and the structure of your foot, and since you're not in the computer, the second step will fry you to a crisp."

"Then how do we get up there?"

"There are three ways. Two will be guarded: the main staircase, and an airlift right next to it. The third way I discovered when I was a little girl—a secret stairway that I think he put in as an escape route—but I don't know if it's wired too."

"If it is, we won't have any warning before he activates it," said Nighthawk. "We'd better use one of the public routes and take our chances with the guards."

She nodded her agreement and set off down the corridor. When they reached the summer kitchen she stopped as Nighthawk destroyed yet another camera. He turned and saw her standing hesitantly, her face troubled.

"What is it?"

"Something's wrong," she said.

"What?"

She frowned. "There are always staff members here. This is where they cook their own food when it's not being used for some big ceremonial dinner."

"Nothing's wrong. There are dozens of alarms going off. They're all out looking for the bad guys— meaning us."

"Cooks don't carry weapons," she said. "*Someone* should be here."

As if on cue, the heavy metal door to the walk-in freezer opened and two middle-aged men walked out, each carrying slabs of meat.

"Freeze!" said Nighthawk softly.

One of the men was so startled he dropped his meat noisily to the floor and held his hands up. The other simply stared at Nighthawk as if he was the latest in a long line of minor irritations.

"Can you regulate the freezer's temperature from the inside?" asked Nighthawk.

"Yes," said one of the men.

"Okay. Go back inside."

"But—"

"No arguments. Just do it."

When both men were inside the freezer, Nighthawk began shutting the door.

"You're going to be here for a few hours, so raise the temperature and relax."

Before they could protest he had shut and locked the huge, gleaming door.

"So much for your missing men," he said, turning to Cassandra. "Now where do we go?"

"Follow me."

*"No!"* he said sharply. "I'll go first. You just tell me where."

"Out this door," she said, pointing, "then follow the corridor to the right, pass through the sitting room, and we're at the grand foyer."

"That's where the staircase is?"

"Yes."

"Okay, let's go."

He walked out into the corridor, a pistol in each hand, alert for the slightest noise or movement. Suddenly he heard the sound of footsteps coming through the country kitchen. He stepped back, passing Cassandra, waited with frightening calm until three men burst through the door, and fired. All three were dead before they hit the floor.

"Damn!" he muttered.

"What is it?" asked Cassandra.

"We should have set off more alarms inside the house. With only one sounding, they'll know security has been breached."

He walked back into the kitchen and blew out a window. The alarm went off, adding its whine to all the others.

Then he reentered the corridor and led the way to a large sitting room. He blew away the camera and gestured her to join him. As she did so, he shot out yet another window and activated the room's alarm.

"The main entrance is right past that door, you said?" he asked, indicating a massive door at the far end of the room.

She nodded. "The staircase and elevator will both be off to the left."

"How many men should be there?"

"Ordinarily there's a color guard of a dozen, plus a few minor functionaries," replied Cassandra. "But with all these alarms, who knows? They could all be outside, looking for enemies—or they could have smelled a ruse and tripled the guard."

A nearby explosion made the entire mansion shake.

"I hope he remembers he's not supposed to blow this place up until we're out of it," muttered Nighthawk.

"My father's got a couple of hundred men on call," she replied. "He couldn't get much closer."

"Never underestimate Friday," said Nighthawk. "He can blow them all to hell before you know it." He walked to the door. "Are you ready?"

She pulled her pistol out and nodded.

"Then let's go."

He ordered the door to open and burst into the grand foyer. There were eight uniformed men and a pair of robots standing guard. Five of the men were dead before they knew he was among them, and Cassandra downed two more. Nighthawk quickly turned his fire on the robots, melting the first with a laser blast and disrupting the circuits of the other with a solid burst of sound from his sonic pistol. The one remaining man turned and raced to the airlift.

"Get him!" snapped Nighthawk, still concentrating on the second robot, which was firing lethal pulse blasts from a finger that had been created for that purpose. He kept his sonic pistol trained on it, decided that the first robot was no longer a threat and added his laser fire to it, and heard a scream from the direction of the airlift just as the second robot finally collapsed, its limbs moving aimlessly, its weaponry no longer functional.

"Jesus, you're good!" said Cassandra admiringly. "You didn't need me at all, did you?"

"I needed you to stop that last one from warning your father or calling for reinforcements."

"He's stopped—but my father has to know *someone's* here by now." She paused. "I destroyed the airlift controls. We're going to have to climb the stairs."

"Doesn't make much difference," replied Nighthawk, staring at the dead bodies and deactivated robots. "We've protected our rear, and what's waiting for us will be waiting no matter which way we approach it."

"Yeah, we're okay unless someone enters the house," she agreed.

"No one will," he said, walking over to the entrance and fusing the lock with a blast from his laser pistol.

"Don't you think that will just alert them?" she asked.

"Probably."

"Then won't they immediately break the door down?"

"They can try," said Nighthawk. He checked his timepiece. "There's a six-foot lady who's going to have something to say about it in forty seconds or so," he added with a smile.

"Pallas Athene?"

"That's right," he said, starting to ascend the sweeping staircase.

"I was wondering what she was doing."

"Pretty much what we've been doing the last couple of minutes, but on the outside."

Nighthawk stopped at a landing, looking into every nook and cranny, peering into every shadow. When he decided it was safe, he climbed the rest of the stairs, then waited for Cassandra to catch up with him.

"So far so good," she said.

"That was the easy part," he replied. "Your father's no fool. You can bet the last hundred feet will be a hell of a lot harder than the first hundred."

He began walking cautiously along the corridor to Hill's outer office. Twice men emerged from rooms to stop him, and twice he shot them before they could take aim at him.

A robot emerged from the outer office and confronted them. Nighthawk turned his laser and sonic pistols on it, but with no discernible effect.

He looked around as the robot approached, spotted an overhead chandelier, and shot it loose from the ceiling. It fell heavily on the robot, which staggered and spent a moment getting free of it. During that time Nighthawk, no longer worried about keeping his presence secret, pulled out a projectile gun and fired a bullet into each of the robot's eyes. The sensors began smoking, and Nighthawk crouched down against a wall of the corridor, motioning to Cassandra to do the same. The robot continued walking in a straight line, crashed through a railing that overlooked the grand foyer, and fell some thirty feet to the marble floor below.

"Why the hell didn't my other weapons stop it, or

even slow it down?" muttered Nighthawk, as much to himself as to Cassandra.

"It was made of a titanium alloy with a super-tight molecular bonding," she answered.

"I've seen titanium before," he replied. "But I never saw one that a laser couldn't even char."

"There have been a lot of advances in the last century," she said. "Don't count on your memories, because if it's a state-of-the-art security device, my father owns it."

"I'll keep it in mind," he said seriously, finally straightening up. He tucked the sonic pistol into his belt and kept the projectile gun out. "I think I may need this one."

"You'll need them all before you're through," she said. "My father's a dangerous man. I wish you'd kept the molecular imploder."

He shook his head. "Fire it at a man standing against a wall and you not only turn the man to liquid, you do the same to the wall. And, sometimes, the trees beyond the wall." He smiled. "You really don't want to use it on the second floor of a house with high ceilings. Besides, Ito has to get back to the ship. It's better that he has it."

He turned back to the outer office, approached it silently, and burst into the room, weapons at the ready, only to find that it was empty. He waited until she caught up with him, then went through the doorway to the inner office. A robot stood at attention, staring at him.

"Good evening, Mr. Nighthawk," it said. "How nice to see you once again."

Cassandra turned her gun on it, but Nighthawk held up a hand.

"He's just an office robot. He's not programmed for violence."

"But he'll warn my father we're here!"

"He already has."

"Governor Hill has no idea you are inside the building, Mr. Nighthawk," said the robot.

"You're lying, right?" said Nighthawk.

"That is correct, sir."

"Sit down behind a desk and keep your mouth shut."

"I think I should remain at my post, sir."

"If you don't sit down right now, I'll melt you with a laser," said Nighthawk. "Consider that carefully and then make your decision."

"I will be of greater use to my master if I sit down," announced the robot, walking over to a desk and seating itself behind it.

"How many men and robots has Cassius Hill got behind that next door?" asked Nighthawk, indicating Hill's office.

"None, sir."

"You're lying again."

"That is correct, sir."

"How many?"

"Three thousand and fourteen."

Nighthawk pointed his pistol at the robot. "If you lie once more, I'm going to blow your goddamned head off. Now, how many men and robots has he got protecting him?"

"Quite enough, sir," said the robot. "You may fire when ready."

"If you insist." Nighthawk squeezed the trigger and melted the robot from the neck up.

"What was that for?" asked Cassandra. "It was only a machine."

"No sense giving it a chance to tell every other robot on the grounds exactly where we are. Pallas Athene's good, but she's not *that* good."

"It probably told them already."

"Then that's what it gets for telling them," said Nighthawk irritably.

He cautiously approached the door to Hill's office. As he reached it, it dilated before him, allowing him and Cassandra to pass through.

Cassius Hill sat at his desk, flanked by four Security robots. He was elegantly dressed, and was smoking an Antarrean cigar.

"Good evening, Widowmaker," he said. He turned to Cassandra. "How very nice to see you too, my dear." Back to Nighthawk. "To what do I owe the pleasure of this visit?"

"You owe me five million credits," said Nighthawk. "I'd like it in cash."

"Nonsense," said Hill. "I told you I didn't want her back. I want Ibn ben Khalid."

"I know. You still owe me five million credits."

"I just told you, I—" Suddenly Hill's eyes widened and he stared at Cassandra. "*Of course!* What a fool I've been! No wonder I could never find out anything about Ibn ben Khalid's past! No wonder he always seemed to know my next move!" He stood up. "I commend you, Cassandra. I couldn't ask for a more exceptional daughter. You have everything it takes to succeed me in office." He paused, then added with mock sadness: "What a shame that I'm going to have to kill you."

"You're not killing anyone," said Nighthawk, leveling his pistol at Hill.

"Don't be a fool, Widowmaker. I'll admit you showed enormous resourcefulness to reach my office, but you'll never leave here alive if you kill me." He placed his hands on the desk and leaned forward. "You've fulfilled your commission. You've returned my daughter *and* presented me with Ibn ben Khalid. You're free to leave Pericles. The money will be transferred to your lawyers' account."

"What happens to *her*?"

"What happens to her is going to happen whether I kill you first or not."

"I don't think we have a deal," said Nighthawk. He pointed toward a solid-looking safe that stood in a corner. "Open your safe."

"No."

"I can open it whether I kill *you* first or not."

"You agreed to fulfill my commission," said Hill. "I was given to understand that the Widowmaker always honors his contracts."

"A lot can change in a century," said Nighthawk. "Open the safe."

"And then what?" said Hill. "You'll kill me anyway."

"I have no intention of killing you."

"You just admitted that you break your word—so why should I believe you?"

"Once I've got your money, what purpose would be served by my killing you?"

"If you let me live, I'll hunt you to the ends of the galaxy."

"I doubt it," said Nighthawk. "If I let you live, you'll be grateful for the gift of life and won't chance losing it by following me."

Hill stared at Nighthawk. "I could order my robots to kill you right now."

"I don't think so. They're programmed to protect you." He raised his voice. "The instant I see a robot move, I'll shoot Cassius Hill at point-blank range." He smiled at Hill. "All right, give them the order."

"This isn't over, Widowmaker. Every man has his weaknesses, including you. You've just signed your death warrant."

"I've been dead for a hundred years," replied Nighthawk. "There's no future in it." He pointed to the safe with one of his pistols. "Get busy."

Hill turned to Cassandra. "Have you nothing to say, daughter? No word of regret for turning against your father? No plea for forgiveness?"

"Just get the money," she said.

He shrugged, walked over to the safe, and rapidly touched a combination, then whispered a trio of code words so softly that Nighthawk couldn't hear them. The door swung open.

"There it is," said Hill, indicating the tall piles of crisp banknotes. "Little good may it do you."

"Step aside," said Nighthawk.

"This is your last chance, Widowmaker. You can still walk away."

"You're in no position to be giving orders."

"I'm Cassius Hill," he said, walking back to his desk. "I'm *always* in a position to give orders."

"Keep your gun trained on him," said Nighthawk. "If he or the robots make a move, shoot *him* first."

Nighthawk approached the safe, peered into it, then holstered his gun and reached in for the money with his left hand—

—and the door slammed shut—

—and the safe suddenly sprouted legs and grew to a height equal to Nighthawk's—

*—and the safe developed arms that reached for Nighthawk's throat.*

"Poor, stupid clone," said an amused Cassius Hill. "A lot can happen in a century. Meet the newest, finest security device on the market—a weapon that can assume any shape that I choose for it."

Nighthawk pulled out his laser pistol, but the safe—the Weapon—slapped it away.

"Call it off or she'll kill you!" he yelled as one of the metal arms clamped shut on his left shoulder.

"Call *her* off or I'll have *it* kill *you*," countered Hill.

Cassandra fired, and her father grabbed his right arm.

"The next one will take your head off," she said coldly.

Nighthawk uttered an involuntary groan as the metal hand crushed his shoulder. He continued bobbing and weaving to keep his head away from the second hand—but now the Weapon had sprouted three more arms, each longer than the first two.

*"Now!"* shouted Cassandra.

"All right," said Hill. He turned to the safe. "Kiss!"

Suddenly the metal arms flowed back into the walls of the Weapon, though the door still pressed against his left arm, holding it motionless.

"Kiss?" repeated Nighthawk, almost amused despite the agony of his crushed shoulder.

"I wanted a word an enemy wouldn't think to utter," said Hill almost conversationally, as if being confronted in his office by an armed assassin were an everyday occurrence. "What now? Do you kill me or do I kill you, or do we find some common ground?"

"Make it let go of my arm," said Nighthawk.

"I don't think so," replied Hill. "You're a very

dangerous man, Widowmaker. Much better to keep you incapacitated until we've reached some understanding."

"Kiss," ordered Nighthawk.

"It only responds to *my* voice," explained Hill. "And 'kiss' is the command that makes its limbs vanish. It requires another word to make it let go of you—a word I have no intention of uttering."

Cassandra took a step nearer to him and aimed her pistol at a point between his eyes.

"No melodramatics, daughter," said Hill calmly. "His life isn't being threatened now, so you have no reason to threaten mine. And if you shoot me, my robots will kill you even faster than the Weapon will kill him."

"We can't stay like this forever," said Nighthawk.

"Then it's time to talk business," agreed Hill.

"Okay."

"But my business is only with you, Widowmaker. My daughter may inherit my paltry little estate someday, but what you and I have to say is of no concern to her."

"Fuck you!" snapped Cassandra, extending her arm so that her pistol was even closer to her father.

"Such language in a refined young revolutionary," said her father with mock distress.

"My arm's getting numb," said Nighthawk. "We've got to start talking soon."

"As soon as we're alone," said Hill.

Nighthawk turned to Cassandra. "I don't know how much longer I can stay conscious. You'd better do as he says."

"No goddamned way!" she protested.

"I'm in no position to argue!" he snapped. He

looked back at Hill. "She can't go back to the outer office. She'll be a sitting duck if any of your men show up there."

"What do you propose?" asked Hill.

"I don't know," grated Nighthawk, grimacing in pain. "Is there some other way out of this room?"

Hill looked around. "Well, there's always the balcony."

"Fine. Lock her out there till we're done."

"What if she jumps down and runs away?"

"She'll break a leg, or your men will kill her."

"I'm not going anywhere!" snapped Cassandra.

Nighthawk stared at her. *Will you stop being tough and stop being noble and just remember who's waiting downstairs and what he's holding?*

"I suppose we'll have to wait until you pass out and she gets tired of pointing her gun at me," said Hill. He shrugged eloquently. "I never could do anything with her."

*Jesus! You still haven't figured it out!*

"Get the fuck out of here, you dumb bitch!" he yelled.

She glared at him, her face reflecting her fury, and stalked out onto the balcony without another word.

*Good. Now just get over your mad long enough to look down before I pass out.*

Hill closed the door behind her. "Well, here we are, Widowmaker," he said easily. "My offer still stands: you can walk away safely, and the money will be in your attorneys' account tomorrow."

"Fuck my attorneys," said Nighthawk. "I'm doing this for *me*, not *him*."

"Ah!" said Hill with a smile. "Enlightened self-interest. That certainly makes you more comprehensible to me." He paused. "Let me make sure we understand each other. I release you, I pay you off, and you leave my office. I don't know how many men you have out there"—he waved his hand in the general direction of Friday's bombs—"but you call them off and take them away with you." He paused and stared at Nighthawk. "Ibn ben Khalid you leave behind."

"Agreed."

*Where the hell are you?*

"Good. Now all that's left to discuss is your fee. I think three million credits sounds exceptionally generous."

"What happened to five million?"

"That was before you threatened my life. Besides, you've surely done a couple of million credits' damage to my property this evening, don't you think?"

"Probably."

"Well, then?"

"I'll give you two options," said Nighthawk. "You can pay me three million or eight million, it's up to you."

"What's the difference?" asked Hill, curious.

"For eight million, I don't come back and kill you."

"More threats? You are a very slow learner, Widow-maker." Hill sighed and stared at him for a long moment. "I'll tell you what I'm going to do," he said at last. "I'm going to accept your proposition and pay you the eight million. I truly don't relish spending the rest of my life looking over my shoulder for a man of your abilities."

"Good," said Nighthawk. "Then we have a deal."

"That's right." He lowered his gaze to the Weapon and uttered a single word: *"Bite!"*

Nighthawk bellowed in pain as he felt his hand severed at the wrist. He almost passed out as Hill ordered the door of the safe to open.

Nighthawk, finally free, rolled on the floor, then tore off his belt and wrapped it around his wrist to try to staunch the bleeding. As he did so, Hill reached into the safe and withdrew red-stained stacks of currency.

"To coin a phrase, here is your blood money, Widowmaker. And while I believe that you intended to keep your promise not to hunt me down, I think a little encouragement is always beneficial."

Nighthawk reached for his laser pistol, which was lying on the floor, but one of the robots pointed a deadly finger and shot it away.

"Breaking your word already?" asked Hill.

"The bleeding hasn't stopped," mumbled Nighthawk. "I've got to cauterize the wound!"

"Allow me," said Hill, reaching into his desk and withdrawing a laser pistol. He aimed it at the blood-drenched stump and fired. Nighthawk bellowed again and doubled over in pain. "Number Four," said Hill to one of his robots. "Go out onto the balcony and kill my daughter."

"Yes, Governor," replied the robot, walking to the door that led to the balcony.

There was a brief humming sound, and the robot became a small gray puddle on the floor.

*"You remembered!"* muttered Nighthawk as Cassandra strode into the room, fired the imploder at the other three robots, and then turned the Weapon into jelly.

"What the hell did he do to you?" she demanded, finally noting Nighthawk's arm.

"Don't worry about it!" grated Nighthawk. "Let's just get the hell out of here!"

She turned the imploder toward her father, who pointed his laser pistol at her.

"It's still a Mexican standoff," he said calmly.

"You think so, do you?"

She fired the imploder, and he was a puddle of liquid and juices before he could fire back.

"I forgot all about Kinoshita until you cursed at me," Cassandra said, helping Nighthawk to his feet. "That was so unlike you that it startled me and made me think."

"I must be weaker than I thought," he said unsteadily. "It feels like the whole room is shaking."

"Oh, shit!" she said. "It is! That bastard must have tied his life readings into the house system and rigged it! Now that he's dead the whole goddamned wing is falling apart!"

"Grab the money!"

She pulled a pair of bags out of her pocket, opened them, and quickly tossed one pile of money into one and a smaller pile into the other, as the room began shaking more violently. "Now what?" she asked.

Nighthawk staggered to the balcony door. "Throw the bigger bag down to Ito! And give him the imploder, too!"

She raced to the railing of the balcony, threw the money and imploder over it.

"What now?" she asked.

"That secret passage you mentioned. Where is it?"

She was about to lead him to it when the floor vanished beneath her and the office wing of the mansion collapsed.

# Chapter 33

*Nighthawk groaned and pushed a piece of timber off his chest.*
He reached down to remove another one from his leg,
then realized that he was missing his left hand. As badly as
that hurt, the pain in his crushed shoulder was worse.

Suddenly a tall, lean figure was standing over him,
pulling timbers off his torso and legs.

"Cassandra . . ." he mumbled.

"She's all right. Don't waste your strength. Just lie
still and I'll have you out in another minute."

He tried to focus his eyes, and finally realized that
he was looking at Pallas Athene.

"What happened?" he asked, confused.

"The goddamned house collapsed," said Pallas
Athene. "I assume you killed Hill?"

"Yes."

She nodded her head. "I've heard of this baby before. It's called the Vengeance System. You're lucky to be alive." She pulled the last piece of lumber off him and stared at him. "What the hell happened to you? You didn't lose your hand from *this*."

"It's a long story." Suddenly he sat up. "Where's Blue Eyes? We left him on the roof."

"Dead. He's about forty feet off to your left. Broke his neck in the fall."

"Damn!" He leaned back, exhausted from the effort. "Where's the rest of your team?"

"Scattered from here to my ship," replied Pallas Athene. "All dead."

"Too bad."

"They knew the odds." She paused. "So you got Cassius Hill!"

"*She* got him."

"I'm glad you left it to her," said Pallas Athene. "After all, she's Ibn ben Khalid. It was a damned generous thing for you to do."

"Generosity had nothing to do with it," replied Nighthawk. "She saved my life."

"Sure."

"She did!" he said heatedly.

"Okay, she did. Keep your voice down and don't waste your strength. You haven't got a lot to spare."

"Pull out my communicator," he said.

"Where is it?"

"One of my pockets, or inside my belt."

She frisked him gently and produced it.

"Activate it. Band 1193."

"Done."

"Johann, how's it going?"

No response.

"Johann, are you there?"

Silence.

"Are you sure it's on the right band?"

She checked again. "1193, just like you said."

"Shit. Try Band 2076."

"Okay."

"Eddie, come in. Tuesday Eddie, come in, damn it!"

No response.

"Is anyone else alive besides you, me, and her?" he asked weakly.

"Beats me. Where's Kinoshita?"

"He'd better be halfway to the spaceport by now," rasped Nighthawk. "Or the whole thing was for nothing."

"What do you mean, nothing?" she said. "We killed Cassius Hill, didn't we?"

"Right," he said. "We killed Cassius Hill. Get me onto my feet. If I stay on my back for another minute, I'm going to pass out."

She helped him up, and braced him for a moment until a wave of dizziness passed.

"Where's Cassandra?"

"Over here," said Pallas Athene, walking over to a crumpled body.

"I thought you said she was all right!"

"She is, considering. She has a major concussion and maybe a few fractured ribs. She was awake a couple of minutes ago; she could be a lot worse."

"Friday!" said Nighthawk suddenly. He adjusted the radio band. "Friday, are you there?"

"Of course I am here," said the alien's familiar voice. "This has been a wonderful night. A glorious night. I *knew* I was right to team up with you, Jefferson Nighthawk!"

"Is Melisande all right?"

"She is dead."

"How did it happen?"

"They swept the area with lasers. She never saw it coming, and I doubt that the man who killed her ever saw her. These things happen." There was a pause. "Have you any further orders, or should I return to my ship?"

Nighthawk swayed as he surveyed the carnage around him. "Stand by," he said at last. "I'll get back to you shortly."

He deactivated the communicator.

"The best killers survived," said Pallas Athene. "That's usually the way in war."

"At least it's over," he said. "The enemy's dead."

"You're not thinking clearly," she corrected him.

"What are you talking about?"

"The *general* is dead," she explained. "The army's still intact, minus a few thousand casualties, and tomorrow there'll be a new general."

"No," he said. "It wasn't a war. It's done."

"It won't be done as long as you're alive," she said. "Even those who hated Hill's guts will still try to hunt you down. You came onto their turf and you killed them where they lived. That requires vengeance."

"I don't plan to spend the rest of my life running," said Nighthawk.

"Then you'll make a stand and fight," replied Pallas Athene. "After all, you're the Widowmaker."

"I'm just his surrogate," answered Nighthawk. "What we did tonight was save the *real* Widowmaker."

"I don't understand."

"It doesn't matter; *I* understand." He looked around once more. "You killed everyone out front?"

"For the time being," she replied. "There'll be

thousands of reinforcements bearing down on this place once they know what's been going on."

"They won't know until sunrise," said Nighthawk. "We jammed their signals and destroyed their transmitters."

"Okay, they won't know until sunrise," she said. "So what?"

"That's all the time we need."

"For what?"

"To end the war forever." He pulled out his communicator. "Friday, how far are you from the governor's mansion?"

"Perhaps a mile," answered the alien.

"Get here in the next half hour and blow the damned thing to smithereens. Then make it back to Sylene any way you can."

He tossed the communicator onto the rubble, then turned to Pallas Athene. "I left a vehicle about a mile up the road, behind some shrubs. Do you think you can find it?"

"If it's still there."

"Go get it and bring it back here."

She turned and started walking away without a word.

Nighthawk rummaged through his pockets and pouches with his remaining hand until he found what he was looking for: his metal ID card and passport cube. He placed them on the ground, reached for his laser pistol, suddenly realized that he didn't have it anymore, and walked over to Blue Eyes' corpse, where he appropriated the dragon's laser.

He returned to the card and the cube, put the weapon on a low-intensity setting, and fired it at them. The card turned black, and its edges curled from the heat, but when he took his finger off the trigger he could still make out part of his name and number. The cube melted, but he aimed the beam away from it before it was totally destroyed.

He waited a few minutes for the card and cube to cool, then picked them up and put them in a pocket. Finally he walked over to Cassandra, knelt down next to her, and gently stroked her hair.

She opened her eyes. "You're alive," she said.

"I'm a hard man to kill."

"When we couldn't find you, I thought you were buried under half the house," she said. "Then . . ." She frowned. "Then I can't remember anything."

"You passed out."

She was silent for a moment, and then looked up at him. "We did it, didn't we?"

"Yes, we did."

"I *knew* we could. And now it's finally over."

"Not quite. But soon."

Pallas Athene pulled up in the darkened vehicle. "There's no one on the roads yet," she said as she got out. "But that can't last long. We'd better get to the spaceport immediately."

"My ship won't be there," said Nighthawk. "Kinoshita's probably taken off by now. Where's yours?"

"A couple of miles south of here."

"Take Cassandra there and go back to Sylene." Suddenly he began looking around on the ground.

"You looking for this?" asked Pallas Athene, holding up the bag of money.

"Yeah. Take it with you."

"What about you?"

"I'll wait for Friday."

"Why not come with us?" she persisted. "My ship can handle a dozen men."

"I've got one last thing to do before I leave the planet."

"What?"

"I've got to kill the Widowmaker."

She frowned. "What the hell are you talking about?"

"After Friday blows the place," said Nighthawk, reaching into a pocket and removing the card and cube, "I'm going to bury these in the rubble." He forced a grim smile to his face. "And *that* ends the war."

# Epilogue

• • • • • • •

*In an orbiting hospital far out on the Rim, more than half a galaxy from the Inner Frontier, Nighthawk slowly opened his eyes and peered out through the bandages.*

"How are you feeling?" asked Cassandra.

"Like a new man."

"Good," she said with a smile. "Because there's not very much of the old one left. New hand, new shoulder joint, and now a new face."

"The old one was a little too well known," replied Nighthawk.

"I can't wait for the bandages to come off, so I can start getting used to this one." She paused. "By the way, your surgeon took me aside and told me he thought he could detect the first signs of eplasia."

"I wouldn't be at all surprised if he was right," replied Nighthawk, wishing the bandages would allow him to smile.

"He says that they're within months of a cure."

"Good. Then the money will be enough to keep *him* alive."

"And to cure you."

"Medical science has managed to cure everything else," he said, flexing his artificial hand. "Why not eplasia?"

She sat down on the edge of the hospital bed. "Do you ever wish you could meet him?"

He considered the question for a long moment, then shook his head. "No. The younger one, the one who died on Solio II, *him* I'd have liked to have met, because I might have been able to help him. But the original? No, once they cure him, he won't need anyone's help."

"He'll be sixty-two years old in a world he won't be able to recognize," noted Cassandra. "Don't you think he'll need help adjusting?"

"He's the Widowmaker," said Nighthawk, as if that answered everything.

Which, in a way, it did.

# ABOUT THE AUTHOR

◆ ◆ ◆

*Mike Resnick is one of the major names in science fiction,* both as a writer and an editor. He is the author of almost 40 novels, 8 collections, and more than 100 stories, and has edited 23 anthologies. He has been nominated for 15 Hugos and 8 Nebulas since 1989, and has won 3 Hugos and a Nebula, as well as scores of lesser awards. Among his best-known works are *Santiago*, *Ivory*, *Soothsayer*, *Paradise*, and the Kirinyaga stories, which have become the most honored story cycle in science fiction history. He lives with his wife, Carol, in Cincinnati, Ohio, where he is currently at work on the third book in the *Widowmaker* trilogy.